Mary F Nixon-Roulet

With a Pessimist in Spain

Mary F Nixon-Roulet

With a Pessimist in Spain

ISBN/EAN: 9783337239831

Printed in Europe, USA, Canada, Australia, Japan

Cover: Foto ©Andreas Hilbeck / pixelio.de

More available books at **www.hansebooks.com**

WITH A PESSIMIST IN SPAIN

BY

MARY F. NIXON

CHICAGO
A. C. McCLURG AND COMPANY
1897

TO MY MOTHER

CONTENTS.

LIST OF ILLUSTRATIONS.

WITH A PESSIMIST IN SPAIN.

CHAPTER I.

GIBRALTAR.

THE Pessimist is my most intimate friend. I have summered and wintered her, and while she is at times depressing, still she is a very good balance for my flightiness, and she has a nice admixture of the sugar and spice of which little girls are made.

I have deliberately planned many tests fearful to so brittle a thing as feminine friendship, and the Pessimist and I have even liked the same men, without hating each other.

At last I determined to make a final effort.

"Pessimist," I said, "but one thing remains. We will travel together."

The Pessimist smiled her sad, sweet smile. (Sad, sweet smiles may be poetic, but poetic things are sometimes very exasperating.)

"We will go to Spain," I said, emphatically.

"Spain!" she gasped.

"We 'll be captured by brigands and in-quisitioned and stilettoed and vendettaed and—"

"Nonsense, Pessimist! You 're sadly mixed," I said.

"Vendetta's Corsica, stiletto's Italy and the rest are relegated to the Middle Ages. We are going to the land of the Hidalgo and Low Dago. It takes nine days to get there and you land at Gibraltar," I added practically.

"Nine days!" sighed the Pessimist; "I shall be sea-sick nine whole days."

"You won 't be, and if you are I 'll take care of you. Moreover the ship's doctor is sure to be adorable. He always is on the North German Lloyd Line. We can sail early in March," I remarked serenely.

The way to manage the Pessimist is to take a great deal for granted.

"You seem to have it all arranged," she said resignedly. "Perhaps you can tell me what I am to wear as a traveling dress?"

"Certainly," I replied, with that cheerful insolence which forms so large a part of my character, and to which I owe my name of Optimist.

"You 'll travel in your tweed suit and take a silk waist and three print shirts. We are going to see sights and not to carry luggage. Our entire paraphernalia will consist of two hand-bags, two umbrellas, one Kodak and ourselves.''

''Have your own way about it,'' said the Pessimist solemnly. ''*But*, if anything happens to me, cholera infantum, or anything,'' (vaguely) ''I shall never go any place with you again.''

''No, probably not; but nothing's going to happen, certainly not cholera infantum.''

(The Pessimist is usually truthful, and she *says* she's thirty-eight. I think she's forgotten the first five years of her life, but as I wasn't there until twenty years afterward, I never remind her of them.)

Thus it was settled that we go to Spain; and go we did.

Over the events of the voyage let us draw a veil. The Pessimist assures me that the table was excellent. She sampled it after the fifth day, and she also relaxed her pessimism sufficiently to say that there were pleasant people on board.

I cannot dispute the fact with her. I was not on board, and there were no pleasant people in *our* cabin.

There were two fiends for a part of the time and a wretched atom of humanity for long days and nights of torture.

Suffice it to say that I did not fulfill my promise to take care of the Pessimist.

Fortunately for Europeans who depend largely upon travelers for their existence, one always reaches port a few hours before committing suicide.

On the morning of the tenth day I was able to sit up and notice things, and went on deck to find we had sailed by the Azores in the night, that Cape Saint Vincent was long passed, and Gibraltar a surety by four in the afternoon. I found, also, that the Pessimist was engaged in studying the guide book. This is something I never permit. If information is desired I prefer to have my traveling companion receive it in a diluted form after it has filtered through the sieve of my cerebrum.

If she reads the Murray or Bädecker herself, she is likely to get it into her precious head that there is one particular thing she wants to see, and there is no rest for the weary until she has seen it.

"Gibraltar is a rocky promontory three miles long and three-fourths of a mile wide, and its northern portion stretches to the province of Andalusia," read the Pessimist solemnly. "There are fifteen thousand inhabitants, consisting of Spaniards, Arabs, Jews, and English. The Bay of Gibraltar contains a great deal of fine shipping. The straits are fifteen miles wide and—"

"Pessimist," I interrupted, "do you mean

to say that you intend to read that guide-book in preference to talking to *me?* I am surprised at you. Why do you care to know all those stupid details?"

"I wish to know everything," she replied, stretching out her hands embracingly. I took advantage of this gesture to possess myself of the guide-book, remarking:

"Very well, then, I will give you a few items of interest:

"The Barbary ape is a small and very festive animal who disports himself in the crags and peaks of Gibraltar. He is not found anywhere else in Spain. As he is not amphibious he must have come over from the Barbary States by means of an underground passage beneath the straits."

"That's very interesting," said the Pessimist. "I mean to see a Barbary ape."

I gasped in despair. It served me right for insisting on having my own way. I knew my friend well enough to feel sure that no one could induce her to leave Gibraltar until she had seen an ape. Unless I could secure an organ-grinder's monkey to pose as the only original Barbary ape, I was lost.

"They are seldom seen by strangers, being of a shy and retiring disposition," I said hastily. Then, to my delight, a timely interruption occurred.

The day had been cloudy and a heavy fog obscured the way, but suddenly the sun burst through a bank of clouds, and without a moment's warning the great rock seemed to spring at us with such a bound as to almost make me jump back.

At first I saw only a huge, dark mass, rearing its haughty head even above the clouds which drifted across its rocky sides like dissolving snow-banks. Then—as we drew nearer and nearer, the clouds disappeared entirely, things began to assume form and comeliness, and what had seemed a shapeless mass assumed the bold outline of the well-known mountain.

The green patches on its sides proved to be trees, stone-pines, aloes, and rough *cacti*, and below this, as the last shimmering cloud raised its wings like a great white dove and floated heavenward, I saw the town, the wonderful, many-hued, strange, fascinating town of Gibraltar.

There was the moss-grown ruin of the old Moorish castle, built by Abu-Abul-Hajes in 725 A.D. Gibraltar is supposed to take its name from Tarik, the "one-eyed Berber" who took it in 711, Gebel-Tarik, or Hill of Tarik being the derivation.

Below there were houses set on the hillside one above another like stair steps, their flat roofs in soft shades of terra-cotta tiling, their walls painted in warm hues of blue, pink, lavender, rose, tawny brown, and cream, with lattices and vines and a bewildering variety of color.

Beneath the houses was the wall, rising sternly from the wharf, and then came the water of the bay, of that indescribable blue which must be seen to be realized. With the sun glancing upon it and the whitecaps dancing until they fell from sheer exhaustion into a watery grave, and the blues of sea and sky melting into each other in perfect loveliness, I wondered how the Straits of Gibraltar could be considered so dangerous as they are.

After feasting my eyes upon all this in silent admiration I turned to look at the Pessimist, who beyond the first surprised "Oh!" had said nothing. I found her seated on her steamer-chair grasping the arms and staring with wide-open eyes and mouth at the rock. (The Pessimist's mouth *is* large, but fortunately the rock is stationary, else it might have fallen in, so widely had wonder distended her lips).

"Well, how do you like it?" I demanded. She gave me a disgusted glance.

"I do n't *like* it at all," she said.

"One does n't expect to like a—a monstrosity! It 's one of the wonders of the world. Do you realize that the highest point, Sugar Loaf, is fourteen hundred and thirty-nine feet above the sea?'' And she craned her neck to get a view. of the very highest pinnacle, during which process her hat fell off and a gust of wind tossed her hair into a *cheval de frise.* When I had righted matters I said very meekly, (for I saw plainly that I had not rescued my friend from the guide-book quickly enough and that she was not to be trifled with):

''Yes, dear, but it was not the rock but the town I wanted to know how you like.''

Then, seeing that she began to relent a little, I went on quickly:

''We are to stay at the 'Calpe,' called after the old Greek name for Gibraltar. The Phœnicians sailed here and called it Alube, and this rock and Ceuta—that queer, dim outline across the straits—were the Pillars of Hercules. These were the western edges of the world.''

I had begun with quite a flow of eloquence, but my oration was cut short by the appearance of the small boat which was to take us ashore, as our great ship dropped anchor in the bay.

There was a great turmoil at the custom house, but we managed to get through in comparative peace, although eyed very suspiciously by the officials, for women without seven trunks, a satchel, shawl-strap, band-box and bundle are unusual in these regions.

The Pessimist had been very quiet, and her sweetly tranquil face with its look of determined disapproval had facilitated my frantic endeavors very much. The Pessimist is one of the women whom every one takes care of, even myself.

They may not like to but they do it just the same. It is this habit of allowing herself to be looked after and her plans made for her which has endeared her to me as a traveling companion. I like making the plans myself and my vanity is immensely pleased at carrying things on successfully. We went smiling up to the frowning gate, where a guard awaited us, and I was about to ask him for the pass or permit necessary to enter this walled town, when the Pessimist grabbed my arm.

"What is that?" she demanded. "Is that a—a prince or the governor, or what?"

I looked quickly in the direction indicated by her glance and then smiled.

"No, Miss Columbia, whose foot has ne'er before been off her native heath," I answered, as I saw the straight, military figure, his chest protruding like that of a red Shanghai. He had gay, gold decorations upon his tight jacket, an unmistakable swagger, and a pill-box hat perched upon the side of his head over his left ear.

"He 's neither prince nor nabob, but just a male animal of the species Tommy Atkins."

"What 's a Tommyatkins?" she demanded with something closely resembling a sniff.

I regret to say that the Pessimist frequently views the valuable information which I impart as to be taken with a grain of salt.

"A *Tommy Atkins*," very slowly I continued, "is the name given to a private in the British army. Why? There was once a private who did something. (This is a *very* unusual circumstance. They generally do nothing but swagger.) I do n't know what the 'something' was, but it was either very fine or very much the reverse. I can make up a story if you like. His name was Tommy Atkins, and since then all privates have been called thus. With the Queen's shilling comes a nineteenth century accolade and a sort of 'I dub thee Tommy Atkins in the name of the Queen, a shilling and the British lion.'"

Here I stopped for breath, and we received our permit, were forbidden to use our kodak inside the walls under pain of fine and imprisonment, and were at last inside the gates of the great fortress which has for centuries been the key of the Mediterranean.

The Calpe is a small but very delightful hotel built in the pretty Spanish fashion round a square marble court with palms and flowers, and a fountain splashing coolly in the center.

The Pessimist had intended to rest, but when an obliging waiter told us the band played in the Alameda from five to six, she said she was not tired, at least I said she was n't, and off we started.

Gibraltar has three streets running parallel the whole length of the town, intersected once or twice by alleys, but oftener ending in a *cul de sac*, and starting on again, seemingly without rhyme or reason. The main street, Water-port Street, leads from the city gate straight through the town and past all the public buildings, far too pretty and home-like places to be dignified with any such high-sounding titles.

The houses and shops are long, low buildings nearly all with gardens, and the architecture a strange mixture of dainty Moorish lattice, cheerful Spanish *patio*, and English solidity.

Through the main street the Pessimist and I wandered slowly, too absorbed in the sights about us for even an attempt at conversation. Here passed an English soldier in all the bravery of scarlet and gold. There was a dark-browed Spaniard, his cloak thrown about him in picturesque folds, and there an Arab in flowing burnoose of gray—a veritable Shylock.

There are hundreds of Jews in the city notwithstanding that the Treaty of Utrecht read:

"No leave shall be given under *any* pretence whatever to Jews or Moors to reside or have their dwellings in the town of Gibraltar."

Nevertheless, here they are with their greasy faces and unctuous smiles, and in the shops are their beautiful wares, all of which they sell to *you*, in consideration of the fact that you are the loveliest of your sex, for exactly half what the things are marked.

And although the loveliest of her sex knows full well that the villainous old Moors are cheats and humbugs, and the wares not worth all the *pesetas* she cheerfully pays, still the Maltese lace, Arabian gold embroidery, inlaid boxes, and Bolero jackets are so fascinating and so cheap compared to what they are at home that she promptly buys them all.

The Jews gloat over the *Americanas*, but then, let them gloat, for after all, one's only regret is that one did n't (or rather *could n't*) buy more. The Pessimist and I dragged our

reluctant feet past many of these shops, and in and out of the maze of wonderful sights and strange peoples, and finally, attracted by the stirring music, reached the Alameda.

Up to 1814 Gibraltar was one of the dirtiest towns in Europe and the most unhealthy. Then the English took it in hand, and now it is well-drained and neat.

Once in ten years they have Gibraltar fever and the English sometimes find it hard to become acclimated, for the summer heat is intense, but the spring and fall are charming in this latitude, and the months of March and April are especially fine.

The Alameda is a great garden, laid out eighty years ago.

And such a garden!

There is but little attempt at arrangement, no mere formal landscape gardening, where often innocent trees and shrubs are tortured into the shapes required by so-called civilization.

It is a wilderness of flowers, some familiar, some unknown, and all blooming in a brilliance and luxuriance hitherto undreamed of.

Here were gay scarlet geranium bushes, eight feet high, their great heads fully twelve inches in diameter and each separate flower as large as a silver dollar.

Over a wall clambered a heliotrope, its

heavy lavender flowers in huge clusters scenting the air, which was fragrant, too, with jasmine, orange flowers, and violets, which purpled a carpet for our hesitating feet.

Pure callas, white and ghostly, were standing in stately rows, and over them the flaunting roses flirted and nodded at the demurer primroses, while the red-bud trees, in full bloom, blushed deeply at such flower pranks.

There are over four hundred native flowering plants besides all those not indigenous to the soil. Neat walks led through this tropic fairyland, and there were grottoes and caves and rustic seats.

The Pessimist sat down on one of these, under a huge lemon-verbena tree. I regarded that tree viciously. What business had it to grow tall enough to shade a stranger hospitably from the glare of the sun? At home, I had painstakingly nursed its second cousin once removed through a whole winter of its discontent, only to have it die when it had grown a foot and a half high!

The music was playing softly in the distance, and I could hear the strains of ''God Save the Queen,'' which translated into Yankee means, ''God Bless Our Native Land.'' Then the band began on ''Home, Sweet Home,'' for which I had no longings, and my native land, though very desirable as native lands go, did not seem specially so just then. I closed my eyes in dreamy peace, soothed by the sights and sounds and delicious perfumes.

"I am the Sleeping Beauty," I remarked *sotto voce*, "and I am never, never going to wake up, but I am going to sleep here for ever."

"May I be allowed to remark that a gnat is biting the end of your nose and that you 'll not be a Beauty to-morrow?" said the Pessimist in her most dampening tones. "Also that I 'm extremely hungry?"

"Now, that you mention it, so am I," I answered cheerfully, and we made our way homeward with the alacrity which attends the footsteps of those who have satisfactorily seen their sights.

The Pessimist and I spent three days at Gibraltar, and although in that time we saw everything that was to be seen—for it contains very few show places compared to other cities in Spain—we were by no means ready to leave.

We were guided through the fortifications by a delightful English private, to whose splendor my companion could not grow accustomed, and whom she insisted on calling "Sir."

This embarrassed him extremely, for it compelled him to raise two fingers to his pill-box hat every time she did it, besides making him generally uncomfortable.   He was n't used to it, and John Bull hates anything new.

It was a hard climb to those fortifications. First a narrow street up a steep hill, then steps up, up, up; steps cut right into the face of the rock, over two hundred of them, and then we came to a stand-still at the guard-house where our permit, already obtained from the governor (for everything in Gibraltar is tied with red tape in hard knots), had to be ratified, and a guide procured.

Gibraltar is sometimes called the Hill of Caves and there are natural tunnels and caves through the rock.   The most famous of these is St. Michael's cavern.   This extends from a thousand feet above sea-level to several hundred feet below, where the waves can be heard dashing overhead and the air is so bad that no one has ever dared to penetrate farther.

Besides the natural fortification of its almost impregnable position, Gibraltar has had everything which human ingenuity could devise expended upon it to make it the best fortified town in the world.

Mines and countermines, tunnels and sen-tries and signal stations — these are common sights.   The great tunnels were blasted out of solid rock, and by the way, the war prisoners were forced to work to construct them as an illustration of the irony of Fate.

Within openings at set distances along the route, huge cannon which it takes twenty men to move are placed to gaze serenely upon the harbor and the neutral ground stretching between Gibraltar and Spain. The rebound from firing these cannons is so great that the gun carriages are placed upon a sharp incline, so that after rebounding they will run back into place instead of jumping out of their hole and falling over the rock.

There is a regular honey-comb all through the rock with peep-holes for the guns, but the exterior is the most innocent gray rock, covered with shrubs, aloes, fig-trees and many flowers. Visitors are allowed to go only to the last of the open galleries, and thither the Pessimist and I toiled in the charge of our private. Beyond this point no one but a British officer is allowed to go, and not he— unless in uniform. When we reached the last opening we sat down to breathe for a few moments, having neglected that in our last hard climb, and the private pointed out the different points of interest.

"There, mum, is the market and the custom 'ouse, and that's a German man-of-war in the 'arbor. Over there where those white 'ouses begin is Spain. This we 're hon, mum, is Hengland, and that's Spain. Linea or Linctown's the name because it's just on the line. That long, low strip between's the neutral ground. It's neither country's and is guarded by both, and neither Henglishman nor Spaniard can move a foot off his own ground without permission."

It was a glorious view!

Rock, town, harbor, bay and straits were all before us—the neutral ground stretching into sunny Spain, and across the blue water the dim outline of the Dark Continent. I was oppressed by so much grandeur and the Pessimist spoke first.

"When was this given to England?"

Tommy Atkins smiled as broadly as his politeness and his chin-strap permitted, then said:

"It wasn't hexactly given, mum. You might say, was taken in the year 1704."

"I know about that, Pessimist," I said glibly. I love to talk and had been quiet a good while.

"Gibraltar has belonged to all sorts of people, and they say has never been taken except by treachery. Besieged alternately by Christians and Moors, it was finally wrested from the Moslems in 1462.

"In 1704 a force of English and Dutch, under Sir George Rooke besieged it, and although there was a garrison of only eighty men, they killed two hundred and seventy-six English before they finally surrendered.

"Rooke had been fighting for Charles, Arch-Duke of Austria, but the British government forgot this interesting fact and attached Gibraltar to their own Empire, neglecting to reward in any way the man who gained it for them."

The private had listened, much edified, and as I stopped, too indignant at the thought of poor Rooke's unremembered services to talk, he remarked sententiously:

"Hingland requires hevery man to do 'is duty, miss! Do you 'appen to know about the great siege?"

"Yes, indeed," I said. "The one which lasted from 1779 to 1783. The Spaniards made a last effort to wrest the rock from the English. The besiegers had an army of forty thousand, while the English had only seven thousand men.

They held out against assault and storm and starvation for four long years. The history of that siege would fill a book, and General Elliott is one of the heroes of all ages. There are few springs in Gibraltar and the water supply threatened to fail, for they had only rain water to depend upon, and the seasons were unusually dry; but the splendid fellows held out and at last a treaty ended the war of which the struggle at Gibraltar was only a unit."

"It was a big fight, mum," said Tommy, with some of that pride in his nation which makes even the commonest private a bulwark of safety to the British Empire.

"Do you like being here?" I asked him, as we descended the stairway in the rock.

"Oh, yes, miss," he answered cheerfully. "You see it's this way, mum. A private gets a shillin' a day an' rations, and Gibraltar ain't such a bad billet. Much better than Hindia with the dirty niggers."

"What are 'rations' and what do you do with your shilling a day?" demanded the Pessimist.

"Rations means food, mum; a pound of meat and a pound of bread, and some vegetables hevery day. We 'ave to pay four-pence a day for mess, mum, where our food is cooked, you know, and we buys our own pipe-clay and boot-blackin' and it leaves us about three-pence a day for tobacco and— well, and *sweeties*, mum," with an irresistible twinkle in his eye.

This way of designating his pot of ale was entirely too much for even the Pessimist's gravity and she gave our festive Tommy a large fee to add to his puny "shillin' a day" as we descended from the fortifications to finish our sight-seeing.

There was not much left. The Cathedral, —a poor specimen of imitation Moorish architecture,—the old Franciscan convent now used as a government house, and the fine hospital at Rosia are the main objects of interest. We drove across the neutral ground guarded on one side by a stern British soldier and on the other by a picturesque Spaniard in cloak and cocked hat. Linea is a squalid, dirty place, full of brown children, dogs and low gray houses, once white.

It is not picturesque, and there is an advertisement of the Singer sewing machine on the first Spanish house.

We drove back just in time to avoid remaining outside the gates all night, as no one is allowed to enter the sacred walls of Gibraltar after sundown.

We wandered a little about the streets teeming with varied human life, and therein lies the main charm of Gibraltar; not in picture galleries, nor monuments, nor churches, nor buildings, but in the strange commingling of old world and new, English civilization and Arab picturesqueness, and in the fact that it seems to unlock the Orient to our wondering eyes.

"Well, Pessimist," I said that night; "what do you think of Gibraltar?"

"I think," she replied with the decisiveness which marks her fiat, "that the British Lion grabbed a pretty big bone and held on to it. It is likely to spoil and be very much in his way, but it's too big to bury, and he would n't give it back to the Spaniards for anything."

CHAPTER II.

TANGIER.

ROM out the corner of my eye I looked at the Pessimist and saw that she was uncommonly low in her mind. We were en route for Tangier, and it rained dismally, dripping into the small cabin of the Ghib al Tarik, which was crowded with passengers of every variety. We were to reach Tangier in a few moments, and I saw plainly that if I was to rouse the Pessimist from her trance of disgust I must be quick about it. Really, I could n't altogether blame her, for the passage was rough, the cabin stuffy, the decks slippery, and our fellow-travelers anything but agreeable. We had not been ill, but other people had, and altogether we were uncomfortable. Even my enthusiasm was dampened.

I made a hasty visit to the door and returning, remarked, "We 're almost there!" No response. "It looks as if it would clear," I hazarded.   Still that Sphinx-like expression of countenance.   "Tangier is a very old place."   (I tried statistics in desperation.) "It was a Roman settlement under the Cæsars and they called it Tingis.   Augustus made it a free city, and since then it has been ruled by Vandals, Phœnicians and Arabs.   In the fifteenth century the Portuguese possessed themselves of it, and when the Princess Catharine of Braganza married King Charles II., in 1662, Tangier was ceded to England as a part of her dowry.   The British found it undesirable, and in 1684 abandoned it to the Moors. It has—" but here my eloquence was interrupted by a shriek, loud and prolonged, which came from the Pessimist at my side. She was aroused at last, but not by me.   Following the direction in which her finger pointed I saw on the floor at her feet a meeklooking covered basket, from the side of which protruded the head of an enormous snake.   The creature evidently liked the Pessimist's looks for it waved its head, with its sly, blinking eyes, back and forward, with each movement swaying nearer and nearer the unfortunate woman.   She shrieked again and again and a crowd gathered in an instant, a *mêlée* of jabbering Spaniards and Arabs, all gesticulating and acting as though their one desire was to tear everybody into bits.

Suddenly the hamper was snatched up by a Moor in the national burnous, a long white robe, with a hood like a Capuchin's at the back, and girded with cord at the waist. He spoke to the snake, which, after shooting out its tongue at him, drew its head back into the basket. It was a tame cobra from which the poison had been removed, the Moor explained with apologies in excellent French, which all Moors speak more or less.

I accepted his explanations as best I could and turned to reassure my poor Pessimist.

"If I had been bitten by that reptile, I suppose you would have been satisfied," she remarked with that stony dignity which brings terror to my soul.

"I would n't," I replied hastily. "I would n't have been satisfied at all!"

"Indeed! Did you wish him to destroy my mangled remains?" she demanded, still more reproachfully.

"Mangled fiddlesticks!" I cried, my temper getting the better of me. "He could n't bite you. He had n't any—any—biter!" I concluded lamely, at a loss for a word.

"You did n't know that, and you laughed!" said my friend.

"I did n't," I hastily disclaimed. "But if I laugh at myself and everything which happens to me, you ought not to mind my laughing at a snake! That's doing unto others, is n't it? That is the gong for landing and there's a gleam of sunlight. It is really going to clear. Come on, Pessimist," and I hurried her up on deck.

As is often the case in small harbors, we had to go ashore in boats; and as we stood on the gang-plank awaiting our turn to be held over the side by one Moor and dropped into the arms of another, I whispered to my companion, "There's the Barbary ape at last, or the Missing Link at least."

She turned quickly and examined carefully the object to which I had drawn her attention. It—for the sex seemed uncertain—was a Moor, about five feet high and stooping so as to appear almost hump-backed. He was dressed in a gray burnous like a bath-robe, his bare feet were thrust into heelless slippers, his head bound with a white turban, his brown face was wrinkled and seamed, and his small slanting eyes looked out from under a pair of shaggy eyebrows.

To our surprise this object came up and spoke to us, saying that he was a guide. As he spoke fair English and a good deal of French, and showed us a recommendation which assured the reader that "Abul Islam" was no worse than any of his kind, we engaged him for our stay in Tangier.

The sun had chased away the last vestige of cloud, and the city lay before our entranced vision. The houses of the town rose from the strip of golden sand upon the seashore, in the form of an amphitheater guarded by white walls and a castle.

Gibraltar was brilliantly colored in all the hues of the spectrum, but Tangier gleamed pale-hued between blue sea and bluer sky, like a bank of soft sunset clouds. Then, there was a sensation of being rushed through waves of the sea and more turbulent human waves, that dashed and rolled about us in wildest confusion. We were hurried up the steep landing stairs, through the custom house, and into the street, arriving hot and breathless, a few moments later, at our hotel, another "Calpe," named for its brother across the bay, and equally good.

We ate a marvelous luncheon, a strange combination of perfect French cooking and Moorish service.

The table was long and very narrow, and all the way down the middle were low glass dishes containing different fruits—fresh figs, dates, oranges, olives, pomegranates. We were waited upon by an Arab in loose Turkish trousers and a blouse of vivid scarlet with gold belt and embroideries. He wore a spotless turban, and was not darker than a Spaniard, with a smooth, olive skin, and melting brown eyes set a trifle aslant under perfectly marked brows. Altogether, Hassan was a fine specimen, and a more perfectly trained servant I never saw.

Abul Islam, disreputable as he doubtless was, knew his duties as guide thoroughly. The first of these was to *make* people see everything whether they wanted to or not, and Abul appeared immediately after lunch and insisted that we go to see the prison. He would take no denial, so we meekly followed him through the streets. Those streets! Picture to yourself the bed of a mountain brook with the water running in a steady stream down the middle and in unexpected little trickles everywhere else. This was the main street (there is but one), which runs from Bab-al-Marsa (the Gate of the Port), to Bab-al-Sok (the Gate of the Market Place). The by-ways and alleys are a mass of black mud which comes to the ankles always and frequently over the shoe-tops.

Several times the Pessimist opened her mouth to object, but Abul strode sternly on in front, refusing to listen to any remonstrances. She was a sight as she picked her way through that horrid slime and filth, her gown held up in both hands, her face a study.

I laughed till I nearly sat down in a mud-puddle, when it suddenly dawned upon me that I probably looked the same.

> " O, wad some power the giftie gie us
> To see oursel's as ithers see us,"

I murmured as I caught a smile on the face of a handsome Englishman as he passed me. "Pessimist, you are avenged!"

The prison is unspeakable. My acquaintance with prisons is not extensive, but if my opinion were asked I should say that the one in Tangier is the worst in the world.

If there are worse I do n't wish to see nor hear of them. At the entrance court sat the jailer, smoking a long pipe filled with *Kief*, a sort of opium, one whiff of which will send a European to sleep. He watched us furtively. Then we came to a hole in the wall, heavily grated with iron, and at this appeared a face. Poor wretch !

Had he ever known happiness? If he had, it was long since ground out of him, for the shriveled parchment of his skin was like a sombre mask of misery. What had he done? Oh, nothing probably, except have an enemy who denounced him to the Pasha as having a few *duros* which the Pasha thought he could extort from him in ransom. He is there in that dark, ill-smelling, cramped room, with dozens of other unfortunates exactly like him, writhing in chains and groaning with sickness and misery, until friends can collect money enough for ransom, or the charity of strangers throws a few silver coins in his way.

It was hard to be optimistic over such a scene as this, and harder still when Abul waved his hand toward an open court and said, "Ze hospital!" I tried very hard to see it, having visions of neat buildings filled with spotless white beds and all the comforts our blessed nineteenth century affords to the sick.

Upon further inquiry Abul informed us that the Sultan disapproved of sick people, and the aged, and liked to have them killed, but the Pasha was very kind and allowed them to lie in that open court all day. Kind Pasha!

I could stand it no longer.

"For pity's sake, take me to some more cheerful place!" I cried at last, as the Pessimist turned a grieved countenance toward me, and I knew she was on the point of saying, "I told you so!"

Abul understood and quickly guided us to El Sok, the market. It was a confused mass of Arabs, negroes, Moors, Spaniards, and nondescripts.

"This *is* cheerful," I cried delightedly.

"Look at that camel. He certainly looks like the ship of the desert with all sails set, as

he comes steering down the street, scattering everything before him.

Donkeys, pigs, sheep, ducks, vegetables, fruits—did you ever see such a mixture?

There, see that leather. I read somewhere that there are tanneries here, as one would expect in Morocco. What quaint pottery!

What wonderful mats!

"What is that?" I asked of Abul.

"*Koos,*" he said, taking up some stuff which looked like bran.

"We use it to cook, like curry," he added.

"And this is soap," showing us a mass which resembled liquid dates.

"Are those women?" demanded the Pessimist.

"Yes, Señora," said Abul. "They always wear the *haik.*"

"Are they as beautiful as their eyes?" I asked looking at the slender forms in their white draperies, held so as to cover all the face but the eyes.

"Oh, some of them," said Abul. "Would you like to see some?"

"Yes, indeed," we both exclaimed.

"I will take you to a harem," he said, and started proudly away. We held our breath, scarcely daring to breathe lest we dispel our good fortune.

"A real harem!" I whispered. "Pessimist, are we in the Arabian Nights?'' but she gave no answer, for Abul stopped abruptly at a low, white door in a wall and knocked loudly.

The door swung back and a brief parley ensued, and then he motioned us to enter. We did so, and found ourselves in a long, low hall with tiled floor, and doorways opening on each side.

We seemed to be alone, when a voice said softly, in French:

''Here, please,'' and we saw a tiny slave girl, who beckoned us to follow her through one of the curtained doorways. We followed with a pleasurable excitement not unmixed with fear, and entered a cool marble *patio* with a fountain in the center, ferns and flowers and the twitter of birds mingling with the splash of the water.

Here we waited a moment while the noise-less slave glided away to call her mistress. ''Do you like it, Pessimist?'' I asked.

''Ye-es,'' she said slowly and dubiously. Then she edged up to me and whispered,

''Do you think we 'll get out?''

''Out?'' I exclaimed. ''What on earth do you mean?''

''Are we quite safe? Would there be any danger of—'' she hesitated.

''Of the master of the house wanting any

more wives?'' I queried. "My dear Pessimist, there are a great many women in Tangier. Still, if he should happen to be here it
might be awkward. You know they prefer
them plump. Up in Tetuan slaves are made
to stand all day and throw bread pellets into
the favorites' mouths so they 'll grow stout.
Two hundred is a nice weight there, although
a hundred and fifty will do.''

The Pessimist looked uncomfortable, for her
plump figure was one of her trials. Just then
the little slave came back with the chief wife,
who greeted us pleasantly. She was a tall,
handsome creature, dressed in a marvelous
salmon silk robe, covered with gold-em-
broidery. In her black hair were numbers of
gold bangles.

There were fifteen wives altogether, some
were embroidering, some talking in whispers,
and one, the youngest of all, a girl about fifteen, stood a little apart, glancing shyly at us.

She was a lovely creature, shy and modest-
looking, and stood there, clad in a pale blue
silk robe with *haik* half drawn about her face,
and one bare foot with nails dyed red, slip-
ping nervously in and out of her pink san-
dal.

The house was built around the *patio;* on
one side were the cooking and eating rooms.
In one of these a brass kettle was simmering

over blazing charcoal, and the fragrance of rich coffee filled the rooms.

Beyond was a long chamber with low couches at intervals along the walls, and at the end a huge couch piled with pillows, draped in gorgeous colors. But, alas for the unity of the picturesque! It was curtained off with cheap, imitation lace curtains from Nottingham.

This was the bedroom and next it a smaller one filled with scarfs and *haiks* and materials for embroidery—the great occupation of the Oriental.

The chief wife gave us a thick liquid, called coffee, but more like a black, sweetened syrup, and she bade us cordially "*Maraba bickoum*" (welcome). The pretty little wife insisted on kissing our hands. We smiled liberally upon all who could not talk French, gave the patient slave a fee, and our visit to the harem was at an end.

The Pessimist gave a huge sigh of relief as we heard the heavy door clang behind us, and we saw Abul serenely waiting in the mud.

"I 'm glad we 're out of it," she remarked. "It was very interesting, but I was scandalized to see that they looked happy. Think of being married like that!"

"But they 're so little married." I said, flippantly. "You must remember that each has only one-fifteenth of a husband. If there are many more things in Tangier as interesting as the harem, I shall stay two weeks instead of two days!"

Fortunately for me, in view of this decision, there is not a great deal which *must* be seen, and the charm of the place lies in the fact that one can wander at will, guide-bookless, yet always seeing something interesting.

There are twenty thousand people in Tangier, only four thousand of whom are Europeans, and the street scenes present a human kaleidoscope. The houses, which line the streets close together and are all painted white and pale colors, are low, flat-roofed and windowless.

One can stand in the middle of the street and almost touch the doors on each side with both hands.

There are few shops visible, for nearly all the buying and selling is done in the market-places and the curio shops are behind walls, up alleys, and in various impossible places.

The Pessimist and I visited a café under the guidance of Abul, and found it apparently harmless. It was a long, low room, with pillars painted in gay colors, and in the middle sat the musicians playing extraordinarily inharmonious harmonies.

There were guitars, mandolins, banjos, an

accordion and several *rhebugs*, curious instruments between violin and guitar. The musicians sang a weird accompaniment, making horrible faces, especially one gigantic negro, coal black, who showed every gleaming ivory tooth in his exertions to sing.

Groups of men sat about on the floor, smoking *kief* pipes, playing cards and drinking tea and coffee out of tiny glasses.

I started to make a little sketch; but a murmur arose, and Abul said quickly.

"Tear up that paper!"

This I did at once, and he hurried us away, past the pile of shoes at the door (for all the natives are compelled to take off their shoes when entering), down the steep steps into the open street.

Then he explained that the Mohammedans resent bitterly any attempt at sketching. It was forbidden by the Prophet to draw any likeness of anything, according to a literal interpretation of the Holy Scriptures.

Moreover, an Arab thinks that a picture must have a soul, and if he allows his likeness to be made, at the day of judgment there will be no soul for *him*, since his own will have gone into the portrait.

The sun deigned to shine during the rest of our visit to Tangier; the mud in the streets dried up; the city took upon itself an air of pleasant life and activity, and even the Pessimist withdrew the anathemas she had breathed. She developed a marked admiration for the nose of the modern Arab, perhaps due to the fact that her own is an engaging pug.

These noses are unusual, and I have never seen such a perfect shape,—neither Aquiline nor Grecian, but a medium between the two; and the delicate curve of the nostrils, which dilate with every emotion, is statuesque. The Arabs are handsome fellows, with straight, lithe forms, graceful in every curve, sleek, clear skins of a rich olive, eyes full of a dreamy tranquillity, and crisp black hair. Their faces wear a pensive expression and for the most part an enduring agreement with the ways of Providence, very different from our Western unrest. This comes in part from their natural indolence, but largely from their firm belief in Fate.

Our last night in Tangier was ideal. We had seen everything, been everywhere, even to taking a long donkey ride among the neighboring villages, scattered like dots upon the hill-sides.

The Pessimist looked irresistible upon her donkey. Her dignity was painful, for it induced her to try to sit upright and ride gracefully. I have conquered the proper way of riding a donkey, and do it to perfection. The science of it lies in allowing yourself to wobble as much as possible; not to sit up, not to be dignified, not to mind falling off over his ears or tail, as the case may be. In short, have a complete disregard for appearances, and so shalt thou fare better and have fewer bruises than thy more dignified neighbor.

The Pessimist suffered, and retired early, but it was my last night on the Dark Continent and I was determined to make the most of it.

Warmly clad, for the air crept in a little chilly from the sea, I lingered on the iron-latticed balcony of my room, which almost overhung the city's wall.

Far to the right, "*le sable etait comme une mer sans limites,*" stretching away to the grim desert. The sea rolled on in restless fervor, and I could hear its waves lap the cool strand, and see the outline of the citadel against the sky.

As the moon rose high in the air it sent a shimmering path of light across the water.

From the white towers of the citadel the houses, seeming like ghosts of dwellings in the still night, sloped down to the stern walls which guard the city.

The towers of the three tall mosques, in the daylight such strange and wonderful hues of greenish, purplish, bluish gray, now were dark and eerie, and beside them rose the date-palm trees, their huge serrated leaves clearly outlined in the brilliant moonlight. All was silent, still as the night indeed, and gazing upon this perfect scene my soul was filled with a sense of its beauty and with memories of long ago. As I dreamed of the days of good Haroun-al-Raschid, suddenly in the street beneath my lattice there was a sound of steps, the monotonous beating of a drum, the call to prayer, for it was the month Ramadan, and all good Mohammedans rise and pray at midnight.

''God is Great! God is Great! There is no God but Allah, and Mohammed is his Prophet!''

This was the cry, and it broke upon the night air with a sharpness which brought to mind fearful recollections of that creed which has been disseminated by blood and warfare.

Here it was, on this very coast, now so tranquil in the moonlight, that the Mohammedan conqueror, having laid waste and devastated all in his path and converted at the point of the sword all whom he did not kill, with his sword dripping with blood, waded into the sea and swore that the sea should be the only boundary of the religion of Mohammed.

As I mused, lost in thought, a voice from the interior of the room remarked:

"Would you mind telling me what you are doing?" and starting guiltily I beheld the Pessimist in all the glory of crimping pins.

"I 'm—well I 'm looking at the moon," I said, lamely.

It always puzzles me to give any legitimate excuse for sentimentality to the Pessimist.

"Is there anything peculiar about the moon?" she asked, sardonically.

"It 's the only African moon I ever saw," I replied.

"Hum!" she said, contemptuously.

"It 's so nice out here," I added. "Won't you come and see?"

"Thank you. I fail to see any difference between an African moon and any other kind. There is also such a thing as African fever and plain American influenza, and you 'll get one or the other if you stay out there any longer —not to mention the fact of how cross you 'll be at the breakfast table!" she remarked.

"Good-night, Pessimist," I said, humbly.

There are times when pessimistic common sense is very trying.

CHAPTER III

CADIZ, THE CLOUD CITY.

HE approach to Cadiz from the sea is very beautiful, especially, if like the Pessimist and myself, you sail from Tangier on a clear day with the March sun shining in Southern brilliance. We had left the African coast, picturesque and gray in the morning light, and had caught just a glimpse of Tarifa, the most Moorish town in Spain. It was named from Tarif Ben-Malik, the first Berber Sheik who came to Spain, and the modern word tariff is said to be taken from the fact that the Moors made every one who passed pay a tax at Tarifa. It was once a Roman colony, called Julia Traducta (because the Romans peopled it with Spanish women stolen like the Sabines), and under the gray walls of the town the son of Alfonso Perez de Guzman, ancestor of the Empress Eugenie, was put to death by the Moors, in the very sight of his father, in order to induce him to yield the city to save his child's life.

"Better honor without a son, than a son with dishonor," said the splendid old Don (called *El Bueno,* or the Good), as he tossed the Moors the very dagger with which to kill his son, and the Moors were forced to retire and Tarifa was saved. Cape Trafalgar, which means promontory of the cave, and which teems with memories of Nelson, came next, and this is called the "Waterloo of the Sea." As every one knows, here it was that in 1805, Nelson died in all the triumph of his wonderful victory. Gravina, the Spanish admiral, having received a mortal wound in the same engagement, said as he lay dying, "I go to join Nelson, the greatest man the world has ever produced." Poor Nelson! So great, and yet so weak!

After Trafalgar came the Isle of Leon and lovely glimpses of the coast, wooded and sloping gently to the sea. Cadiz lies upon a peninsula stretching far into the sea, and seems like a snow-white cloud on the horizon, for sea and sky are shades of deep lapis-lazuli blue, while the city is quite white.

To those accustomed to smoke-begrimed towns, Cadiz is a revelation, and De Amicis says of it, "I can only describe it by writing the word 'white' a thousand times with a white pencil on blue paper."

"Pessimist, my dear," I remarked, as we looked upon the harbor and quays, and drove through the white gateway, up a white street, to a white hotel, the Fonda de America, "I don't think I should like being a servant in Cadiz. The houses are whitewashed inside and out every year, and a servant who cannot whitewash need not apply for a situation here. The Spaniards call it '*tazita de plata*' or little silver cup.

"Is it not beautiful and dazzling?"

"Very dazzling. I should like a pair of blue glasses. My eyes are nearly put out with the glare," said the Pessimist.

"It 's rose-colored, and not blue glasses you need. You 're blue enough now," I said.

"Did you know Cadiz was eleven hundred years old, and Cæsar made it a free city with five hundred Roman *equites*, of which number only Rome and Padua could boast? In those days it was the market of the world, a wilderness of marble palaces, amphitheaters and aqueducts, teeming with shipping; spoken of by Cæsar; sung of by the Roman poets and praised by Juvenal as the 'City of Venus,' with its *improbæ Gaditanæ*, or ballet girls, whose wonderful grace of movement turned the heads of all the Roman youths, who came to Cadiz in stately galleys o'er the Mediterranean or by that *Via Lata* which stretched from the white city by the sea, to the imperial one where the yellow Tiber sweeps along."

"What is that over the door-way of that large building?" asked my companion. "Those are the arms of Cadiz,—Hercules with his lions and the pillars, and the motto, *ne plus ultra.* How strange to feel that this was the limit of the world, and that it was the Tarshish of the Bible!"

"It does not look as old as that. It 's the newest thing we 've seen," grumbled the Pessimist.

"It 's no use pining for real antiquity in Cadiz," I answered, "for the old Roman remains were long since destroyed by the Goths; theirs by the Arabs; the town was rebuilt by Don Alfonso the Learned, in 1262; burned by the English in the sixteenth century; bombarded in the eighteenth; ravaged by 'the pestilence that walketh in darkness;' desolated by the keen Levanter and the fierce Sirocco, and the center of the Spanish resistance during the Peninsular war.

"Wars and rumors of wars have left little of old Cadiz, the Iberian region sung by Homer. Rather we have flowers, palms, white, fresh streets, and houses neat and clean.

"Cadiz has whitewashed the woes of centuries and left no trace. It 's a regular whited sepulchre!"

"It strikes me," said the Pessimist dryly, "that the proverb about people who live in glass houses must have originated here. Look at those mansions on the right. They have three tiers of balconies inclosed in glass, and look like glass houses."

"The houses are high and straight and there are no *patios*. It does n't seem like Spain," I answered, "but we 've only a little to see before we hurry on to 'fair Sevilla,' where one may find Spain in its element, if what the guide-books say is true."

The first thing we went to see in Cadiz was the old cathedral, called the Palladian. It was built in the thirteenth century and handsome chapels were added in the fifteenth and sixteenth, but it was nearly all destroyed by fire when Lord Essex sacked the city in the reign of Queen Elizabeth. The rebuilding was not a success from an architectural point of view, for the edifice is low, and as an English writer expresses it, "in the Moresque south it screams like a harsh note of music."

From the dreary old church the Pessimist and I wandered to the convent, Los Capuchinos. Over the high altar of the little church is Murillo's last painting. We passed before it in silence. The light was dim, yet a shaft of sunshine lighted up the faces in the wonderful painting, "The Mystic Marriage of St. Catherine."

"There she kneels, Pessimist," I said, "in her robes of velvet and gold, for Catherine was nobly born and of an old Sienna family. The sword at her feet signifies the way she died, for she was beheaded, and on her face is the earnest purpose of her noble soul to lead the life of purity and zeal for our Lord, of which the ring that He extends is the symbol. Murillo must have loved this picture, for he has put much of his very best work into it."

"What are the cherubs to represent?" asked the Pessimist.

"One has the martyr's crown, the other the celestial wreath. Poor Murillo! How sad for him to lose himself in his work so completely that he stepped backward, fell from the scaffolding, and died soon afterwards, leaving this to Meneses Osorio to finish."

"Such is life," said the Pessimist, gloomily. "Where is the St. Francis?"

"There at that side altar. Is not the coloring of the head perfect? The hands seem to stand out, and the expression of St. Francis as he receives the stigmata is marvelous. What a wonderful study the mind and heart of a painter must be! It always seems hard to believe that men who could paint such perfect things, with such deep religious sentiment in every stroke of the brush, could be anything but saints themselves."

"Well, I do n't think they were saints, judging from Raphael and his posing La Fornarina for so many Madonnas. There was n't much religious sentiment in that. Are we going to stay here all day?" asked the Pessimist.

"No, certainly not. We 're going to climb to the very top of the Torre de la Vizia and have the view of the city, and we shall need all our breath for it, so a truce to conversation."

We were repaid for the climb and for holding our tongues so long too, for the view we had was superb and novel. Not content with whitewashing streets and walls and houses, regarding a pencil scratch as an abomination and a fly-speck as a monstrosity, it seemed as if the people of Cadiz even whitewashed their roofs.

It is impossible to imagine anything more curious than the white town lying on the bosom of the sea and from above looking just the same as from below. The houses are flat on top, and the roofs covered with terraces and gardens surrounded with whitewashed walls, and these in turn surmounted by white cupolas or sentry boxes. At the time of a great eclipse of the sun, De Amicis says, the population of the whole city betook itself to the roof to watch the phenomenon, and the white city was turned into a revolving kaleidoscope of color with waving fans and gay shawls and gowns brightening up the whiteness.

The Pessimist did not like Cadiz. She sang a little tune, plaintive and sad, the words of which consisted largely of references to "glare" and wonders which route we were to take in leaving. However, I turned a deaf ear, for while I was forced to admit the glare I meant to see all there was to be seen, if possible.

"We are going now," I said firmly, "to see the Casa de Misericordia."

There is nothing which impresses the Pessimist more, when she is obstreperous, than to hear very large words in a language which she does not understand.

"The Casa de Misericordia," I went on glibly, "is the hospital and poor-house, and it holds one thousand persons. There it is, with that fine marble portico. There are no finer hospitals in the world than here at Cadiz. Nearly all are in charge of the sisters, and some of the heroism of these simple souls in times of pestilence has been marvelous."

"Humph!" sniffed the Pessimist, "You may poke into all the pestilential places and admire all the fine pestilential deeds you want to, but as for me, I am perfectly contented with something more pleasing. I 'm going to find a garden and wait there for you."

"Oh, very well! There is the Paseo de las Delicias, and behind it is the Jardin Botanico. We will go there," I said, for when the Pessimist does rebel against my authority, there's nothing for me to do but yield. So we went to the famous garden and saw the queer plants. Here was the Dragon Tree of India (*Dracæna Draco*) five hundred years old, its limbs twisted and gnarled into fantastic shapes like some uncanny demoniacal creature, and there was a phalanx of *cacti* and tropical plants.

The Pessimist liked the garden and relented a little, but she would not let me hunt up the house of José de Cadahalso, a poet, born in Cadiz, in 1741, and killed at Gibraltar, in 1782, and she utterly scorned the idea of the picture gallery, and Gallio-like, she "cared for none of those things." Although I did not like giving up, I confess that I preferred rambling down to the old fish-market, where the gay fisherman flourished around with a dagger in his glaring waist-band, his head tied up in a gaudy cotton cloth.

Altogether Cadiz is a queer little city and there are some pleasant sights, but a day is long enough to stay there. Its great beauty lies in its situation, as it seems to float like Venice, between sea and sky; and in the memories of ancient times with which it throngs the mind.

There are several routes to Seville, and my friend and I had a vigorous discussion as to which one we should follow.

"Shall we go by Jerez, where the fine sherry comes from?" I asked. "That is the frontier keep of Andalucia, and so was called Jerez de la Frontera by Alfonso the Learned."

"What is there to see at Jerez?" asked the Pessimist, intent as ever upon getting the worth of her money."

"I don't know," I said vaguely, searching my cranium for guide-book lore. "We might run up to Utrera where the old Moorish system of irrigating still exists. The whole country there is a luxuriant wilderness of tropical vegetation, and explains why wise old Peter the Cruel wanted to ally himself to Mussulmans and Jews, since they understood irrigating the country.

Catherine of Aragon brought Jerez sherry to England when she married Prince Arthur, brother of Henry VIII. The sherry is delicious, and there are the finest wine-cellars in the world—regular palaces of Bacchus, some of them containing fifteen thousand barrels.

The whole process, from pressing the grape to bottling for exportation, may be seen in these *bodegas*.

"*Bodegas!*" said the Pessimist, "I call them breweries, and I can see breweries at home."

"Then we 'll take the other route and go to Seville by the Guadalquivir. The boats are good, passage lasts only eight hours and costs three dollars," I replied.

To this my friend agreed, and we started in the morning, sailing off from the white town, which looked unspeakably lovely in the early morning sunlight.

When the sun was well up, we sat on deck enjoying the gentle motion, for the sea was tranquillity itself; and passing close by the mouth of the Guadalete we saw fertile fields and valleys and the river flowing peacefully to the sea. Once it ran red with blood, for it was near here that the great battle was fought that gave the Moslems their hold on Spain.

" Whilome upon his banks did legions throng
Of Moor and knight in mailed splendors drest,
Here ceased the swift their race, here sunk the strong;
The Paynim turban and the Christian crest,
Mixed on the bleeding stream, by floating hosts op-
    pressed."

All the trouble came from a woman, for Don Roderick saw Florinda the Beautiful, and stole her away from her father Count Julian. In revenge the latter went over to the Moslems, and came with Tarik the One-Eyed, and Muza-ben-Nozier, a Berber sheik, to invade Andalucia and despoil the Goths. On the great battlefield Taric cried to his soldiers, "Ye are conquerors of Africa, O followers of Mohammed; back ye cannot go! The sea lies at your backs; the waves of your enemies —Christian dogs—are lashing your faces. Follow me," and he led them valiantly against the Gothic host. Two days the warfare endured, and when the sun shone on the third, it rose over a bloody field, with stained banners and heaps of slain, and Roderick the Goth, his kingly head laid low in the dust, had felt the vengeance of Count Julian. "All the Goth's silks and riches did not prevent his being cut off," says Sancho Panza, and thus died Roderigo, last of the Gothic kings of Spain.

Sailing along at the rate of ten miles an hour, we passed Rota, famous for its Tintilla wine, and Bonanza, a Frenchy port, making one wonder about the origin of the modern slang, "striking a bonanza." The river winds in and out, and half way between Cadiz and Seville branches off so as to form two islands, Isla Major, forty kilometers long and Isla Minor, seventeen kilometers.

The water was remarkably limpid, the reflections wonderfully distinct. In the distance were hills crowned with cypress trees and clothed in flowers, peasants in gay costumes, fields of grain and a luxuriant vegetation.

As the setting sun gilded the river into glory and lighted up the sky with rainbow hues, a sudden turn of the boat gave us our first glimpse of Seville, and we almost held our breaths.

There was a huge, dark pile which we recognized as the cathedral, built on the site of an old temple of Venus, once a Gothic church, then a mosque, and after many vicissitudes of fire and sack, made a Christian cathedral by St. Ferdinand.

Little of this remains, save the Giralda, and the present edifice dates from 1402.

It is a magnificent specimen of the style of the best Gothic period of Spain, and looms up above everything in a grandeur which made me exclaim to the Pessimist: "The cathedral of Seville! oh, we must see more of it! Think of all the things which have happened here,—the pageants of Holy Week and all the splendid celebrations of Ferdinand and Isabella. There is the Giralda, all that is left of the mosque of Abu Jusuf Jacub, whence the Muezzin's call to prayer sounded over Moorish Sevilla. I can even see '*la girardilla*,' the bronze figure of faith, on the top."

"What is that, close by the water's edge?" asked my friend, who, in the marvelous beauty of the scene, forgot even her pessimism.

"La torre del Oro," or golden tower. It was named from its peculiar orange coloring; and here Columbus' treasures were kept when he brought them from the New World. Oh, is it not perfect? See those gypsies and muleteers! Do you remember in Childe Harold?—

> " How carols now the lusty muleteer!
>   Of love, romance, devotion, is his lay,
>   As whilome he was wont the leagues to cheer,
>   His quick bells wildly jingling on the way,
>   And as he speeds he chants *Viva el Rey!*"

Proud Sevilla triumphs unsubdued, Seville at last! Seville the fair, the city of fans and guitars and dances and gayety and love and romance and song, Seville the Marvel!

"LA MARAVILLA."

UIEN no ha vista Sevilla No ha vista maravilla," I quoted to my friend the morning after our arrival in Seville. "We are to see a marvel, Pessimist. Behold! The first glimpses! Our first day in Seville!" I said dramatically, throwing open our closed lattice, expecting to gaze forth upon a scene of wonder and delight. Alas! nothing was to be seen save the ghosts of some houses opposite peering at us vaguely through heavy mist, and as I searched the sky for some signs of fair weather, down came a quick patter of rain, and I withdrew hastily.

"It 's going to rain every minute of the time we 're here in your Marvel," said my companion, in a thoroughly pessimistic mood. "I am not going to get up or go anywhere today," and she turned over and went to sleep. I dressed dejectedly, for how could I go about alone and I knew nothing would move the Pessimist.

However, fortune favors the brave. At breakfast I made the acquaintance of an English curate, with a reliable cough, and Mrs. Curate spending the winter in Seville, and delighted to show their favorite haunts to a stranger. We started out with galoshes and umbrellas and mackintoshes, and attacked the picture gallery first and foremost. I love fine pictures, and I particularly dote on Murillo. There is something so appalling about a list of famous pictures in a guide-book that I always try to see them first, leaving the rest of the city till later. After one has been to the gallery and walked through its miles of madonnas and saints, frying or broiling as the case may be, one knows exactly what one wishes to go back to see.

The picture gallery is on the Calle de las Armas, close to the Puerta Real, and was formerly the Convent de la Merced, founded by St. Ferdinand, in 1249, and here one fairly feasts upon Murillos, Zubarans, Valdes, and many others. The finest Murillos, those to which I returned time and again, never wearying of their perfection of coloring and expression, were the "St. Thomas of Villanueva giving Alms," the "Immaculate Conception," "St. Anthony of Padua," and the "St. Felix of Cantalicio." Of the first of these, Sir Edwin Head, a great English critic, has said, "In the saint's face and figure there is a wonderful union of dignity and humility, whilst the beggars in the front are admirable for truth and expression, as for instance, the boy on the left showing to his mother the money he had received."

The coloring is warm and rich, and the whole picture is in Murillo's best style, and many think there is only one of his superior to it, the "St. Elizabeth," in the Madrid gallery.

The "Immaculate Conception," "*De la luna*," as it is called, is one of his largest and finest, similar to the one in the cathedral and the one at the Louvre in Paris.

But the "St. Anthony" is the one which appealed to me the most, and I looked upon it in rapt awe. How the pure saint loved our Lord! It shows in every line of his figure, and the dignity and sweetness of the child-God are indeed a triumph of art.

"This picture," I said to myself, "requires unlimited study;" and during my stay in Seville, scarcely a day passed in which I did not find in it new beauties.

After Murillo every one seems tame, and yet when I saw Zubaran's "St. Thomas Aquinas," I almost held my breath; for this great master has much of the coloring of Titian, the drawing of Corregio and the power of Raphael. Carried away by Soult, the "St. Thomas" was recovered by Wellington after Waterloo, and returned to Spain, and this picture alone has been said to place the artist second only to Murillo. St. Thomas is represented with the four doctors of the church, Ambrose, Augustin, Jerome and Gregory. Above in the clouds are Christ and the Blessed Virgin with Saints Paul and Dominic, while Charles the Fifth and Archbishop Deza (for whom the painting was done, in 1625), kneel below.

"It was an odd way the painters had of putting in their patrons along with saints and angels, and no doubt it largely contributed toward getting them other orders," said my English friends, as they bore me away in triumph to the river-side, telling me charming stories of the streets through which we passed.

"There, in that house close to the San Leandro lived Don Juan Tenorio," said the coughing curate. "He was the Don Giovanni of Mozart, and Byron's Don Juan. Do n't you recall?—

> ' In Seville was he born,—a pleasant city,
>   Famous for oranges and women,—he
> Who has not seen it will be much to pity;'
>   So says the proverb, and I quite agree.

> Of all the Spanish towns none is more pretty;
>   Cadiz perhaps, but that you soon may see.
> Don Juan's parents lived beside the river,
>   A noble stream and called the Guadalquivir.'

"This youth, so wicked as to have his name become a synonym for vice, was a Sevillian of noble family, living in the 14th century. He had adventures enough to fill volumes; and the story of his doings was formulated, in 1625, by Gabriel Tellez, and translated into several languages. Upon this are founded Moliere's "Festin de Pierre," Shadwell's "The Libertine," Dumas' "Don Juan de Mañara," and a famous play by Señor Zorilla, late poet-laureate of Spain."

"So he lived here, gay Don Juan!" I said, looking at the small house with its iron-barred attic windows and Saracenic arches. It was so quiet in the lonely street that I found it difficult to picture Zerlina and Leporello and Doña Elvira frisking about there. Legends say that Don Juan died repentant, and I chose to believe that Satan did not get him upon his excursion into the tomb where the gay, reckless fellow went after the body of his sweetheart, Doña Ines. Sevillians say that he was warned·by a vision of himself in an open grave, and made up with Doña Elvira, his unpleasant but very holy wife, and died in the odor of sanctity."

"You must not confuse him with the Señor Manara who founded the great hospital," said the curate.

"He was quite a different person and lived many years later. Here is 'La Caridad' which he founded. See the inscription over the door:

> " 'Santa Caridad,
> " 'Domus Pauperum,
> " 'Scala Cœli.'

"You must go in, for there are fine Murillos here."

We entered, and the porter led us with the quiet and somewhat stately courtesy one finds everywhere in Spain, through double *patios*, separated by graceful columns. These *patios*, peculiar to Spain, are inner courts with arches and pillars, fountains and beautiful flowers and palms, and a glory of blue sky overhead.

"Don Miguel de Mañara lies buried in the chapel," said my guide. A Sister of Mercy came forward and unlocking a door led us into the chapel, impressive and dark. At the left of the altar was the picture of the miracle of loaves and fishes, one of Murillo's best, and opposite "La Sed" (The Thirst), or "Moses Striking the Rock." What struck me most about the latter, marvelous in coloring and tone, were the types of the characters—men, women, boys, dogs, such as one may see at any moment in the Triana, or suburb of Seville to-day.

The landscape is Spanish, unspeakably rich in tone, and the Moses himself is dignity personified. Murillo and Don Miguel were warm friends, and to the latter is due the preservation of these superb paintings. This and the humility of Don Miguel's epitaph designed by himself makes one have a *tendresse* for this gay, wicked, artistic, repentant "Don Juan," buried beneath the slab of the high altar, on which one reads, "Here lies the greatest sinner that ever lived, Don Miguel de Mañara."

"Near by, just beyond la Plaza de Santo Thomas is the shop where lived the Barber of Seville," said my cicerone. "We must see that and then Murillo's house, No. 7 Plaza de Alfaro, in the Juderio, where the great master died, in 1682," but I cried for mercy.

"No more, I beg. Let me go home and eat luncheon and *make* my friend come with me later on. It is a shame for her to miss it all; and then, my brain cannot hold so much. Is all Seville so full of interest?"

"Every street and nearly every house," he answered, "has some story to it. Do you know the reason one street is called the 'Calle de la Cabeza del Rey Don Pedro,' and another one 'Calle de Candilejo?'"

"Oh, dear me, no; I do n't know what it means even," I cried.

"Peter the Cruel," said my obliging companion, "was well-named, and delighted in nothing so much as catching his servants or officers in some misdemeanor, whereupon he made pin-cushions of them or had them bisected as ornaments for various city gates, or lay awake at night devising some other form of punishment equally pleasing.

"Whether it was that he liked seeing people killed or because he feared the population would decrease too rapidly to fight his battles for him, I do not know, but at any rate Don Pedro forbade duelling, upon pain of death to the survivor.

"Shortly after the edict, however, as the king was wandering in disguise through the streets one dark night, he came upon a cavalier with whom he had long wished to fight, and without a further thought Don Pedro whipped out his sword and promptly killed his adversary. Pushing up his mask, he wiped his weapon, and then remembered that his own edict had sentenced himself to death. Glancing hastily around and seeing that he was still unobserved, he laughed suddenly, as it flashed into his mind what a fine chance he had to make it unpleasant for the Alcalde or Mayor. Then he took his evil laugh back to the Alcazar rejoicing.

"Next day, sending for the Alcalde he demanded, sternly: 'Where is the man who killed the cavalier on the Plaza near the Casa de Pilatos? If he be not found in three days, I shall hang you in his place,' and the poor Alcalde, trembling in every limb, withdrew to search Seville, in despair for the murderer.

"Two days passed and he gave himself up for lost, when his sweetheart, a clever girl and as beautiful as are all Sevillianas, brought to him an old woman who alleged that she knew the murderer.

"'I heard the noise of the weapons, Señor Alcalde,' she said, 'and as my trade is to lay out the dead, I knew I should be needed for one of the duellists; so I raised my window, and holding the candle, I plainly saw the king as he put up his mask. Moreover, I heard him laugh, and no one else in all Seville has such a laugh. I closed my lattice as quickly as I might, I tell you,' and the old woman wagged her head. Then was the Alcalde much rejoiced, and next day in the Plaza de San Francisco, the Alcalde hung the king in effigy, and justice was satisfied.

"To this day the street where the duel was fought is called the street of the Bust of the King Don Pedro, because he placed his bust there to commemorate the event, and the alley from which the old woman peeped is called the Street of the Candle."

"Oh! how charming to have a reason for the name of everything," I exclaimed. "What is happening here?" for a file of people were going into a garden gate.

"A funeral, or rather there is to be one, and the corpse is now on view. Do n't look so shocked. It 's the custom. The furniture of the room where a person dies is all taken to the *patio*, partly to prevent infection and partly to avoid recalling the loss. The body is laid out in the principal room, and all may go and stare. It—the poor body—has to endure it, and is dressed as finely as possible even to new shoes. These are sold before the burial, and one of the worst things to say to a poor person in Seville is, 'You wear dead men's shoes.' The poor often expose their children's bodies openly in the streets, so that some one with money will buy them coffins; otherwise they must put them into the ground with only shrouds."

"Ugh!" I exclaimed, "That's not a tale for gay Seville. It seems as if there must be no ugly doings in so fair a city. Tell me something else."

"You know of the martyrs, Rufina and Justina, two Christian girls, sellers of earthen jars, when the cathedral was a Roman temple. They refused to worship the goddess Venus, and were put to death near the Puerta del Sol, after the fiercest lions had refused to devour them. Murillo has made them more famous by his fine painting of them." But he had no time to say more, for we had reached the hotel and I rushed up to the sleeper and awakened her noisily.

"Oh, what you have missed!" I exclaimed. "The sun has come out, and everything is glorious. Do get up and come and see things!"

The Pessimist sat up in bed, rubbed her eyes, then remarked calmly:

"I do n't see what I 've missed. I 've had a good nap, am quite rested, and ready to have you tell me all about everything. You always want to see things a dozen times, and it wont hurt you to go back again to all those places with me. You 've only gotten your feet wet and tired yourself out," she added, provokingly.

"My feet are n't wet and I 'm not tired," I exclaimed, glancing guiltily at the mud which covered my overshoes and then in the mirror at my disheveled locks. "At any rate, I saw them first," I added, in child-like spleen.

"He laughs best who laughs last," said the Pessimist. Somehow, now and then, the Pessimist and I seem to change places.

CHAPTER V

SEVILLE, THE FAIR.

IRST the cathedral!" I said, as we emerged from our charming hotel, the Madrid, to begin our sight-seeing.

"Tell me about it," said my friend in the calmly authoritative manner with which she turns me into a guide-book.

"You know when it was made, but perhaps you 've forgotten that when Saint Ferdinand had captured Seville the chapter said, 'We will build such a church that people will call us mad.' And they built it and called it La Grandeza. Spanish-Gothic in its exquisite architecture, it is massive and grand without, but the interior beggars description." As I spoke we entered the grand portal, and I went on softly:

"See the clustering columns, airy pillars, colossal arches, and feel the awesome mystery which makes the heart stand still. Ah! *La*

Grandeza indeed! The pillars were from the old Roman temple of Hercules and the Saracenic mosque, and there are nine entrances vying with each other for beauty, the door of San Miguel being especially noted.

The Portal de los Naranjos is one of the finest specimens of the Mudejar style, with its high horse-shoe arch, built by Alfonso XI. The many chapels, with their simplicity and perfection of detail, make this cathedral one of the finest in the world though it is much to be regretted that the many earthquake shocks have injured the building.''

''Who is buried here?'' asked the Pessimist, pointing to a plain slab let into the floor behind the choir. On it was a Latin inscription and two small caravels were carved, one on either side.

''Fernando Colon, son of Columbus,'' I answered. ''He died in Seville in 1586, and the inscription says, 'Of what avails it that I have bathed the entire universe with my sweat, that I have thrice passed through the New World discovered by my father, that I have adorned the banks of the gentle Beti and preferred my simple taste to riches, that I might again draw around thee the divinities of the Castalian spring and offer thee the treasures already gathered by Ptolemy, if thou, in passing this stone in silence, returnest no salute to my father and givest no thought to me?"

"What does it mean?" asked my friend.

"Ferdinand Columbus sailed everywhere, and with infinite pains gathered a library of most valuable books, which he willed to the cathedral, and which library is called La Columbiana. '*À Castilla y à Leon nuevo mundo dio Colon,*' the slab says. In the library are Columbus' note-books in his own handwriting and all the details of the voyage. Just think, if it had n't been for him you and I might have been Spaniards or French or even Danes!" I exclaimed enthusiastically.

"You might have been anything you like, even a Hottentot, but I could n't have been anything but an American," said the Pessimist, sternly.

"I do n't see how you 'd have managed it if America had n't been discovered," I returned, as we went into the chapel Royal to see St. Ferdinand's tomb.

"His was not the age of great kingly virtue, and his character stands out all the more in brave relief against the vices of his day, for he was saint as well as king, and showed his Christianity in more ways than by conquering infidels.

"There he lies, in his crystal coffin, his sword in his hand, that sword which was never raised in unrighteous warfare, and from the handle of which Peter the Cruel, took all the precious gems, lest, as he said, 'the hand of the ungodly might take them.' Oh, godly Pedro!"

"We have n't seen the pictures yet," said the Pessimist. "Where are the famous ones?"

"Here in the sacristy major is the 'Descent from the Cross' by Pedro Campana. It is an awfully grand thing. Murillo used to stand here and gaze, the tears running down his face, saying, 'I am waiting until those holy men have taken down our Lord.' In the chapter-house, just there where the shaft of purple light from that window strikes the column, is the 'Conception,' not so fine as the one in the museum or that in Paris.

"The gem is in the Baptistery,—the St. Anthony. This is the one from which the figure was cut, stolen and carried to New York in 1874, but it was finally recovered and faultlessly replaced. It was of this picture that Antonio Castello, nephew of the great Castello (Murillo's master), said, "It is all over with Castello. Is it possible that Murillo, my uncle's imitator, can be the author of that grace and beauty of coloring?"

"He looks as if he did n't have enough to eat and would take cold in his bald spot," said the Pessimist.

"You are incorrigible." I answered, "I sha' n't take you to see the 'Guardian Angel,' though it 's one of the most exquisite of all Murillo's. We will go to the Alcazar, through the Court of Oranges, all that is left of the old mosque.

"Are not the orange-trees beautiful? There is the Giralda again. Oh! how I wish Geber, who built it, had spent all his life in making such airy, graceful, perfect things, instead of inventing Algebra with which to torment unhappy school girls. I never saw a more perfect rose color than the walls of the Giralda. There, that bare, square-looking façade is the Alcazar."

"I can 't say much for it then," said the Pessimist, grimly. "Do you mean to say *that* is the palace you 've been raving over?"

"Wait, wait, Pessimist!" I said, as we entered the gate and the matchless palace was reached.

Even the Pessimist was silenced at the entrancing vision of Moorish work.

"Tell me about it," she commanded, and delighted, I began:

"It was the House of Cæsar, and then an old Moorish fortress, and is so preserved as to give a perfect idea of the palaces of the Arabian Nights. Long before the Alhambra was finished at Granada, the Toledan architect,

Jalubi, built the Alcazar, but it was Don Pedro el Cruel who rebuilt and beautified it.

"Portals and arches and door-ways and floors and courts, tiles and *patios*, all are Moorish and blazoned like gems in a golden crown.

"Memories throng each court, and spectres crowd from every nook and crevice, each with a tale of love or woe.

"Here in this open court sat Peter the Cruel, posing as El Rey Justiciero—the Dispenser of Justice. His was justice of a rough and ready sort, to suit his own will.

"From that quaint patio so fragrantly clothed in flowers, I see step an array of maidens, two hundred in all, and as their snowy mantles are lifted and their eyes gleam forth, I see the Moorish king smile, well-pleased.

"This is the Patio de los Doncellos, and those maidens are Andalucian beauties made to pass before the Saracen ruler that he may choose fifty rich and fifty poor, of all the fairest, for his harem. Were they glad or sorry to be left—those Andalucian girls? Is vanity stronger than love of country in the feminine breast of Spain?

"From behind that lace-like marble screen peers a face; Venus or Juno or Undine or all together were not more fair. Such glorious eyes, dark as night, such luxuriant hair, lips proud and sensuous, languorous grace, and witching smile!

"Who is she, Queen or Princess? Neither, unless both by right of royal beauty, for this is Maria de Padilla, mistress—some say wife—of Peter the Cruel. No wonder Pedro forgot even his pet delight of cruelty for her.

"For her he built these rooms and fountains. This water, pearly white and flowing between orange and citron-trees, was where la Padilla bathed, and the courtiers drank the water to show their gallantry.

"What is there left of her now—this woman so fair, and yet who loved her cruel lord so well and tried to wield a gentler sway over him? Nothing but dust and a stately tomb within the cathedral. Not even an unstained memory. Alas, poor Maria!

"Here is yet again a memory of the Alcazar, and on this dark night no Moorish beauties peered into the Hall of Ambassadors. Don Fadrique, brother of Pedro, was sent for in brotherly friendship to come to a tournament at Seville.

" 'We cannot joust without your knightly arms, my good brother,' wrote *el Cruel*, and trusting Don Fadrique came. Alas! he found no welcome, no gay and joyous festival, only a darkened hall, and then he felt a sudden onslaught.

"He tried to grope his way to the *patio*. The assailants closed upon him. His good sword laid them low, as he stood with his back against a carved pillar. Then his sword hand caught—perhaps entangled in his badge as Grand Master of Santiago, perhaps hampered in his *caballero's* cloak, and he fell, and there his blood stains the tesselated pavement to this very day, and there the king spurned the body with his foot.

"Don Pedro, you have much to answer for, yet naught more dastardly than this foul and treacherous murder.

"Surely this is the fairest *patio* in all sunny Spain, here with the arabesques and lace traceries and latticed casements with close *jalousies* (or jealousy-s) from which the fair Padilla looked down upon her lord. No such deeds should have been done *here*. There should have been naught but love and chivalry.

"Yet, once more, I see Don Pedro, with his boyish, smiling face, too fair to belong to so vile a heart. Once again he violates the laws of chivalric hospitality.

"This stately figure in scarlet trousers and silken vestments, with the calm tranquillity of the Orient in his liquid eyes, is Laban Bermejo, the Red King of Granada. In his orange turban he wore many priceless gems— the greatest a Saracenic Kohinoor or Balax, a priceless ruby, as red as his life's blood, and with his very blood he paid for his visit of friendly homage to the king. Pedro saw and coveted the jewel, slew Laban, and stole his gem.

"After Maria de Padilla had decked her regal brow with it Don Pedro gave it to the Black Prince at the battle of Navarreta, and until this day it shines in the regalia of England."

"Let us go somewhere else," said the Pessimist at last. "Ugh! you make me shudder," and she urged me forth, into the wonderful gardens, looking over her shoulder as if expecting to see a ghostly figure stealing behind her.

Sunshine of the tropics; huge banana-trees waving their rough, green leaves like the sails of Don Quixote's windmills; palms in a fine frenzy; stately cypress-trees sternly pointing aloft; cedars fragrant with Eastern perfumes of Lebanon or Nazareth; box-bordered walks and beds; a tangle of jasmine, sweeter than odors of Araby the blest, and overhead a sky of matchless blue. This is the vision which the memory of the Alcazar gardens brings to one's mind. The Giralda in the distance towers over the town, the stern profile of the cathedral peers over the tops of the walls and trees, and the scene has such a sweet tranquillity, it seems scarcely possible that the city lies without, teeming with life and activity.

"What has happened here?" said my friend, as she sat down leisurely on a bench where a fountain splashed coolly in the shade.

"There, in that corner where it is so sunshiny and bright, is the labyrinth of Charles V. I can see his strong face which Titian painted in such wonderful color, with the rugged features, and the prominent under lip—a plain face, yet he was every inch a king. Down that path, he stepped. There glistened upon his finger the single ring he always wore, the one given to him by Isabella, his wife.

"I can see the purple of his velvet cape drawn close about his frail form; for he was always chilly, this poor, gouty king. There he sought his gardener and there they consulted about the famous labyrinth—how the statue should be in the center and the plan of the maze engraven on the floor of the pavilion, done in finest bronze. 'Here in this Alcazar where I have been so happy, I wish to leave my mark when I am gone,' murmured Charles; and here it is to remind us of the great emperor, when he is moldering to dust in his dark sarcophagus in the Pantheon at the Escorial.

"A pleasant memory is this of the mighty king, crowned with the title, ' Emperor of the Romans ' by the Holy Father himself; ruler of Austria through his father the archduke; ruler of Spain by virtue of his mother, poor mad queen Juana, and liberator of twenty-two thousand Christian slaves by his own prowess at arms.

"Near by is the bath of his poor mother, queen though she was, yet unable to reign on the one throne she coveted, the heart of the man she loved, Philippe le Bel, Duke of Burgundy.

" I see the mad queen now, her eyes flashing fire at her unfortunate maid of honor, whose only crime was that Duke Philip had admired her luxuriant hair.

" ' Cut it off!' shrieks the queen.   ' Cut off her hair!   Not a word, minions, be thankful it is not her head.'

" Poor, mad Juana!   Ah! what avails it to be a queen and wealthy and fair, too, in your wild dark way, since you may not have the love you crave so sorely?

" Then, here, creeping down that path, holding in his slender hands five oranges, I see our old acquaintance, Don Pedro, him of the bust and the candle story.

" He is smiling, well-pleased, and well we know that smile bodes no good for those within his thoughts. How his lips curl back from his strong white teeth, and how like a fox he looks!

" How carefully he cuts the oranges in halves and floats them, the flat side down, upon the limpid water of the fountain! How pleased he looks that the reflection is perfect! He calls the guard and they bring in four judges, trembling in every limb.

" 'How many oranges are there?' says Don Pedro, smiling in their affrighted faces.

" 'May it please your most gracious majesty. There are ten,' they stammered.

" 'It does *not* please my majesty to have four fools as judges,' he screamed. 'Liars, knaves! There are five!' as he flung the oranges in their faces.

" 'Off with their heads!' his oft repeated cry, and there at that cornice the heads hung for days and weeks.''

" Ah!'' sighed the Pessimist. ''It makes one feel that nothing pays. Wealth and triumph and fame, all are buried in the grave, and all is over at last.''

"Oh, no, Pessimist!' I exclaimed, ''The best of all is left. See these gardens. All who made them are long since dust, yet the flowers are fair and sweet these hundred years. And as to a good name, only think of being handed down to posterity with such a reputation as Don Pedro el Cruel. It 's worth being good, if only to prevent that.''

'' 'The evil that men do lives after them, the good is oft interred with their bones,' '' quoted the Pessimist dismally.

''Oft, but not always. Who would n't rather have been St. Ferdinand than Don Pedro? Would you rather be remembered as Maria de Padilla with all her fame and grandeur, or as the pure, beautiful, ill-fated Donna Urraca Osorio, whom Pedro had burned to death? She was so spotlessly pure and modest that her little maid (when she saw the flames fan aside her mistress' robes at the stake), rushed in to cover her form from the gaze of the idle crowd, and died with her.''

''Only one more memory of the Alcazar, and this shows truly the sternness of retributive justice. Do you see, in your mind's eye, Horatio, that tall figure—in his face so much of stern valor, dignity and pride, such intensity of will?

'' 'Who are you?' demands Charles V., as the courtier tries to press through the crowd to obtain audience of the king.

'' 'Hernando Cortez, sire. A man who has given your majesty more kingdoms than your father had towns,' was the reply of the haughty old Don.

''Charles turned from him in stern displeasure, poisoned against him by slanderous tongues, and Cortez's great heart broke at his king's ingratitude. Silently he went home, to die seven years later, still unforgiven and unhonored. Did the screams of one hundred thousand slaughtered Mexicans rend his ears, and the innocent faces of the vestals of the Mexican Sun-God appear before him?

"Did he hear the dying words of Montezuma as he lay upon the bed of coals—'Am I reposing upon a bed of roses?'

"Ah! Cortez—lonely old man—was *your* death-bed one of roses?"

"I must say you have a collection of the most grewsome tales I ever heard," said the Pessimist. "I did n't know Cortez was here."

"He died at Castileja de la Cuesta, just outside Seville, but he and Pizarro and Columbus all sailed from here down the Guadalquivir," I answered. "As for the grewsomeness of it, those were grewsome times. The history of Seville would fill volumes.

"Cæsar conquered it 45 B.C., and Roman relics are constantly being found. Vandals and Goths lived here; the Moors reigned with the noted Umeyyah family, and under them were established the silk factories, and the greatest prosperity existed. St. Ferdinand conquered it in 1248, and the Moors, and later the Jews, were sent away to Africa.

Such a mistake it was, for they were its most thrifty citizens. It was an awful blow to them, too. In the cathedral are some of the keys they gave up to the king, but that of the Puerta del Sol has never been found, for the Moors were so sure of returning that they took it away with them.

"The African Jews still call themselves 'descendants of the catastrophe of Castile,' and their important Hebrew documents are signed, '*Hachol Beminahry Castilla*' (according to the usage of Castile).

"Alfonso the Wise gave lands to the nobles and this was called '*El Repartimiento*,' and Seville was always faithful to him; so he granted them the motto, '*No 8 Do*'—(It has never deserted me)—and this, with the three silk skeins, is their badge to this day.

"Now let us go to the house of Pilate. It belongs to the Duke of Medina-Celi, was made by Pedro Enrique and finished in an exact copy of Pilate's house at Jerusalem by Don Fadrique, Marquis of Tarifa, on his return from a visit to the Holy Land. It was a regular salon for *literati* in the time of the Duke of Alcala, who was the Mecænas of Spain and rivaled the Colonna in Italy.

"Cervantes, Gongora and Rioja were all frequenters, and also Pacheco, who wrote the lives of the artists.

"Here it is. It's rather dingy on the exterior, but that's a nice motto for a house, '*Nisi Dominus ædificaverit domum in vanum laboraverunt qui ædificant eam.*' What is that Spanish motto? There are the three crosses of Jerusalem, the Medina Celi arms and '*en 4 Agosto in 1519 entro in Hierusalem.*' He must have been a pious old soul. Come, let us go in," and we entered the hall, tiled in various colors, with busts of the Roman emperors gleaming from niches, and a magnificent Minerva in one corner of the *patio*.

"There is the *Credo* engraved on the door, more piety, and there's a bust of Pallas and one of Venus. Strange mixture, isn't it, Pessimist?"

"I should say so," she said. "Speaking of piety, where was the Inquisition held?"

"It was first established in the Moorish castle in Triana, but the *Quemadero*, or burning place was on the plain outside the town.

"It had to be in a large place, because the Spaniards love a spectacle, cruel or otherwise, and always flock to an execution.

"There never was in all the world such a political mesh as the Inquisition.

"Political intriguers cloaked and hooded under the garb of religion their private spite and revenge, proclaiming to the world that they were actuated by motives of religion."

"Do n't preach," said the Pessimist. "Let us go and see something pleasant."

"I think, my dear Pessimist," I replied, "that I have found a sure cure for your lugubriousness. After this, when you 're gloomy I shall tell you all the weird tales I know, and see if you do n't re-act as you have done to-day."

CHAPTER VI.

SPANISH DANCES.

E have n't seen a single Spanish dance and we 've been in Seville a week," grumbled the Pessimist.

"We are going to see them this very day, for the famous boys' dance takes place in the cathedral. It is held only two or three times a year, and we are fortunate to be here at Easter to see it. Come, we must hurry off at once or we 'll not be in time," and the Pessimist and I wended our way toward *La Grandeza*, reaching its massive portals as the peasants, in mantillas and sombre dresses (for they always wear plain clothes to church), were returning from an early mass.

How still it was within this grand temple. The throng of people was quiet and the service not yet begun, and as we sat waiting, amidst nobles and peasants, old Don and plainest cigarette-maker, the beauty and grandeur of the scene was past telling.

93

"All sorts and conditions of men, women, and children, all nations and races in seeming harmony; surely this is the millennium," I whispered.

"I hope the millennium won't be as chilly as this," said the Pessimist, shivering. "What are those things on the altar?"

"The famous relics, St. Ferdinand's cup, King Roderick's cross and the keys of Seville, surrendered to St. Ferdinand. One says, 'May Allah render eternal the rule of Islam in this city!' The other was given by the Jews, and says, 'The King of kings will open; the King of all the earth will enter.' There come the boys," I whispered, and there began a strain of music so piercing sweet as to take one's breath away. Flutes, hautboys, the grand organ, and violins mingled with boyish, flute-like voices, sweet and clear, and suddenly out of the great darkness appeared a troop of boys.

They formed into lines before the altar and began the dance, *de los seises*, as it is called, and never was there anything more exquisite. The grace of the boyish figures in their plumed hats, silk hose, white satin clothes and mantles of the Blessed Virgin's own blue over their shoulders; the sweetness of their voices, the earnestness of their faces, for they evidently regarded the dance as a solemn religious rite—and the rythmic movement of the minuet they danced, all produced an impression not easily forgotten; and as they disappeared as quietly as they had come, I gave a great sigh of pleasure.

The Pessimist arose and motioned me to come out, and I followed her silently into the Court of the Oranges.

"Is n't it awful?" she said. "Dancing in church!"

"That depends upon how you look at it. I thought it charming. Did n't David dance? The Holy Scriptures say so. Surely the natural thing for a child to do is to dance for joy, and is not Easter the time for rejoicing that our Lord is risen from the tomb? You would have agreed with the old archbishop, two hundred years ago."

"What did he do?" she inquired.

"He objected to the dancing and forbade it. The people rose in wrath at having their customs interfered with. Spaniards are great respecters of antiquity, and 'What our fathers have done is good enough for us,' they say constantly.

"Well, there was a great to do about it, and at last they appealed to the Holy Father. He—being a sensible man, as well as the Pope, promptly replied that he could n't disapprove or approve of what he had never seen. Whereupon a rich merchant of Seville transported the whole company, boys, costumes, and musicians to the Vatican. There the children danced and sang, to the extreme delight of His Holiness, who remarked, 'Our Lord called the little children to Him. Would He make them walk on stilts and wear long faces? Let the boys dance so long as their costumes last.'

"Every one went back to Seville very well satisfied; and as care has been taken to renew first one part of the costume and then another, they have been miraculously preserved, and the dance continues."

"That 's what might be called 'beating the devil around the stump,' " said my friend. "Where did you say Murillo's 'Virgin of the Napkin ' was?"

"In the picture gallery, where we cannot go to-day, but I 'll tell you about it if you like.

"This picture of the Virgin is not one of his best. The Virgin is not the ethereal, shadowy being that he usually paints, but an Andalucian beauty, with a wonderful skin, gypsy face, and rippling hair.

"The baby is a darling, though not Christlike, only a genuine flesh and blood *niño*. Murillo lived then in the Capuchin convent, near the Cordova gate, and was painting one day when a lay brother came in to bring him his dinner.

" 'Ah, *Maestro!*' cried the poor monk, 'What a gift *el buen Dios* has given to you! Could I but have *one* of your Virgins I could die happy.'

" 'Money cannot buy them, but friendship may,' said Murillo. 'Bring me a canvas that I may paint for you.'

" 'Alas! I have not even a *peseta*,' said the Capuchin.

" 'But this will do,' said the painter, taking up his napkin and beginning to paint rapidly. Then glancing out of the window, he exclaimed: " 'Is it she? The *gitana* I loved so long ago?' as he saw a gypsy girl with a child in her arms.

"He painted her portrait and that of the baby upon the rough dinner napkin, and that night an angel came to him in a dream and said, 'Murillo, the picture of the gypsy girl thou usedst to love give thou to the brother, for she belongs not to thee but to another. To keep her portrait is a sin.'

"And when the morning broke he gave the portrait to the monk, who cherished it carefully in the chapel of the monastery."

The Pessimist always receives legends as if she were being forced to believe them, and she gave quite an audible sniff as I related the story; then asked:

"Where did Carmen live?"

"There was no real Carmen, but there are dozens of just such girls over there in the great tobacco factory.   Only think, that huge building cost $1,850,000.

"The cigarette girls are usually very pretty, and we 'll probably see many of them to-morrow night at the dance in the Café Ojeda."

And so we did, for our guide, a most obliging youth, who seemed to speak every known language and several unknown ones, took us down to No. 11 Sierpes, where the national dances are to be seen.

One hears a great deal of the beauty of Spanish women.   I should call it rather fascination. Their features are not perfect, their figures seldom are, but they are always charming.

Of course, it goes without saying that people with such eyes and such lashes must use them.

Their manners, their laughter, their gayety, their languorous or their vivacious grace, all these are charms far beyond the beauties of those who are "faultily faultless, icily regular, splendidly null."

> There ne'er was born a Spanish woman yet,
> But she was born to dance,

and when one adds to these charms, a pair of arched feet, slender and tiny which, "beneath her petticoat, like little mice " twinkle and dance, and an undulating grace of rhythmic movement, then one understands why men and women from the days of Pliny down, have raved over Spanish dancing. Describe it?

Certainly not. One can merely say, "Go to Sevilla and see Señorita Mercedes dance an *Ole*, or with three others a *Cachucha* and then sing a few *coplas* of the *Seguidilla*.

Do not flatter yourself that you will wait until she comes to this country, as Señorita Mercedita, the great Spanish *danseuse* from "*La Follie*" in Paris.

When she does, she will be merely another skirt dancer, tiresome as are they all. She will have gone to Paris, from Seville, and will have learned to kick instead of to glide, to jerk instead of sway, and to wear ballet tarletan instead of *mantilla* and *bolero* jacket.

"What else are we to see in Seville?" asked the Pessimist, as we strolled about the streets toward the end of our stay.

"We are going now to the old Cartuja convent, which is now a porcelain factory, and then into Triana to study gypsies.

"This suburb of Seville was named from the Emperor Trajan, who was born near here, and it is one of the most picturesque spots in Seville.

"Then we 're going to take a peasant's cart, a donkey harnessed to it, with bells and ribbons, and drive about the environs."

We carried out our programme to the letter. A gay Spaniard acting as guide, we drove out to Italica, founded by Scipio Africanus in B.C. 547.

It was the birthplace of Trajan and Theodosius, and the Roman ruins are fine, and the landscape is magnificent.

"Near here was the great battle of the Cid, Pessimist," I said.

"Tell me about it," she commanded, and I complied.

"Don Alfonso sent the Cid (the Spanish Bayard, living in the eleventh century) from Burgos down here to Seville to receive the tribute which was owed by Almucanis, Arab king of Cordova and Seville.

"Now Mudafer, Saracen king of Granada, aided by Count Garcia Obdonez, Castilian foe of El Cid, was at odds with Almucanis, and the Cid threatened vengeance if they assailed Almucanis, the 'friend of the king and the breast-plate of Castile.'

"Notwithstanding this, the foe entered the territory of Seville, and put it to fire and sword. The Cid, hearing of their depredations, upon his war-horse Babieca, met them at Cabra, and there ensued a bloody fight. The Cid cried :

"'Smite, smite my knights, for mercy's sake. On boldly,
    on to war.
I am Ruy Diaz de Bivar, El Cid Campeador!'
Three hundred lances then were couched with pennons
    streaming gay,
Three hundred shields were piercèd through, no steel
    the shock might stay;
Three hundred hauberks were torn off in that encounter
    sore;
Three hundred snow-white pennons were crimson dyed
    in gore;
Three hundred chargers wandered loose—their lords
    were overthrown;
The Christians cry, "Saint James for Spain!" the Moor-
    men cry, "Mahoun!"

"But in all the fearful fray, the noble Cid, called the 'Beauteous Beard' was foremost, and he conquered in the end.

"However, the Castilian knights prejudiced the King Alfonso against him and Ali Maimon, Arab king of Toledo, complained that Ruy Diaz had laid waste his territory, though this had been done by the Arabs themselves. So King Alfonso banished the Cid in disgrace. Alas! poor Cid, but he said, only:

"'I obey, O King Alfonso,
    Guilty though in naught I be,
    For it doth behoove a vassal
    To obey his lord's decree.
    Prompter far am I to serve thee
    Than thou art to guerdon me.
    I do pray our Holy Lady
    Her protection to afford

That thou never may in battle
Need the Cid's right arm and sword.
Well I wot at my departure
Without sorrow thou canst smile,
Well I wot that envious spirits
Noble bosoms can beguile;
But time will show, for this can ne'er be hid,
That they are women-knights, but I — *El Cid.*'

"He was a splendid old fellow, Pessimist, and we 'll see him again at Burgos and at Barcelona."

CHAPTER VII.

FROM THE TORRE DE LA VELA.

" The Moorish King rides up and down
Through Granada's royal town,
From Elvira's gates to those
Of Vivarambla, on he goes.
    Ay de mi, Alhama!

Letters to the monarch tell
How Alhama's city fell;
In the fire the scroll he threw
And the messenger he slew,
    Ay de mi, Alhama!"

HEN when the King of Granada, poor Boabdil, heard from the messenger that the Marquis of Cadiz had taken the city of Alhama, the stronghold of the Moors and key of Granada, he would not believe the terrible news, and sore he wept, and all within the Red Castle, men and women cried, '*Ay de mi* Alhama!' But it was long, long before that the Alhambra was built. In the reign of Suwar Ibn Hamdún the first tower was made, and it was Ibn-l-Ahmar, the founder of the Caliphate of Granada who built the real palace in 1238. Each Moorish king took pride in beautifying some portion of it, and the gold for the gilding was procured from Africa in huge nuggets and beaten into strips before using.

Never anywhere in Moorish Spain has there been such a combination of airiness and lace-like traceries, such mosaic pavements, and such clusters of arches as here in our Alhambra. No wonder the Moors wept to leave it. It was cruel."

"You are Spanish, are you not?" I asked as we sat upon the stone parapet, just outside the Gate of Justice, before entering the Alhambra.

We had just arrived, the Pessimist and I, had eaten a delicious dinner at the Hotel Siete Suelos and had been sent out in the charge of a young Spanish friend to have our first glimpse of the wonderful Alhambra by moonlight.

"Spanish, yes, señorita, but on my mother's side, far, far away there is a Moorish ancestor. You know the old saying, 'Once a Moor to love them ever,' and I have much feeling for them. Perhaps it is because I so much love all this," with a little gesture around.

"It must have been terrible to leave it. No wonder the old chronicle says, 'Boabdil wept like a child over the kingdom he could not keep like a man.'

O, my city of Granada! that never had a peer,
The pride of every Moorish land, to all the Moslems dear,
For seven hundred years has the crown been worn by
   thee
Of the famous line of monarchs that now must end with
   me;
I see thy fields and meadows, thou Vega of renown,
And thy fragrant flowers are withered, thy stately trees
   are down,
O woe betide the luckless king, who such a crown has
   lost,
'Tis his to feel the bitter shame, 'tis his to pay the cost.
No more to ride a horse of war, or rank amongst his
   peers,
But live where none can see his shame, and end his life
   in tears."

"Why is this called the Gate of Justice?" asked the Pessimist.

"It was the beginning of the fortress and some say it was built for a seat of judgment. The Arabs had many customs from the Jews, and they were used to sit in the city gates.

"The Caliph had to see all who came to ask justice, and he received them here. Over the pillars is carved, 'There is no God but Allah, and Mohammed is his Prophet;' and this motto you will find all over the palace. Then the hand over the door is to ward off the evil eye, and the key is a symbol that the Prophet has power to open and shut the gates of Heaven.

"But, to-morrow, you will see all this, señorita. To-night, you must see the view from the Torre de la Vela by moonlight," and Diego de Gonzalez led us down the court, where eerie shrubs peered at us and strange flower scents were wafted to us, up to a huge tower.

"Can we enter to-night?" I asked.

Diego laughed gayly.

"Señorita, I have lived close to our Alhambra ever since I was a child. Save the three years I was in Gibraltar at the English school, I have never been away. I know every nook and corner of this place and all the custodians know me. Old Dolores would let me into the Vela at midnight if I wished," and he knocked heavily on the iron-bound door.

A step was heard, a light crept through the chinks, and a quavering voice said:

"Who comes?"

"I, Diego. Let us enter, Dolores *mia*," said the boy.

The heavy door swung back on its hinges, with a creaking as of a dungeon cell, and the light of a candle flamed in our faces.

"*Bien venido*, Diego *mio*," said an old woman, her hair quite white under her lace mantilla, but her eyes dark and soft. She added something in Spanish, at which Diego smiled.

"She says thrice welcome to the friends of

her friends," he explained as he led us up the steps,—narrow, winding steps, dark and steep, with small platforms and grated windows,—up and up till, breathless, we reached the summit and stood upon the flat top of the Torre de la Vela.

"There!" cried Diego, triumphantly, "Is it not a view?"

We stood speechless. Rising from the center of the roof, against the sky stood out the famous watch-tower of the Moors, from which rang forth the great bell of the fortress, pealing weal or woe to the people.

From the distance came sounds of guitars and castanets in the Albaicin or gypsy quarters below on the right, while in front of us sloped down to the Darro the wooded hills, and beyond lay the town, snowy and silent. The pure heights of the sierras in the far distance and the plains of the Vega, the sapphire sky—even at that hour blue and dotted with countless stars, brilliant and gleaming—and the soft haze of the moonlight, all this made a scene so perfect that one's senses could only yield as a harp played upon by fairy music. And when the gypsy music died away, and through the stillness there came the sweet and wonderful song of the nightingale from the chestnut woods below, we felt that the climax was reached, and as the bird's clear notes died away upon the pure night air, I exclaimed:

"Sevillians say their city is a marvel, but it seems to me Granada is one, too."

"Ah, señorita, do n't you know what the Granadino replied to the Sevillian boast about La Maravilla?" Diego said—

> "*Quien no ha vista Granada*
> *No ha vista nada.*'

"See, there are the towers. Do you know the history of that one close by the walls? To it came King Alfonso El Sabio, when Ibn-l-Ahmar was Caliph of Granada. This was after the war with Prince Sancho *El Bravo*, who rebelled against his father and deprived him of his throne.

"All his wisdom and mildness did not help *El Rey* Alfonso to regain his lost kingdom and he sought the help of the Moors.

"They revered him much, for he was a scholar and had written many books, and the Saracens esteemed knowledge highly.

"He it was who wrote 'The Great Conquest Beyond the Sea,' and well the Moors knew that it told the history of Mohammed, and of the struggle of Saracen and Christian at the Holy Sepulchre.

"Alfonso had compiled the '*Partidas*' or law-book, modeled after the old Roman law. These were well spoken of by those Moors who had been at the court of the King at Valencia, either as hostages or envoys.

"The rules for the upbringing of princesses must have seemed very curious to the Moors, who brought up their women for harems, not for courts.

" 'The king's daughters,' says the *Partidas*, 'must endeavor to be moderate in eating and drinking, in their carriage and dress, and have good manners in all things, especially that they be not given to anger, for besides the wickedness that lieth in it, that is the thing in all the world which most easily leadeth a woman to do ill. They must be handy at performing the works which do belong to noble ladies, since it becometh them much and they obtain by it cheerfulness and a quiet spirit.'

"It was this Alfonso who came to Granada two years before his death in 1282, to ask aid from the Caliph. Perhaps it was here, too, that he wrote that curious letter to his kinsman, a Guzman, in favor at the court of Fez—

" 'Cousin Don Alonzo Perez de Guzman,' the letter begins, 'My affliction is great and I find no protection in my own land, neither champion nor defender; and since they of Castile have been false to me, none can think it ill that I ask help among the Benamarin.

" 'Consider of what lineage you are, and, my good cousin, do so much for me with my lord and your friend Abn Jusef, that, on the pledge of my jewels, he may lend me so much as he may hold to be just. And so may God's friendship be with you.

"'*El Rey*, Alfonso X.'"

"He may have visited here, Diego," I said, "but I think that letter was written at Seville. At any rate it 's very interesting, and I wish the poor king had gotten back his kingdom, instead of dying at Seville crownless, while his rascally son reigned in his stead.

"Where is the tower of La Cautiva?"

"There, the square tower to the left. There pined Doña Isabella de Solis, Zoraya or Morning Star, favorite Sultana of Abul Hassan. To her was due the fall of the Alhambra," said Diego.

"Why is that blame laid on a woman?" asked the Pessimist.

"Muley Abul Hassan, King of Granada, in 1465 refused to pay tribute to Castile, and brought upon himself the enmity of the Spaniards," said Diego.

"Hassan's Sultana was the Princess Ayxa la Horra, and her son Boabdil was heir to the throne.

"Isabella de Solis, the Christian captive, became Sultana, and she had a son for whom she wished the throne, and incited the king against la Horra and Boabdil.

"Hassan then confined them in the Tower of Comares, there, in the center, over the Hall of the Ambassadors. But the Sultana Ayxa was not one to stay a captive. The walls of the Tower of Comares are thick, and there are small windows barred with iron. On three sides of the tower are stone balconies below the windows, and from one of these balconies the Queen lowered Boabdil with scarfs knotted together, and he escaped with a few faithful servants to the mountains of Alpujarras.

"There, later, he allied himself to Ferdinand; at least he promised tribute to the Spanish king, if he himself ever regained Granada.

"Muley Hassan, however, was of a different nature. 'Tell your sovereign,' he cried, when ambassadors came to demand from him tribute,' that the Moorish kings who pay for their thrones are all dead! My mint coins only daggers and Damascus blades.' And so the bloody war went on.

"The Moors must have won, or at least have held out much longer had it not been for the dissensions among themselves, caused by the rival factions at court, the friends of the two queens."

"Has every tower here a legend?" I queried.

"Very nearly, señorita," the boy said, "and I know them all. Am I not a child of the fortress? Your Mr. Irving calls one of his guides 'a son of the Alhambra,' and that I am too, since my people have lived here and my ancestor was governor after the French left. That tower on the outer wall is the Torre de las Infantas.

"Do you know the story of Zayde, Zorayde, and Zorahayda? The three sisters dwelled there with their nurse, the 'Discreet Kadiga,' in the reign of Muley Hassan, the Left-Handed.

"A Christian bride whom he had captured bore him three daughters, and a wise man had prophesied that great trouble would come to him unless he guarded them carefully when the time came for them to marry. So Muley shut them up in the tower; but alas for his calculations!

> If she whom Love doth honor
> Be confined from the day,
> Set a thousand guards on her,
> Love will find out the way.

"The three maidens, looking from their window saw three Christian knights, captives, working in the ravine below,—saw and loved them; and the knights too, loved in return.

"How it came about only the discreet Kadiga could ever tell, but two of the princesses let themselves down from the window, with Kadiga, and escaped to Cordova with the knights. The youngest, her father's favorite, fair, timid Zorahayda, remained behind, and pined away and died.

"They say she haunts the tower yet, señorita," and Diego's voice fell.

"All this is very interesting," said the Pessimist, "but I fear we 'll meet the fate of Zorahayda if we do n't stop haunting these towers, and go to bed. Is there any legend about the Torre de la Vela?"

"Not a legend exactly," said Diego, laughing, "but any one who rings the bell from this tower on the night of the second of January will marry within a year."

"To-morrow we must see the interior of the palace. It is even more wonderful than my dreams!" I exclaimed. "Diego, you are introducing us to fairyland," and with a lingering look at the wonderful scene, still bathed in the waves of the moonlight, we left the lonely tower.

"Was Boabdil such a wicked wretch, and did he imprison his wife and ill-treat his uncle?" I asked Diego, next morning, as we three rambled slowly along the green lanes toward the Puerto del Pino.

"Oh, no, señorita. He was far better than many of the other kings. It is only that he was unsuccessful, and so all his good deeds were distorted. He was brave but tender-hearted, the latter such a rare virtue in his day as to be considered almost a vice. As for his uncle, he had conspired against Boabdil, usurped his throne, threatened his life, and injured his kingdom.

"What wonder that when he at last fell into the hands of his justly irate nephew, Boabdil cried, 'Call me no more *El Zogoubi* (the Unlucky), for mine enemy is delivered into my hands,' and he drove him from the walls."

"He was lucky to murder his uncle," I said, flippantly.

Diego looked inquiringly at me. Although he spoke excellent English the boy did not understand it sufficiently for irony, and accepted all with a perfect Spanish gravity, irresistibly droll to one so inclined to laugh at everything from a pure overflow of good spirits, as was I.

"Yes?" he said inquiringly, "The señorita has some uncles then that she would like to murder?"

"Tell us about Boabdil's wife," interposed the Pessimist, while I buried my face in a huge spray of lilac, with which the gardens were fragrant.

"Unlike most of the Moorish kings Boabdil

had only one wife, and her name was Morayma. He loved her devotedly, and she
remained with him through all his trials.
When he abdicated the throne of Granada she
was at his side. Her voice was raised in
weeping as Boabdil el Chico left the fortress,
saying to the Spanish chief, Don Gutierrezde
Cardenes, who had been sent to take charge
of the palace: ' Go, señor, and take possession of those fortresses in the name of the
powerful sovereigns to whom God has been
pleased to deliver them in reward of their
great merits, and in punishment for the sins
of the Moors. Morayma pressed close by
him as he handed the keys of his kingdom to
Ferdinand and Isabella, saying, 'These keys
are the relics of the Arabian Empire in Spain;
thine, O king, are our trophies, our kingdom,
and our person. Such is the will of God.
Receive them with the clemency thou hast
promised.' Morayma pressed his hands to
her lips when, pausing on the Alpuxarras the
unfortunate king took his last lingering look
upon the palace he had loved so dearly, for
which he had fought so well.

" '*Allah Achbar!*' he cried, 'God is great,
but when did misfortune equal mine?' and,
turning sadly from the spot, to this day
called '*El ultimo suspiro del Moro*' (The
last sigh of the Moor) he went to his exile in

the valley of Purchena.   There he tarried so long as Morayma lived, delaying his wished-for departure to Africa, and loving her to the last.   He left his land, a melancholy being mourning more the death of his wife than the loss of his kingdom.''

"He was unlucky, poor Boabdil,'' I said, my spirit taking fire at the boy's earnestness. ''People in those days seemed to consider it meritorious to die in a heap of ruins, killing all the innocent commoners, and refusing to yield to reasonable terms of peace.   I think Boabdil was sensible, and showed genuine greatness, to be willing to save his people by abdicating and accepting Ferdinand's treaty. What became of him finally, Diego?''

"He departed from Purchena, where he had lived in happiness some time, and went over to Fez where the Caliph received him kindly, and there he died years afterward, fighting in defense of the kingdom of those who had befriended him.

"But there, señorita, enough of Boabdil.   I always talk too much when I speak of him. My heart is sore for him ever.   That is the Palace of Charles V.   How do you like it?''

Diego watched us anxiously out of the corner of his eye, as we looked at the huge Græco-Roman pile in silence.

"I must say I do n't like it, Diego. It 's an anachronism," I said.

"I do n't know anach-ronism," he said, "but you are right not to like it. It does not belong to our Alhambra. It is too bad to have the Spaniards spoil the Moorish palace. To make this ugly, rough house, the fairest parts of the Alhambra were torn down, the harem with all its matchless decorations, and many more buildings.

Even the Emperor himself was sorry when he saw what had been done. What right had he here, he was half an Austrian?" and Diego's eyes flashed fire. "But, Señorita, now we enter the real Alhambra," as he led us to a door in a rough wall, half smothered in lilac bushes.

"Close your eyes and let me say the 'Open Sesame' and then welcome to our Alhambra!"

CHAPTER VIII

THE PALACE OF THE ALHAMBRA.

E said not a word as we stepped through the portal and stood within the Patio de la Alberca; only a quick, sharp, indrawing of the breath denoted our utter astonishment. Read, talk, think, dream of the Alhambra as you will, the reality is not only unlike your anticipations, it surpasses them.

To be sure, as our eyes grew accustomed to the softened light streaming through arch and lattice, we saw the scene familiar through photograph and illustration.

There were the slender pillars, light and marvelously ornamented, the galleries, the wood ceiling inlaid and carved and painted gold in Moorish times.

There were the quaint doors, the *agimez* windows, the deep niches, and in the center the pond full of gold-fish, and bordered with myrtle carefully trimmed, and giving the

court the name, *de los Arrayanes*, (of the myrtles). There were the stuccoed ornamentations and scriptural inscriptions; but the wonder and surprise lay in the perfection of detail, the marvelous coloring, the almost optical illusions of loveliness.

In the limpid waters of the pond were reflected a myriad of lovely sights; the red towers of the fortress, the colonnades ending in slender arches, and the snowy clouds of the sky above—a whole world within the myrtle-bordered waters. On the walls were the words of Ibn-l-Ahmar, who returning victorious from battle, was greeted by the people with the cry "*Galib !*" (conqueror), to whom he replied, "*Wa la ghaliba illa Allah !*" (There is no conqueror but God).

In silence we went through the Court of Blessing, and reached the Sala de Embajadores (Hall of Ambassadors), and here we halted long, for its loftiness is beyond compare. It was the grand reception room of the Moorish kings, a square hall seventy-five feet high, with deep window recesses overlooking the Darro. From one of these Charles V. cried, as he saw the glories of the view, "Ill-fated the man who lost all this!" The hall (with the tower of which it is a part) is called *de Comares*, because its workmanship was modeled after that at Comerach in Persia.

But, grand as this hall is, it seems to belong to a different period from the rest of the palace; it is more solid, with a number of guipures on the walls and much inlaid wood, and despite thronging recollections of the days of old when the *sala* was peopled with Moor and knight, Christian embassy and Persian poet, a spirit in our feet seemed to urge us on, and through the lovely *loggia*, and the "Queen's Toilette" (so called because made by Bourbon Philip for his young wife, the Parmese Elizabeth), and past gardens, glimpses of which touched the senses as a benediction from Paradise, we entered the longed-for spot, the Mecca to travelers at the Alhambra — the far-famed Court of Lions.

"Barmeja, the Red King of Granada, whom Don Pedro el Cruel murdered at Tablada, was succeeded by Mohammed, who built the Court of Lions in the year 1371," said Diego, but I interrupted quickly:

"Oh, Diego, we want to know all about everything but do wait just a few moments until we take a little of it in!" as I looked about the *patio* in ecstacy. The first impression one received was of pillars, pillars, pillars! Single pillars, carved, and fluted; double pillars, from which sprang horseshoe arches, delicate in outline, fragile in appearance, wonderful in coloring, cloud-like in hue; triple pillars, supporting the airy pavilions surmounted with conical roofs in all the hues of the rainbow.

Lightness, brightness, beauty. Between the pillars were archways of an open-work like Mechlin lace, with the blue sky peering through, and doorways leading into galleries each more marvelous than the last.

In the center was the famous fountain, with its two alabaster basins supported by the lions in white marble, their manes cut like griffin scales.

"What are those words around the lower basin?" asked the Pessimist at last.

"A poem in praise of the founder of the court, written by Abu-Abdillah-Mohammed-Ebn-Yusef-Ebn-Zemric, a small sample of the poetic names of the day," said Diego.

"Over that fountain the children of Abu Hasen were beheaded by order of their own father, all except Boabdil, and on a corner of the arcade stood fiery old Muza, when he answered Ferdinand's herald so sturdily:

" 'Does the Christian king think us greybeards or women with distaffs, that we should yield with swords in our hands? Let him know that sweeter far to the African is a grave in the ruins of the Alhambra than the richest couch in his proudest palace!' "

"It 's all very famous, and I 've no doubt a great many extremely unpleasant things happened here, but," objected the Pessimist, "it seems to me very absurd to have so many pillars that have nothing in particular to do, —nothing but just be pillars. One would do just as well to hold up an arch as three. It 's a waste of raw material. Then those lions are grotesque. They are almost sphinx-like, and fore-shortened until their legs are ridiculous."

"You do not like it?" said Diego. "Then we will go to the Sala de los Abencerrages." (Hall of the Abencerrages) and we entered through an open archway to the right of the Lions' Court.

"Ah! it is the gem of the whole palace, this square hall with its walls of the finest raised work, inscriptions in Arabic,—'Glory be to our lord Abu Abdillah!' and the verses from the poem of the 'Two Sisters.'"

The roof, a cupola in form, is hung with stalactites in blues, browns, red, and gold. Through the octagonal windows at the top peered the blue of heaven, and as we gazed, a tiny bird, disturbed from its home on a carved window ledge, with a quick little twitter and whir of wings, flew across the hall and out, up to the sky above.

> " 'The little birds flew east,
>   And the little birds flew west,
>   And I smiled to think God's greatness
>   Flows around our incompleteness,
>   Round our restlessness, his rest.' "

I quoted.

"The restlessness of the world does not seem to strike this quiet spot. It did in the times of the Abencerrages, for here it was that Muley Hassan, father of Boabdil, jealous of his wife's attachment to one of the Abencerrages, invited thirty-eight of them to a banquet, and slew them all," I said.

"No, not all, for one escaped," corrected Diego, "and there is a story about his family which is a curious one. He was found to be innocent, and permitted to live in Granada on condition that if he had sons they should be educated away from the court.

"Abendaraez was the only son of the Abencerrage, and he was sent to the castle of Certama to be brought up in ignorance of his birth, by a friend of his father. This friend —the Alcaide—had one daughter Xarisa, with whom Abendaraez was brought up, but when he reached manhood he discovered that he was not her brother, and declared himself her lover.

"In fear of the Alcaide they married in secret; the Alcaide suspecting them, however, they were separated, vowing eternal constancy. At length Xarisa, from her captivity in the fortress at Coyn, managed to send Abendaraez word that her father would be away at a certain time. He hastened to see her, but on the road was captured by six cavaliers, commanded by Roderigo de Narvaez, Alcaide of Antequerra.

"To him the Moor told his tale, and Don Roderigo gave him permission to keep his tryst with Xarisa, provided he would return and enter captivity again, which Abendaraez readily promised. He went to Coyn, saw his wife, and she returned with him at the expiration of his furlough.

"'Behold, Alcaide, how an Abencerrage keeps his word!' said the Moor proudly. 'I promised thee a captive, and I bring thee two. This is my wife. Receive us as thine own, for I trust my life and honor to thine hands.' Don Roderigo was much delighted at the honor of Abendaraez, and gave him the castle of Alora in which to dwell until forgiven by the father of Xarisa. The lovers were taken into favor at the court of Granada, and some of the best families in Spain boast the blood of the Abencerrage in their veins."

"Are those supposed to be blood stains or rust on the floor?" asked the Pessimist.

"Blood, of course. You 've no imagination

at all," I exclaimed. "It 's a great deal nicer to be born with a spirit of credulity like mine. I believe there's Scotch blood in you, for it takes you forever to accept a statement. Where do we go now, Diego?"

"To see the Hall of the Sisters, so called from the two equal-sized slabs in the pavement, which are the sisters; then we have a glimpse of the Hall of Justice, where there are the famous paintings, the only pictures of living things in the whole palace.

"They are said to be painted on animal skins, and coated with gypsum to receive the paint. They could not have been Moorish, for the Moors were never permitted, according to the Koran, to represent living creatures. It will always be a mystery how they came here, but the best authorities say they were done by some Christian renegade, and they are portraits of Moorish judges, landscapes filled with birds and beasts, and chivalric scenes.

"Then you must see the great Alhambra vase, enameled in blue and gold, which was discovered full of gold, and on which the inscription, 'Eternal Salvation,' is repeated over and over again.

"There is the wall where all the great people have inscribed their names,—Byron, Chateaubriand, and Victor Hugo. Then we will go to the Sultan's Baths, and the chamber of secrets, where at one end, by placing your ear to an opening in the wall, you can hear every word said at the other end of the room.''

''Diego!'' I cried in despair, ''let us see all these another day, but now show us some quiet place where we can sit down and let you tell us some more legends. My eyes can look at nothing more.''

''Ah, señorita!'' the boy exclaimed, ''I think you begin to love my Alhambra a little, and to see the wonder of it. Let me take you to the gem of it all, the Patio de Lindaraja,'' and he led us through the corridors into the *mirador* of the Sultana, where the *agimez* windows look out into the verdant *patio*, and at last we sat down in the famous garden, and the luxuriousness of the tropics stole over our senses.

Diego sat on the edge of the fountain which raised its shell-like basin in the center of the garden, surrounded by straight cedar trees, box-bordered walks, and orange trees, blooming and heavy with the ripe fruit.

Diego was a picturesque creature. There are few things more beautiful than a Spanish boy of eighteen. As men, Spaniards seem too small, and scarcely sturdy enough, (though some of them are superb), but a boy has just that charm of grace and sweetness which is very attractive. Diego had brown curly hair, a face of great purity and sweetness, blue eyes, almost black, with heavily drooping lids, and a gravity of demeanor, lit up by occasional glimpses of gayety, very charming. He wore a correct suit of light clothes, English in cut,—but Spanish blood will tell, and he had a gay necktie, a *caballero* cloak, black, lined in scarlet, which was flung over one shoulder, while his *sombrero* was tied with brilliant cord and tassel.

"Are you really Spanish, Diego? You are so fair. Our idea of a Spaniard is that he must be as black as the ace of spades," I said.

Diego laughed, showing his rows of even white teeth, as strong and white as a dog's.

"There are very many kinds of Spaniards," he said. "They are all the way from black to white. I am Andalucian, and sometimes they are blondes like yourself, señorita."

At this I smiled. I never saw a genuine blonde in Andalucia, but Diego was entirely too polite to leave me out.

"Do you know why we are called Andalucian?" he went on.

"No; another story; do tell us," I cried.

"All the saints in heaven had countries but Santa Lucia, and she was unhappy. Now, Santiago is very kind-hearted, and also rather busy, for Spain is a great country, and one which takes a good deal of looking after; so he said to her: 'Santa Lucia, go down to my country and choose any part of it you want, and you may have it, and—' he added under his breath—'I 'll have quite enough to do to look after the rest of my Spaniards!' So Lucia started, and as she came to a very fertile spot, round which were snowy mountains, a voice seemed to say to her—'*Anda*, Lucia!' (Go, Lucia!) so there she went, and the province is called Andalucia until this very day.''

''More legends, Diego,'' I cried, ''even the Pessimist likes to hear them.''

''Yes,'' she said, ''so they are not blood-curdling, like yours. I like them very well,'' and we settled ourselves for a comfortable listen, more enticing at times than a comfortable chat.

''I will tell you the legend of the flowers,'' said the boy, throwing aside his hat, and baring his open forehead to the breeze.

''Once, long, long ago, there lived in the Alhambra, a very wise king, Ben Jusef Omreyh, by name, and he had but one child, a daughter, Hafiza, whom he loved as his own soul. Hafiza was of marvelous beauty, with liquid dark eyes gazing wistfully from beneath dark lashes, lips like a scarlet pomegranate blossom, cheeks like the first blush of dawn on the white clouds, and hair soft and long, and dark as night.

"Innocent she was as she was fair, and the old king loved her all the more because she was the only child of his favorite Sultana, long since dead.

"The fairest gardens of the Alhambra were kept for the young Hafiza, and there she grew from childhood up to womanhood, amidst her slaves, nor knew she aught of the world or of men, so carefully shielded was she there in the garden *de las Rosas.*

" 'My father,' said she one day, springing to his side, as the garden door swung to behind him, 'grant me a wish to-day,' and she flung aside her white *haik*, and stood by him in all the loveliness of her fresh girlhood.

" 'What is thy boon, Hafiza?' asked the old king, as with proud and tender eyes he gazed upon her, and gently stroked the dark hair from her temples.

" 'Just beyond my garden wall I see another garden, and in it the flowers seem so rare I fain would pluck them. It is not that my own are not as beautiful, dear father, but only that I weary of them, and long for thine. There, close beside the marble fountain's rim I see a rose, so red in hue, with perfume so far-reaching that even here it haunts my senses, and makes me feel as if the Peris who wait at the very gates of Paradise must have brought it hither. I long to pluck that rose, O king, my father, and call it mine,' and Hafiza laid both hands caressingly upon the stern king's arms, and looked beseechingly into his face.

"As no one else dared, so did Hafiza to *El Rey*, for he loved her dearly, the stern old king.

"He looked sadly into the sweet face raised to his, then led her to a balcony which overhung the garden.

" 'Show me thy rose, my child,' he said.

" 'There it is,' she cried, pointing with a slender finger, its nail dyed with henna. 'There, in the glorious sunlight, and something stirs within my breast, and whispers, "Dear Princess, I have bloomed for you. Ah, pluck me, and wear me on your breast." '

" 'Look closely, child, and tell me what thou seest, my little one, there near to the red, red rose,' said the king, a shadow deepening on his brow.

" 'Beside the rose-tree, trailing its fringed blossoms o'er the fountain's brim, and reflecting their purple hues within the water, its vines clinging close about the red rose stem, I see another flower, strange in form, yet beautiful, and that, too, I would pluck.

" 'Well-nigh hidden by the leaves and vines, yet twined with their tendrils, there grows a third sweet flower, a tiny blossom of palest pink, in its center one deep scarlet spot. It has a faint perfume, yet 'tis sweet. It, too, seems to speak to me and say, "Dear Princess, I live for you. Wear me on your brow, I pray." May I have these flowers, dear, my father?'

" 'Tell me yet again, what else thou seest, beside the fountain, my Hafiza,' said the king.

" 'Ah! a flower so fair, I scarcely dared to hope for it,' she cried. 'It is strong and brave, one blossom upon a single stem, without the grace of the rose, the allurement of the purple fringed flower, or the delicacy of the pink one.

" 'It has a perfume of such penetrating sweetness that its scent haunts me day and night. It is a pure, calm white, yet in its depths, like a beam of imprisoned sunlight, lies a heart of gold, and this flower I long for most of all, O great, good king, my father.'

"The old king sighed again, yet smiled as well, and said:

" 'Each flower has a meaning, my little one. Know then, that the red, red rose thou will'st to pluck, though thorns there be upon its stem, is from all ages the fair flower of love, and twined about it is the purple passion-flower. There, close allied to both, is the sweet, pink cyclamen, which has the crimson stain within its heart for pain—and last of all, my child Hafiza, is the Eastern lily with the golden heart, which is for self-forgetfulness.   It ever comes with a true love.

" 'Yes, my child, thou shalt have thy flowers, for well I see thou art a child no longer, but hast come to maidenhood.'

"So then the king sent Hafiza into the garden, and she flitted about, plucking the flowers and chasing the butterflies and gay dragonflies, singing merrily.

"And as she went it chanced that there came to seek the king a stranger, a noble youth, or an embassy from far Castile, and as he saw Hafiza there amidst the flowers, herself the fairest flower of all, his heart within him gave a sudden bound.   And, as her eyes met his within their liquid depths sprang up a swift fire, and when the stranger knight passed Hafiza dropped her rose, which he quickly took, and hid within his breast.   And when his audience with the king was over, long dallied he by the Xenil, and sometimes hasty glimpses had he of the fair young princess, and many were the stolen glances which passed between them.

"At last, emboldened by his love—which ever makes the heart of man as bold to other men as it is timid to the maid he loves—he asked of the old king, his daughter's hand. Then the king called Hafiza to him, in the presence of the stranger knight, and said to her;

" 'Will my daughter have the rose which brings with it the passion flower and the cyclamen?' And the princess, looking from the sad, kind eyes of her father to the eager, glowing ones of the stranger knight, buried her head upon her father's breast, whispering softly, with shy maiden blushes, 'Yes, my father, an you will.'

" 'Then, see thou hast the lily, too, my child,' said the wise old king, as he placed her hand within her lover's own. So they were married, and the legends say that many were the sorrows of their life, and yet Hafiza was a true and faithful wife always unto Don Juan de Sanchez, and bore her trials with a gracious calm, which made her like a perfect lily. Her husband loved her ever, and when she died, he built for her a mighty tomb, and on it laid her effigy in marble, a lily in her hand, and underneath the words—'The Eastern Lily blossoms now in Paradise.' "

"Oh! Diego, what a charming tale!" I exclaimed. "Is it a real legend, or your own?" but the boy only laughed and said:

"These are the gardens; why should it not be true?" as we wended our way through the gardens and lanes homeward.

CHAPTER IX

THE GENERALIFE.

"UNDAY morning, Pessimist, and I wonder what Sunday is like in Granada," I said as we awoke, and threw open our latticed casement to let the morning sun enter.

"I hope it will be more quiet than Sunday in Seville," she replied. "Such a performance as they had on Easter Sunday! It 's all very fine to have church *festas*, but the Sevillians are too noisy about them to suit me."

"Well, we 're to go to High Mass with Diego, and see the cathedral at the same time, so it behooves us to get our breakfast," I said.

Soon we were walking down the elm-bordered walks, and past the fountain of Charles V., made of stone from the Sierra Nevada, with three crowned genii to represent the Darro, Xenil, and Beiro, which stream through the Vega.

The town of Granada is mournful and quiet, and little like the gay Granada of the Moors.

"It does not seem as if it could be the city of poem and romance," I said.

> "Over all the rest supreme,
>   The star of stars, the cynosure,
> · The artist's and the poet's theme,
>   The young man's vision, the old man's dream—
>   Granada by its winding stream,
>   The city of the Moor.
>   And there, the Alhambra still recalls
>   Aladdin's palace of delight,
>   "Allah il Allah," thro' its halls
>   Whispers the fountain as it falls;
>   The Darro darts beneath its walls
>   The hills with snow are white.
>   The Vega clift by the Xenil,
>   The fascination and allure
>   Of the sweet landscape chains the will;
>   The traveler lingers on the hill,
>   His parted lips are breathing still
>   The last sigh of the Moor."

"Where did Cano, the painter, live, Diego?" asked the Pessimist.

"We do not know just where, señorita, but the cathedral has some of his paintings in the high chapel. He had a curious life. When he was in Madrid he was a great favorite, and the instructor of the young prince, but his chances were all ruined by the suspicion that he had murdered his wife. He was seized and tortured to make him confess his guilt, but his right hand was saved by the king, that he might be able to paint if he survived.

"As he endured the torture without a groan, he was acquitted, and he retired to his native city, Granada. Here he became a priest, and spent the last of his life in decorating and carving the cathedral, dying in extreme poverty, as he gave his all to the poor."

"It seems to have been the fashion in those times to make a good death whatever had been the life. Is that the cathedral?" I asked.

"Yes, señorita. It does not show very well, because it is so cramped in with houses, but the interior is very beautiful."

We entered softly, and Diego procured some little stools for us, for few of the foreign churches have seats, and we gazed about in wonder until the service began. How unlike many gaudily decorated churches was this simple and noble interior, with massive pillars, fine nave, huge dome-like roof, painted in white and gold, and high altar with kneeling figures of Ferdinand and Isabella! Then the notes of the wonderful organ reverberated through the building, and the peasants thronged the aisles.

What a motley array there was! Lovely Spanish women, in black frocks and mantillas—

the church dress of the noble Spaniards—sat
by Andalucian peasants in smart attire, while
haughty old Dons were next to Cook's tourists.   When the service was over we went to
the Chapel Royal, where are the tombs of the
Catholic kings.

"This was built by order of Ferdinand and
Isabella, and here they are buried, and Juana
and Philip also," said Diego.   "We think
Queen Isabella was very beautiful."

"She was," I answered, as we looked at the
fair and gentle face sculptured in marble, which
looks as if she had been, as Bacon says she
was, "one of the most faultless characters of
history, and one of the purest sovereigns that
ever graced a throne."

"But, I do n't like tombs," said the Pessimist, "and I want to see La Cartuja.'

"We are going to drive over there now," I
said, for I had seen lately that the Pessimist
was restive under the legends, and seemed
to be longing for more worlds to conquer.

So we drove out to the convent, now suppressed.   It was founded by the Carthusians
on land given them by Gonzalo de Cordova, *el
gran Capitan.*   It is a quaint white pile; the
approach to it is through narrow streets, with
countless beggars swarming after one, and
demanding money.

"*Señorita una peseta!*" they screamed,

throwing flowers into the carriage, and looking so winsome and gay through all their dirt,
that we had to give them something, and
searched our pockets for coppers. I had nothing but a ten cent silver piece, and started to
throw it to the prettiest child, when Diego,
stayed my hand with horror.

"Señorita!" he exclaimed. "You would
make them nuisances forever to all *Americanas!*
See—this will please them," and he scattered
a handful of coppers. How they scampered
and called down blessings upon us, and then
ran off in glee to show their spoils!

Far in the distance was the bridge of Pinos,
a slender arch over the Xenil, but not so slender as that thread upon which hung the destinies of the New World. Columbus had
been at the court of Granada, beseeching the
queen to help him in his project, but rode
away—disheartened. Here, on the bridge, he
paused a moment.

"Alas!" he sighed, "I must seek help at
the court of France or of England; Spain will
do nothing for me," and he looked back
regretfully upon the fair town, from Vega to
Alhambra bathed in sunlight and beauty.

His kind, keen face was furrowed deep with
care, and yet the steadfast purpose of one who
believes in his own aim glowed in his eyes.

What was that cloud of dust which arose

upon the road, and came nearer and nearer. Ah! Fate was kind, and pausing on the Pinos Bridge, Columbus heard the messenger of the queen, riding full tilt, cry out, "Hold! The queen has sent me. She bids you return to Granada," and thus the destinies of the New World were decided.

The interior of La Cartuja is wonderful, for seldom does one see such marbles in shades of green, red and gold, all from the sierras; and such inlaid work of tortoise-shell and porcelain, nor such horrible pictures as those of the Carthusian martyrs, executed in England during the reign of Henry VIII.

Near La Cartuja is the quaint old church of San Geronimo, where Captain Gonzalo de Cordova is buried.

"What a splendid old Bayard he was, Diego," I said, as we gazed at the church, begun by the king in honor of *El Gran Capitan*, and completed by his widow, and which is one of the finest examples of the Gothic in Spain.

"Ah, señorita! If one could only be a soldier, as he was, one would not mind serving in the army. He was magnificent! Think of him when the Biscayans leveled their pikes at his breast, mutinied and demanded more pay. All he said was:

" 'Higher, men! Raise your weapons

higher, lest they prick *El Gran Capitan!'* Think of his being the one to negotiate with Boabdil for Granada, of his gaining Naples, sending the French from Italy, and taking Zante from the Turks! Oh to have served under him! He was so kind, so knightly, so brave, so stern to the wicked, such a comrade to the good. He said he'd rather step forward into his grave than make one backward step on the field of battle to save his life. No wonder the inscription here reads:

" 'Gonzalo Ferdinando de Cordova, Hispanorum duci, Gallorum ac Turcorum Terrori.'

"Oh to have lived then with the second Cid, and to have served under him!" and the boy's delicate face glowed, and his eyes gleamed. The blood of fighting ancestry coursed in his veins, and he looked like a young Saint George.

"Why, Diego! Why are you not in the army, if you are such a fighter?" I asked.

His face clouded and fell.

"Oh, now, it is very different. Next year it is my time to serve, and if I get a low number when the lot is drawn I shall buy a *permiso.* The army is a hard school, señorita. The pay is but three of your cents a day, and the discipline is frightful for the private. He cannot marry, for he is allowed no rations for his family, and his mess is very poor.

"If a soldier is drunk once, he has two months in prison, and there he gets idle and lazy. He cannot go to church or to work. He is shut up with wicked men, and even if he is a good country lad, he soon grows wicked like the others.

" Then he must serve in The Islands (Cuba and the Filipinas) and there he has a fever, or is murdered by the negroes. The officers are better, but I will not serve if I can get my *permiso.* It is not all gay uniforms, and cocked hats, and brass buttons, and the leaders, although brave men, are not all like *El Gran Capitan.*"

As we drove home Diego pointed out to us the barracks, and on the training green before the rough fortress-like walls, there were a large number of soldiers taking the oath.

"What do they do, Diego?" I asked, as we saw the long file of men slowly moving forward, while bands played the royal march.

"They each must pass under the flag," he said.

"See, there in the center is the standard-bearer holding the Spanish flag, and opposite, a captain raises a drawn sword. Each new recruit must pass between the two, swearing to wield the sword and defend the flag with the last drop of his blood."

"Are Spaniards patriotic?" asked the Pessimist.

"I think I do n't quite know what 'patriotic' is," said Diego, "but if you mean do they love their country, it is more that they love their own place. They say, 'I am Catalan,' 'I am Andalucian,' more than, 'I am a Spaniard.' "

"Very much as I revel in being a Hoosier," I said, as we reached the hotel.

The next thing on our programme was a ramble to the Generalife, and Diego took us there on an afternoon unrivaled in the annals of beautiful weather.

The villa belongs to the Marquis de Campotejar, who acquired it by marriage, Philip V. having made it a perpetual inheritance to the house of Granada and Venegas.

A permit is required for entrance, but Diego always had permission to go everywhere, and indeed the boy's smile ought to prevail upon Saint Peter to unlock the gate of heaven.

"Tell us about the Generalife, Diego," the Pessimist asked as we passed the gate, and through the magnificent avenue of cypresses which leads to the palace.

"Abu-l-Walîd built it in the 'year of the great victory of Religion' or 1319, and it was called the Garden of the Dance. It is smaller than the Alhambra, but before it was ruined

with white-wash, was even more perfect as to its decorations," he said, ringing the bell as we entered the patio.

"How those old Moors understood water! They must have had sea-kings or mermaids for ancestors, for they seem always to have known just the right way to procure water, and the most beautiful ways of using it," I exclaimed as we stood looking through the long, narrow patio.

The water lay like a silver thread through the center of the court, reflecting the gallery's slender arches, and the railed balconies of the palace, the shrubs and vines and the cloudless sky above; while through the grated doorway at the other end we caught a lovely glimpse of perfect blue, framed by the arched corridor.

Diego was whispering earnestly to the portress, and as I spoke, he came toward us smiling.

"Come to the other end of the patio," he said, "and I will show you something that few strangers see," and we followed him curiously, and stood waiting, noticing the sunlight sparkle on the water, turning it to silver.

"I would give a good deal to see the fountains play, Diego," I said; and he smiled, for at that instant there sprang into the air showers of silvery spray, from each side of the canal, the slender jets rising high in single streams, then mingling with each other, and falling like mist, while the gold-fishes flashed like imprisoned sunlight in the water.

"Oh, how lovely!" was all we could say, while Diego fairly danced at our delight.

"They play only three times a year," he said, "but I have begged Carmen to turn them on for you, so you can say you have seen the fountains of the Generalife, señorita."

Then, as we thanked him earnestly, he continued:

"I like to show you everything, señorita, because you *feel* it all, and you do not laugh at the stories of the places that I love so well. So many Americans smile at everything. We call them often, 'The men who laugh, and believe nothing,' but you are more Andalucian with your eyes and hair, and you and your friend, I think, love my country."

"Indeed we do, Diego," I cried; and we wandered through the lovely gardens, saw terrace after terrace of beauty, fountains, statues, box-bordered walks, old cypress trees, orange and lemon trees in bloom, and the pomegranate, from which Granada is named. There was a wilderness of flowers, myrtles, heliotropes, primulas, wall-flowers, violets; fleurs-de-lis—purple, yellow and white—callas and wonderful roses, and over all the sky of that brilliant turquoise hue of which Byron says that it was

> " So cloudless, clear, and purely beautiful
> That God alone was to be seen in heaven."

Many were the stories Diego told us of that Fatima, wife of Muley Hassan, who was here found dallying with one of the Abencerrages, and condemned to death unless she could find four knights to fight for her. There, from that tower, she watched and waited until the messenger she had sent for aid might return; watched and waited in vain for days, until she was to be burned at the stern king's command; but at the very last, as she well-nigh despaired, she saw a group of horsemen ford the stream, dash up the hill-side, and clang for admission at the palace gates. Her champions had come; and well they fought the Moorish knights, and vanquished them, and saved Fatima; and I daresay, old Muley Hassan wished often that he had burned her after all, for with all her beauty and witchery, she was a troublesome captive.

We wandered slowly homeward, our hands laden with flowers, for Diego spoiled the fairest gardens for us; and as we reached the Concela de Fuentepeña, a sudden storm arose, a pelting rain which seemed to come from a crack in the blue sky, and we were driven for shelter into a neighboring cottage, Diego assuring us of welcome. It was a quaint little place, a narrow, white-washed cottage, with tiled roof, low rafters, and stone-paved floor. The peasant and his wife were at home, and the pretty children ran to us in a friendly way, seeming to have no idea of begging, and surprised when we gave them coppers.

The room contained a table, some chairs, a stove, and beyond, an alcove where all slept on two rough beds. The mother, a pretty, blackeyed peasant woman in dark skirt, white *camisa* and scarlet jacket, insisted upon lighting coals in a *brasero* to dry our feet, and treated us with a simple hospitality that was very beautiful.

On the wall was a crucifix—a beautiful piece of carving—with some bright pictures of the saints, while a tiny lamp burned before a statue of the Blessed Virgin.

A girl sat spinning with an old-fashioned wheel, and the *madre* showed us, with great pride, the linen she had made for her daughter's bridal, which was to be after Corpus Christi. As the rain ceased as suddenly as it had begun, and we arose to go, all showered upon us blessings and entreaties to come again, and the father of the family followed us to the door, and completely paralyzed the Pessimist by kissing her hand with the air of a courtier.

As we escaped, smiling, I exclaimed:

"I wonder why we never see common people in our own country so simple and natural."

"It's because they're all trying to be something different," said the Pessimist, "instead of being content to be the very best they can in their own station."

"The reason you never see good Spaniards in America," said Diego, sagely, "is because only the discontented ones go there, and if a man is discontented at home he's likely to be so every place else."

"'A Daniel come to judgment,'" I exclaimed. "'Out of the mouths of babes, etc.' Where did you learn your wisdom, Diego *mio?*"

"The señorita laughs now," said the boy, laughing gayly himself.

That night, as I leaned from my balcony in the moonlight, and watched the white towers of the Generalife, I lapsed into verse.

Now, as a rule, I do n't think much of my poetic effusions, but this was very fine. I apostrophized the Spirit of the Past, and requested it to return and do something, I was n't quite sure what.

In an evil moment I showed these chaste lines to the Pessimist, with the result that they are lost to the lyrics of the ages.

Her practical mind saw no reason for addressing any such misty individual as that I referred to, when she herself was there wanting to be talked to and to find out by what route we were going to Cordova.

Moreover, she thought it highly improper to be hankering after harems and their inmates, and gave it as her final opinion that traveling in Spain bade fair to have a very deteriorating effect upon my character.

It was all very well for Diego, a poor boy who had been brought up in a foreign land, and who had never seen even a cable car or anything modern. He had almost a right to believe in all the queer stories which he told. Indeed, he would be abnormal if he did n't. But as for *me*—oh, well! she supposed it was only what she should have expected.

The Pessimist is not always consistent, but that is a small matter, for people who are may become tiresome as traveling companions. So, I forgave her the tirade, remembering how angelically she had yielded to all my whims, and consoled myself by thinking that my poetry was over her head.

I arranged to her satisfaction as to the train which was to bear us away from our beloved Granada, and then said:

"We are to have a serenade to-night, Pessimist. Diego and a friend of his are coming with mandolin and guitar to play Spanish airs

under our window.   Hark! I hear them now.
Yes," as I ran to the window and peeped
out, "I see a figure.   Now, listen!" ex-
citedly.

We listened and we heard, and after the
first glance at the Pessimist's face, I sat down
and laughed until I could have cried; for the
figure which I had mistaken for that of our
boyish cavalier was four-footed, and the music
which greeted our ears was nothing more nor
less than an ear-splitting bray from an innocent ass, who had paused a moment to give
vent to his feelings before climbing the hill.

"I have always thought," said the Pessimist severely, when I stopped laughing from
sheer exhaustion and sat looking at her, "that
the Spanish cavalier beneath his lady's case-
ment was a donkey.   I am glad to be proved
in the right."   But, as she spoke, there came
our real serenade, and the tinkle of that mandolin and guitar in the sweet night air, laden
with flower scents and the fresh earthy smell
of the tropics, made our last evening in Granada more like fairyland than anything else.

"Lovely the moonlight was as it glanced and gleamed
  on the water,
Gleamed on the columns of cypress and cedar sustaining
  the arches,
Down through whose vaults it fell as thro' chinks in a
  ruin,
Dreamlike and indistinct and strange were all things
  around them."

> " Los cipresos de tu casa
>   Están vestidos de luto,
>   Y es porque no tienen flores,
>   Que oprecerte por tributo,"

sang the voices, and the dreamy music mingled with our memories of long ago, and seemed to bear us upon its lyrical wings to the far-away times when all was beauty and minstrelsy and song.   As the sweet boyish voices, mingling with the music of the stirring *Marcha Real*, died away in the distance, I sank to rest, murmuring even in dreams:

"Viva, España!   Viva Andalucia!"

CHAPTER X

LEGENDS BY THE WAY.

HE Pessimist and I were *desolées* at leaving Diego, for the boy had proved such a delightful companion that we felt as though a real friend had been torn from us, as the train sped away from the station, and we left him on the platform.

"Adios! Adios! señoritas!" had been his cry as he kissed our hands, and our last glimpse of him, as we leaned far out of the carriage window, was of the knightly figure in its huge cape, outlined against the blue sky, his *sombrero* pressed low upon his forehead, as he watched the train leave the station.

We were still in Andalucia, garden of the gods. The Spanish *ferro-carril* has to the full extent the national trait of indolent calm, and generally arrives *mañana*, *mañana*, and we crawled through fields of wheat, with palms, citron trees, sugar cane and orange groves.

We were in no hurry, and were quite willing to alight at every station, and pluck flowers and chat with the peasants, for the spirit of Andalucia had infused itself into our veins, and we felt light-hearted and lazy.

"Tell me about the Vega," said my friend, as Granada faded from our view.

"The Spanish king beleaguered Santa Fé," I said.

"'Full many a duke and count was there, the noblest in
　　the land,
And captains bold, that swelled the host of good King
　　Ferdinand,
For they were men of valor bold and now had drawn the
　　sword,
To win Granada's kingdom fair in battle for their lord.'

"One morning at nine o'clock, so the poem of Perez de Hita says, a Moor appeared, riding a black charger, and in red, white and blue petticoats (but underneath all these vestments, 'a coat of armor true'), carrying a double-headed lance and a buckler of buffalo hide. He gave a very cordial invitation to any knight to come and perch upon the end of his lance.

"'Come one, come two, come three or four, it matters not
　　a jot,
Or let the captain of the youths, he is a man of note,
Let Count de Cabra sally forth (in war a potent name),
Or Gonzalo Fernandez, whom Cordova doth claim.'

"The cavaliers all were anxious to avail themselves of the Moor's kind invitation, but

a youth named Garcilaso arose, and begged that he might go.

"Now the Spanish youth of 1490, seems to have been quite similar to the youth of the present day, for when he was told he was too young, and must wait till he was older, Garcilaso retired to his tent and sulked. However, he got over his temper, disguised himself, and went out secretly to meet the Moor, assuring him he was sent by the king.

"The Moor refused to do battle with a babe, saying:

"'I am not wont, methinks, to take the field with beardless boys,
Return, rash lad, and tell the king to send a better choice.'

"At this the young man's temper completely got the better of him, and he rushed at the Moor and 'fought with valor true,' vanquishing the enemy, and returning to the camp, with the head of his adversary grinning at his saddle bow,—one of the pleasing decorations of the day.

"'He knelt before the King and Queen, they gave him honor meet,
And marvelled much that such a youth should do so grand a feat,
'Twas in Granada's Vega that thus he won his fame,
And Garcilaso de la Vega thereafter was his name.'

"This Garcilaso de la Vega was the ancestor of the poet and scholar. The camp seems to have been a good school for Spanish poetry, and the soldier poet was born in Toledo in 1503; at the age of seventeen was sent to court, where he was made a *contino* or one of a guard of a hundred nobles, a number of whom were continually about the royal person, and for years he enjoyed the favor of Emperor Charles V., and was sent on diplomatic missions to Naples, France, and Vienna.

"While fighting in Charles V.'s celebrated expedition to Tunis, becoming wounded, he was rescued by the emperor himself. Later, in the Italian war he was killed in defending a difficult post.

"We shall see his tomb at Toledo, where Gongora says every stone is a monument of him. He says of himself that he lived, 'now seizing on the sword, and now the pen,' and some of his poetry is as fine as are the knightly deeds of his life. The versification is uncommonly sweet and tender, as for example in the lines:

> "' For thee, the silence of the shady wood
> I loved; for thee, the secret mountain top
> Which dwells apart, glad in its solitude;
> For thee, I loved the verdant grass, the wind,
> That breathed so fresh and cool, the lily pale,
> The blushing rose and all the fragrant treasures
> Of the opening spring.'

"Garcilaso's success, added to Boscan's, introduced the Italian style of poetry into

Spain, and so he wielded a great influence upon the national literature.

"Five miles away from here is the Duke of Wellington's estate. It was given him by the King of Spain at the close of the Peninsular War, and is called Sota de Roma, and he it was who planted the magnificent elms."

"I want to hear all the legends Diego told you last night, about these places we are passing," said the Pessimist, as she leaned back in the corner of the carriage, empty of travelers save for ourselves.

> "' From Almeria to Granada
>   The Moorish king did ride,
>   And thrice a hundred Moorish knights
>   Went prancing by his side,'

and Almeria, called Al-Mariyat by the Arabs, is on the sea-shore, and upon a hill crowned by a beautiful castle. From this castle the cavalcade sallied, bearing in its train a Christian captive. The Moors were talking and boasting each of his respective Leila or Hafiza or Fatima, when out spoke the captive:

> "' Ye all have vaunted yours, my lords,
>   And now I 'll speak of mine;
>   Her face so fair and ruddy bright,
>   Like morning sun doth shine.'

"At this the Moorish king suggested that so fair a maiden belonged by right to him; to which the youth replied:

> "'I'll give her thee, my Moorish King,
>   If thou my life wilt spare;'
> 'Present her now,' the king replied,
> 'And I will grant thy prayer.'
> At this the gay young Spaniard
> Drew a medal from his breast,
> The Virgin Mary's face;
> The king grew pale to see it,
> And turned him from the place;
> 'Away with him, the scoffing dog
> To Almeria bear;
> Bestow him in a dungeon deep,
> To live his life out there!'

"Further the deponent sayeth not, but the probabilities are that the youth languished there indefinitely. He may be there yet, but we're not going to see," I added, flippantly.

"Go on," said the Pessimist, sleepily.

"Another Moorish knight captured a Christian, who remarked:

> "'My father was of Ronda,
>   My mother Antequera;
> The Moors they led me captive,
>   To Xeres de La Frontera,'

and here he seems to have had a rather unpleasant time. The Moor sat up nights to devise punishments for him, and his fertility of imagination was such that he played horse with him (literally and not in a slang sense), driving him with lash and bit and bridle.

"The Moor's wife, however, took pity on him, and allowed him to escape, and he says:

> "'She sent me to my own country,
> With gold doubloons twice fifty,
> And so it pleased the God of Heaven
> That I am here in safety.'

"There is another delightful ballad beginning:

> "'O Valencia! O Valencia!
> Valiant city of renown,
> Once the Moor, he was thy master
> Now thou art a Christian town,'

and it goes on to tell a very unpleasant legend about a Christian girl who entrapped a Moor, beguiling him until her father could come to bind him in chains.

"Of course, the Moor would have carried her away to his harem, and murdered her father, but a treacherous woman is such a horror to me I cannot bear the story."

"Is there no Spanish literature but Moorish ballads?" asked the Pessimist.

"Indeed there is. Have you forgotten Cervantes, and Calderon, and Lope de Vega, Boscan and Guzman?" I said, indignantly.

"If I wanted a list of Spanish writers, I daresay I could look in the encyclopædia for them," said she, fretfully. "Can't you tell me something about them? And why are there not more of them at Granada?"

"Because when the Moors left Granada its greatness died away, and they took their peculiar type of literature with them. The Moors of Cordova and Toledo were more amalgamated with the Spaniards, and so more remains of their scholarship are left to us," I said.

"There were only two places for literature to thrive in those days,—the monasteries and the court.

"The kings were large patrons of learning, and the scholarly who were not in the church drifted to the royal seat of government, and this was not at Granada. Very few of the old authors ever settled down at home. Take for instance the ancestor of Garcilaso de la Vega, Fernan Perez de Guzman. Born in 1400, he was knighted by King John II. for unusual bravery at the battle of Higueruela, near Granada in 1431.

"He wrote in a grave, Castilian style, a charming book called, 'Praise of the Great Men of Spain.'

"His pen portraits of Juan II., the great Constable, and many others are well drawn, and he writes fairly and in good faith, though sometimes one detects a trace of the disappointed courtier. He says: 'No doubt it is a noble thing and worthy of praise to preserve the memory of great families, and of the services they have rendered to the king and to the commonwealth, but here in Castile this is now held of small account.   To say truth it is really little necessary, for nowadays he is noblest who is richest!'

"O, *tempora !* O, *mores !*   Even in 1430 the corruption of money-getting had begun to corrode the simple dignity of Castilian life."

"Long before that we 're told that the 'love of money is the root of all evil,' " said the Pessimist.

"Look there!" I cried, pointing out of the window.   "Is not that exactly what Long- fellow paints in his 'Castles in Spain?' "

> " 'The long straight line of the highway,
>   The distant town that seems so near,
>   The peasants in the field, that stay
>   Their toil to cross themselves and pray,
>   When from the belfry at midday
>   The Angelus they hear.'

"We 'll soon be at Cordova, the last of the Moorish cities.   Toledo is nearly all Gothic, and the architecture there has scarcely a trace of the Moor."

"Tell me something about Moorish archi- tecture," said my friend.

"It 's no wonder the architecture in Spain is so varied and so beautiful," I replied.

"The many climates produced diverse peo- ples, and they each showed their trend in the buildings.

"The wild, free Goths have columns like

lofty tree-trunks, and arches like interlacing branches. The Castilian school is grave and somber; the Aragonese proud and dark; the Andalucian softer and gayer, the Moorish luxurious and brilliant.

"In a land where quarries of wonderful stone abounded, where mines were full of treasures, and where forests yielded woods of oak or pine, buildings must have been numerous, and as the climate is one which is peculiarly favorable to preservation, the specimens of antique and modern are about equally preserved. There, among those clustering trees is a glimpse of a typical Moorish house. Is it not charming?

"The Moors founded their architectural schools upon those of Persians and Byzantines, preserving the salient points of each.

"Their mosques had the Basilica of Byzantium, and their palaces boasted of arches, columns, stalactite ceilings, horse-shoe windows, and mosaic dados.

"The splendor of the buildings often outshone the originality of conception. One thing is peculiarly noticeable about Moresque edifices,—they never overtop themselves, that is, the proportions are so adjusted that they always appear solidly founded, and never top-heavy. Their ceilings are light in tone, and their minarets seem to spring heavenward.

"The interiors are particularly noticeable in the beauty and minuteness of detail displayed. It seems well-nigh impossible to believe that what looks like wonderful carving on the walls is merely stucco."

"How is it done?" asked the Pessimist. "Was all that in the Alhambra just stucco?"

"Every bit, but a sublimated extract of stucco, the manufacture of which the Moors studied years to attain," I said.

"Plates of plaster of Paris were cast in moulds, and skillfully joined together so that no piecing showed. This method of diapering the walls with arabesques was invented in Damascus, centuries ago. The Moors used much gilding in their work, especially on the cupolas and ceilings. Lapis lazuli was the favorite hue, and only the primary colors were used. It's wonderful how they have kept their tone."

"Why were tiles used so much?" asked my companion.

"They were cool and clean, a *sine qua non* in warm climates. The Spaniards called them Azulejos, from *azul* which means blue, and the use of them descends from Scripture times. Isaiah says, 'Behold, I will lay thy stones with fair colors, and lay thy foundations with sapphires,' and somewhere else it reads, 'There was under his feet as it were a paved work of sapphire stone.'

"The Moors introduced them into Spain, the Dons into the Netherlands. and the old *azulejos* are nothing to-day but Dutch tiles."

"It's wonderful how everything gets somewhere else some time or other," remarked the Pessimist.

"Very wonderful." I replied. "I should like to get to the Land of Nod. just now. for I'm rather tired," and we both subsided temporarily seeking "such stuff as dreams are made of."

When I awoke I found the Pessimist eyeing me reproachfully.

"Next time you go to sleep and leave me alone for hours, I wish you would n't sit on the guide-book," she remarked acridly.

"I was n't very uncomfortable." I returned, with the placidity a good nap insures.

"Is there anything more you'd like to know?"

"A great many things." severely. "Much more than you can tell, probably. Who were the Manriques?"

"There were several Manriques, all descended from the great Counts of Lara. but Jorge de Manrique is the most famous," I replied. "He was a splendid fellow, and a fighter. as most of them were. His coplas were celebrated. so much so that they are always spoken of simply as 'The Coplas of Manrique.'

"He wrote the dainty lines:

" ' Alas! where is the King Don Juan,
    Each royal heir and noble prince of Aragon?
  Where are the courtly gallantries,
  The deeds of love and high emprise
    In battle done?
  Tourney and joust that charmed the eye,
  And scarf and gorgeous panoply
    And nodding plume,
  What were they but a pageant scene?
  What but the garlands gay and green
    That deck the tomb?'

"Manrique died a heroic death in 1479, endeavoring to quell an insurrection, and in his bosom were found unfinished verses upon the uncertainty of human affairs."

"Do you know about any more Spanish poets?" said the Pessimist.

"I know a great deal," I said evasively, "but do you realize what we are coming to?

"Mountains are giving place to the famous cornfields. That river is the Guadajoz. We are nearing our journey's end, and in an hour we shall reach the spot where

.   " ' Cordova is hidden among
    The palm, the olive and the vine,
  Gem of the south, by poets sung,
  And in whose mosque Almanzor hung
  As lamps, the bells that once had rung
    At Compostelo's shrine.'

CHAPTER XI

CORDOVA AND LA MESQUITA.

"SO this is Cordova!" said the Pessimist as we stood on the famous old bridge over the Guadalquivir, which Arab writers tell us was originally built by Octavius Cæsar.

It was rebuilt by the Caliphs, and is very picturesque with its sixteen arches and Calo-harra tower, which guarded the city so well during Pedro of Castile's siege, and the view was fine from this coign of vantage.

Less Moresque than its southern Andalucian rivals, Granada and Seville, Cordova bears few traces of its magnificent past.

"It is a sad place," I said, "but 'every dog must have his day,' and it's always a consolation to me to think of that."

"I don't see why," said my friend.

"That's because you're a Pessimist," I returned. "No matter if we do get old and worn out, we have had our good time somewhere, somehow."

"Oh!" said she, "I always thought that proverb meant that you were to get old and miserable, and that your day was sure to be over."

"Oh, Pessimist, Pessimist! You're incorrigible!" I exclaimed. "But instead of mourning over the past glories of Cordova it behooves us to be sallying forth to see what is to be seen in the present. Everything else first, and then the cathedral for the last, so we can spend all the spare time within its walls. It's our last sample of Moorish Spain, remember, for we're leaving the Saracens soon."

We wandered about the streets, spotlessly clean, and the first ever paved in Europe (done by Abdu-r-rhâman in 850), and soon reached the opening at the corner of the street of the Great Captain, and street of the Conception.

"There it is, the famous St. Nicholas bell tower. How quaint and curious it is! Read those words, '*Paciencia, obediencia!*' They were put up to reprove the nuns of San Martin, who, living opposite here, objected to having the church obstruct their view."

"Where is the Alcazar?" asked the Pessimist.

"We are going there next, but you'll be disappointed if you expect much.

"It was the Caliph's palace, and was magnificent, but nothing remains now but a few walls and orchards, and the prison stands on the site. The baths and gardens of the Alcazar used to be superb, and the water was brought from the Guadalquivir by a hydraulic brick machine, called Albolafia. The baths were in perfect condition until the fifteenth century, when the water wheel was destroyed because the noise kept Queen Isabella awake when she lodged there."

"Is there a picture gallery?" asked the Pessimist.

"I 'm happy to say there 's none worth seeing. Cordova never produced great painters, and but few *literati* claim her as birthplace.

"This seems strange when one remembers that in the time of the Caliphate it was the seat of learning, the Athens of Spain. Birthplace of Seneca, Lucan and Averroes, who translated Aristotle in the twelfth century, it used to be the *Carta tuba*, or 'important city ' Phœnician times, and was called *Patricia* by the Romans, and made the capital of Ulterior of Spain.

"Because it sided with Pompey, Cæsar put to death twenty-eight thousand of its inhabitants, and under the Goths the city lost all prominence.

"The capital of the Moorish empire, under

the Ummeyâh family, Cordova attained a population of three hundred thousand, with mosques, hospitals, churches, libraries, baths, and a pleasing income of thirty million dollars a year. Quarrels soon put an end to its internal prosperity, and made it an easy prey for the Spanish who, under St. Ferdinand, took possession of the city in 1235.''

"Quite a dose of history," said the Pessimist. "Don't you know any legends or stories about these places?"

"I should think you'd be sick and tired of legends, but I know plenty of them. For before I came to Spain I was brought up on Lockhart's Spanish ballads.

"Do you remember our very unpleasant friend, Don Pedro El Cruel?

"At Montiel he met his death in a way as unpleasant as some of the punishments he inflicted on his enemies.

"His brother, Prince Henry of Trastamara, had stirred up the populace against Pedro, and, incited by the murder of Queen Blanche of Bourbon, the French aided Henry to gain the throne.

"Pedro, although helped by the English Black Prince, and successful for a time, had been compelled to yield, and in La Mancha country was taken prisoner.

"Prince Henry, finding him there, endeavored to kill him, and the old chronicles tell us that he was successful.

"So he died, and as 'of the dead nothing unless good,' we 'll let him rest in peace if he can.

"Cordova was the birthplace of Fernando Gonzalezde Cordova or the Great Captain, and also of his brother, Don Alonzo de Aguilar.

"After the conquest of Granada, many Moors stubbornly unconquered still, hid themselves in the Alpujarras, and harassed the Christian forces beyond words, falling upon them when least expected, cutting off stragglers, and doing deadly damage. Many of the flowers of Spanish chivalry were cut down.

"Don Alonzo went on a desperate venture to plant the banner of Ferdinand upon the Alpujarras; the Moors lay in ambush, and .overpowered the brave Spaniard, who fought like a lion until

" A hundred and a hundred darts are hissing round his
    head,
Had Aguilar a thousand hearts, their blood had all been
    shed,
Faint and more faint, he staggers upon the slippery sod,
At last his back is to the earth, his soul is with his God!"

"The next place we are to go is the Calle de las Cabezas, and there is the house where the heads of the Infantes de Lara were placed. The seven knights of Lara were beheaded by

an enemy at Burgos, and their heads sent to
the Moorish Caliph at Cordova. He—with a
little gentle hospitality of the day—invited
the Count of Lara (father of the seven lords)
to dine with him, and served on the table the
grinning heads. Rather an extraordinary *piece
de resistance* for a dinner!"

"Is there anything pleasant about Cordova?" asked the Pessimist. "It seems to
me it 's as bloody as Seville."

"It is, very nearly," I answered serenely,
unmoved by her fine scorn. "But it 's here
we first have glimpses of Cervantes. He
visited Cordova after his return from Algiers,
and a little later was sent to La Mancha to
collect rents for the Prior of the Order of St.
John.   The debtors refused payment, and
after persecuting Cervantes, threw him unjustly into prison, and there he began 'Don
Quixote,' which was printed at Madrid in
1604. What a wonderful character his was!
Always buoyant, always gracious, always
sweet-tempered, and generous even to Lope
de Vega, who envied and sneered at him.
Brave through misfortunes, sensible in prosperity, vivacious, yet meeting the grim
specter of a painful death from dropsy, with
calmness and sanctity.

" 'Farewell to jesting,' he said upon his
death-bed. 'Farewell, my merry humors,

farewell to my gay friends, for I feel that I am dying, and have no desire but soon to see you happy in the other life,' and with perfect serenity he died in 1616, a lovely old man.

"The convent in which he was buried was removed, and no one knows where the great man's ashes lie, but he is enshrined forever within the hearts of all who love a merry jest.

"Now, Pessimist, we 've seen everything but the cathedral, and I am hungry and tired; let us go into this cool-looking *café*, and seek a *patio*, and have a genuine Spanish luncheon."

"You remind me of a girl I once heard of. Her sister gave her a book of letters, written by an English woman, who was constantly saying, 'The Picture Gallery was fine, but I will not enter into details now. We went to luncheon at a delightful *café*,' and then would follow the *menu*."

"Well, I venture to say, if your friend's sister ever went abroad she was the victim of hunger, as I am," I replied, and we went into the neat little shop and through to the cool, pleasant *patio*.

Such a luncheon! Lamb chops, cooked in a mysterious manner, with vegetables of various kinds decorating the platter. These were followed by artichokes, with a thick butter sauce, and the tender leaves were so delicious

it seemed as if one could never tire of break-
ing them off, putting the succulent green ends
into the sauce, and eating slowly, lest the delicious flavor should go too quickly. Next
came an omelette, a *soupçon* of onion lurking
in its depths, and parsley and cheese to grace
it, potatoes in golden-brown balls, chocolate,
thick and dark, oranges, dates and figs, large,
juicy olives from the finest groves in the world
near Cordova, and Montilla to drink, sparkling Montilla, light, dry and finer even than
Xeres sherry.

The coolness of the fountain lulled my
senses, and I sat in a dreamy content until we
sallied forth, refreshed, into the quiet street.

"We will go to the cathedral, for everybody
else in Cordova is taking a *siesta*," I said.

"There!" as we approached a grove of
trees, "that is the beginning of the Court of
Oranges, and many of the orange trees date
from the sixteenth century. That splendid
pile is the famous Mesquita, or what is left of it.

" 'Let us rear a mosque,' said Abdu-r-rhâman, in 785 A.D., 'which shall surpass that of
Bagdad, of Damascus, and of Jerusalem; a
mosque which shall be the greatest temple of
Islam, one which shall become the Mecca of
the West.'

"For its building, Christian slaves were made
to toil under whip and lash, and even the

Caliph himself worked an hour every day. The walls through which we have just passed contained twenty bronzed doors, magnificent in arabesques and workmanship. Now we enter, and if we act, as De Amicis says he did, we shall be considered mad women.''

The Pessimist gave an incredulous laugh, which, however, was turned into a gasp of astonishment as we saw the vast forest of columns, and the wonderful vistas produced by these arcades of marble pillars. Twelve hundred of them from all over the world, even distant Constantinople; of all styles and shapes, of many-hued marbles, of jasper, green or blood-red, or red Brecia from Cabra.

''Oh, Pessimist!'' I exclaimed, ''look down those rows of pillars. You seem to see nineteen naves one way and twenty-nine the other, and whichever way you look it is down a vast arcade of wonder. Only see the wonderful arches! Are they not in their perfection here? I never saw such roofs before, either. They were made of *Alerce*, the unperishable *arbor vitæ*, and were gilded most wonderfully.

''The cupolas are new. Nobody cares for them. Why could n't the Spaniards have left this mosque as a sample of the Moresque? Let us see the anachronism Charles V. put in the center. He seems to have had a mania for such performances.

"When he saw how much beauty had been destroyed, he did have the grace to be displeased, and rated the chapter roundly. 'You have built here,' he said, 'what any one might have built anywhere, but in doing it you have destroyed what can never be replaced,' and he walked away disgusted."

"That was sensible of him," said the Pessimist, as she followed his example. "It's bad enough to have it here now, but in the days when the Mosque was in its glory it must have been maddening. Where is the sanctuary?"

"Here, beside these peculiarly gorgeous pillars. They called it Mihrab, and there was kept the Koran. The pulpit cost a million and a quarter of dollars, and was studded with gold nails, and made of ivory, and unequaled in all the world.

"This place is just one of those that one cannot talk about," and we wandered silently through the beautiful chapels and arcades.

Never, in all the world, were there such mosaic ornamentations of the Byzantine type, not even at St. Sophia, in Constantinople. They were called by the Greeks *psephosis*, and by the Moors, *sopysafoh*, and the artists were imported from Turkey.

The original wonders are being restored, under the direction of Don Ricardo Velasquez.

We did not seem to care for history, or to

know whose the great tombs were, or anything else, but only wished to gaze and gaze, bewildered and amazed at such beauty and such intricacy. Only one incident seemed to bring us in touch with the Christians rather than the Moors, who, if heathen, had yet done so much for art in the wondrous pile.

Upon a pillar was rudely scratched a crucifix, and it is said to have been done by a Christian captive, chained for life to this marble column because he would not accept Mohammedanism.

CHAPTER XII.

TO THE CITY OF THE GOTHS.

HE Pessimist and I nearly quarreled at leaving Cordova. I always want to stay in every place longer than I can, partly because I 'm indolent, and dislike hurry, and also because a cursory glance at any city is unsatisfactory, if one desires really to know anything about the people.

However, my companion very justly remarked that it would be the same way, no matter where I might be, and if we did n't leave Cordova then, we 'd have to give up Toledo altogether. I wanted to go out to Montilla, the birthplace of the Great Captain. Here it was that the finest castle in Andalucia was built by Gonzalo de Cordova's father, and demolished utterly by Ferdinand the Catholic, to punish the treachery of the Great Captain's nephew.

"Call me not unhappy that my castle is destroyed," said the grand old warrior, "Call me rather most wretched that I am the uncle of a traitor.''

I longed for a sight of this spot, but the Pessimist sensibly remarked:

''What good will it do you to go there, when the castle is destroyed?''

She sternly refused to permit me to visit the unpleasant huts of the hermits.

''They are ill-smelling, and feverish,'' she insisted. ''You can read all about them in the guide-book, and as they won't permit a woman inside the *Ermitas*, that will answer just as well.''

''Then let us go out to Arrizafa, and see the site of the Rizzefah of Abdu-r-rhâman. It was the most beautiful villa ever built, and the palms are superb. Abdu-r-rhâman planted the first in Spain, and wrote lovely verses about the transplanted tree,

> *'' ' Tu tambien insigne palma,*
> *Eres aqui forestra.'*

Or at least let me see the remains of the fairy palace of Azzahia, the Sultana. It was a wilderness of marble and jasper, and is called the Moorish Versailles; and the Caliph was so interested in the work that he missed three Fridays at the mosque, for which Mundhar threatened him with the fires of the Inferno. It cost millions, and was only to be compared to the palaces of the Arabian Nights.''

To all this, however, my chaperon only responded serenely:

"We will go to Toledo by way of La Mancha and Valdepeñas," and I succumbed, inwardly raging, outwardly resigned.

We crossed the Guadalbarbo, left the orange, palm, and olive trees of Cordova, and saw, looming up on our right Almodovar, one of Don Pedro's fortresses, in which he kept some of his treasures, about seventy million ducats. Then came the station of Alcolea, with the superb black marble bridge of twenty arches, and El Carpio, where rises a Moorish tower built in 1325.

Many strange and beautiful sights met my eyes, but I was not to be comforted.

"We are in the province of Don Quixote, but 'what 's Hecuba to me, or I to Hecuba?' " I murmured.

"We 're leaving Andalucia, beloved of my heart. Home of fair women and handsome men, of the gay, bright, and beautiful; of Moorish knight and brave battle. Nothing can console me for that."

A long ride through valleys and plains, and Venta de Cardenas was reached. Hither Cardenio, the curate and Dorothea took the penitent knight, upon his giving up his solitary life. Near by is Valdepeñas, named from *Val de Peñas* (vale of rocks); and here Don

Quixote cut the throats of the wine skins, instead of the throats of the Moors.

The views along the route almost reconciled me to the journey, yet there was a tugging at my heartstrings. I felt that I was leaving the best part of me behind.

"My heart, somehow, lurks in Andalucia,—a section in Granada, another in Seville, a third in Cordova," I said to the Pessimist, who smiled grimly.

"Do n't portion it out in thirds," she remarked. "Wait just a little, and an inch will be apportioned to Toledo, another to Madrid, and another to—"

"Pessimist," I said, "I 'd rather have a sectional heart than have none at all, like you! But, never mind that. Look at the view. See the snow-capped mountains, watching over everything in their pure aloofness; the old Moorish towers perched like dying eagles upon a peak or crag; the winding river, flowing blue and lovely to seek the sea; the valleys, fields, and forests, teeming with scarlet oak, strawberry trees, the purple sage, and yellow Linaria blossoms; and over all, the sky of cloudless blue, and the softest summer haze, which seems to soften all the harder points into beauty, as a filmy veil enhances the charms of a fair face."

"Very lovely!" said the Pessimist.

This was her stock expression. Everything, from an artichoke to a mountain, was "very lovely."

I relapsed into silence and the guide-book, and did not arouse myself until we were nearing Alcazar de San Juan, when the Pessimist asked:

"Where was Cervantes born?"

"No less than six places claim the honor of his birth, now that he is dead," I answered, "but really it was in Alcala de Henares, in the province of Madrid. I cannot think of Cervantes without a sigh; he was so little thought of when he was alive, and his treatment so different from that of his inferior Lope de Vega.

"Nevertheless, Spain is rather more liberal in honoring the living than many nations, as their court chronicles show."

Between Alcazar and Toledo there is little of interest, for the country is treeless, stony, and windy, as it should be from the accounts of El Hidalgo Don Quixote de la Mancha's accounts of tilting at windmills.

One changes trains at Castilejo, and Toledo is reached in an hour and a half. Our first view of the Gothic city was just at sunset, and the golden glow fell upon the stern turrets and battlements, until they looked like gold and silver walls, rather than the grim defenses they are in reality.

Toledo perches insolently upon a high hill, rocky and steep, and below rolls the Tagus, spanned by the famous bridge of Alcantara. This bridge is a marvel.   It was called by the Arabs Al-Kantarah. and built by Al-Manssour, in 997 A.D.   Fortified by Henrique I.. in 1217. the whole structure was swept away by a flood a few years later, and Alfonso El Sabio rebuilt it. in 1260.

The bridge of San Martin dates from 1212. and entwined with its fine arches is a story of how a woman saved her husband from disgrace by a clever strategy.

The architect built the bridge faultily, and feared to remove the scaffolding lest the entire structure fall to the ground.   His wife set fire to the bridge one dark night, so that his poor construction could never be discovered by the king.

As we neared the city walls the Pessimist asked :

"Where was Florinda seen by Roderick?"

"Do you see that Moorish tower open on the four sides?   That is called 'Los Baños de Florinda ' or 'El Baño de la Cava.' and there it was that Roderick saw Florinda. daughter of Count Julian, (called the 'Helen of Spain.') bathing in the Tagus. saw and loved her 'not wisely but too well ' for her own peace of mind, and the peace of his kingdom.   We have heard of the fair Florinda before, and this was the scene of the *tableau vivant* which cost the Goths the kingdom of Spain.

"Near here is the enchanters' cavern or legendary 'Tower of Hercules,' and over its portal were the words, 'Whenever a king shall pass this threshold, the Empire of Spain will fall.' Now, Roderick, being anything but a respecter of persons, laughed at this pre-diction, sought out the cavern, and needing funds badly, penetrated to the depths of the cave, there to find a coffer, upon whose lid was inscribed, 'Open me, and thou shalt see wonders.' Roderick promptly complied, ready to seize the magnificent treasures within, when lo! all that he found was a linen scroll. On this were painted Moorish figures, and the words: 'He who opens this chest shall lose the kingdom of Spain by these armies.' Fatal words!

"A few days later, Roderick, and all his army, met a bloody fate upon the field of bat-tle, and the Moorish dominion in Spain was established. 'Twas of this that Sir Walter Scott wrote his 'Vision of Don Roderick.'

"Toledo looks like a mediæval stronghold, and bears but few traces of Goth or Moor," I said to the Pessimist, as leaving the railway carriage we climbed into an omnibus, drawn by stout mules, to drive to the city. "Everybody has a *navaja* in his belt.   We must buy a Toledo blade before we go.

"Are n't the costumes of the people charming? Look at that man. He has velvet breeches, leggins, a scarlet sash, braided jacket, and looks like one of a stage chorus. Here we come to the *Puerta del Sol* (Gate of the Sun). What a warm, orange color it is, and how beautiful! Ah, that is at least a remnant of Moorish architecture, and what a beautiful double arch under which runs the street! Now, we 're really in Toledo; but what streets! They are nearly as narrow as those in Tangier. I wonder if all the streets are like these."

And they are. Like a fine net-work, they stretch in narrow ways, away from and into each other, so that Toledo, without a guide, is an impossibility.

The streets are all dissimilar, and the houses wonderful. They are covered with coats of arms, arabesques, carvings, and towers; in each corner lurks the picturesque; each stone is replete with memories of romances and legends. One can get but a faint idea of the beauties of Toledo, under Moorish rule, or the glories of it after the Spanish conquest, for, since the court was removed to Madrid, it has become like a silent city of the dead.

THE GATE OF THE SUN, TOLEDO.

"Tell me some stories of Toledo, and what we shall see to-morrow," said my companion that night, as we sat resting after dinner.

I had my mouth full of *mazapan* at the moment, and could not answer Now, all ye who go to Toledo, listen to me! Miss seeing any of the sights you wish, neglect the cathedral, slight the churches, skim the history, an you will, but do not fail to eat all the *mazapan* you can.

What is it?

A compound not peculiar to Toledo, but found nowhere else in such perfection; bewilderingly delicious; also equally deadly, warranted to kill at twelve paces—a concoction of pastry, burned sugar, and almonds, formed into shapes as fantastic as are the quaint little shops where one buys them. Apricots and mazapan are the sights of Toledo.

I bit off the head of a knight in armor, and replied to my friend's demand.

"Do you know the story of King Galafrio's daughter? He was king here before Charlemagne reigned in France, and had a beautiful daughter named Galiana."

"It must have been charming to live then," interrupted the Pessimist. "Mediæval maids were always transcendently lovely."

"Charlemagne was then very young," I

went on, heedless of the interruption, "and he came to visit Toledo, and naturally fell in love with the princess. She, however, was betrothed to Bradamente, Moorish King of Guadalajara, and he adored the princess so much that he had tunneled a way from his city to her palace. Alas for the devoted Moor! She preferred Charlemagne, and the latter challenged Bradamente to combat, and killed him, and, in the pleasing manner of the day, presented the head to Galiana. The gentle lady accepted it, *á la* Herodias' daughter (and Charlemagne with it), and afterward, became Queen of France.

"Then there is the story of Wamba. He and Ervigius were rivals, and the latter poisoned Wamba, and clothed him in the particular variety of monk's cowl which, once on, could never be removed.

"Wamba recovered from the poisoning but could n't get over the cowl, so he retired to the Monastery of Pampliago, and died a monk, as many of the Spanish nobles, and even kings have done.

"He did wisely, perhaps, in retiring while he was in favor, and his name has to this day a pleasant sound to the Spaniards.

"Very unlike this is the reputation of Witiza, more wicked than Nero, in the Spanish estimation, and known in all the old chronicles

as, 'that Witiza who taught Spain to sin.'
The especial sins he inculcated into the innocent breasts of Gothic Spain were murdering
any or all of one's relations, making the
canons of the cathedral marry, and putting
two bishops over the church. 'For,' he said,
'if the cathedral will not yield herself to me,
she shall have two husbands instead of one.'
But Retributive Justice (with capital letters)
sits enthroned on many pages of history, and
with special frequency in Spain.

"Witiza was deposed by Roderick, son of
Theodolfredo, imprisoned, made to suffer as
he had made others suffer, and with his eyes
seared out with red-hot irons, died miserably
in a dungeon."

"What are the people like?" asked the
Pessimist, who had attacked the mazapan, and
was engaged in devouring a large serpent, no
doubt similar to the one which ate Roderick
the Goth.

"They used to be noted for their cultiva-
tion, and Marguerite de Valois, sister of Francis I., and author of L'Heptameron, said, '*Le
langage Castilian est sans comparaison mieux
declarant cette passion d'amour que n'est le
Français.*' Charles V. carried Castilian to
Germany, and Philip II. to the English court
when he married Mary Tudor; and of all forms
of Castilian, Toledan is the purest.

"King Alfonso X. decided by law that in case a doubt arose as to the meaning of any word, the Toledan sense or pronunciation should be accepted. Great learning existed here, and Toledo boasts such names as, Garcilaso de la Vega, Garci Perez de Vargas, and Francisco de Rojas, authors of renown. The people commingle Andalucian grace with northern dignity, and southern vivacity with more sterling qualities. Their loyalty is so noted as to have become almost a proverb. Alfonso VI. said at the Cortes, when a great revolution was pending, 'Let Burgos speak first; I will speak for Toledo, which will do what I wish.'

"Toledo women are quite different from the women of other provinces. They have been called the pearls of old Castile. They are exquisitely neat, and always well dressed in calico skirts, red woolen petticoats, and wear gay kerchiefs over their shoulders. They are graver, more serious, more open, more faithful than the southern Spaniards, more matter-of-fact, less gay. They call a spade a spade, with calm insistency, or as their proverb has it, '*Al pan, pan, y al vino, vino.*'

"As for the Toledans of to-day, they are as brave, as just, as proud as their ancestors. They love music, and poetry, are fond of art, and are alert and bold, notwithstanding a

Spanish poet of a rival city has called them 'a silly people.'"

"Who was the Garci Perez of whom you spoke?" demanded the Pessimist.

"A gay cavalier who disported himself at the siege of Seville in 1248," I answered.

"He was born in Toledo, and fought in St. Ferdinand's army. One day he was riding with only one companion, when he saw seven Moors approaching. The friend of Don Garci took to flight, but

'The Lord of Vargas turned him round, his trusty sword
    was near,
The helmet on his brow he bound, his gauntlet grasped a
    spear,'

and without further ado he walked serenely past the Moors, who did not attack him.

"Having reached a safe place, however, Don Garci discovered that he had lost his scarf, and started back to find it.

'I had it from my lady,' quoth Garci, 'long ago,
And never Moor that scarf, be sure, in proud Seville shall
    show.'

"He rescued it, escaped unhurt, and returned to the Christian camp; and the ballad says,

'That day the Lord of Vargas came to the camp alone,
The scarf his lady's largess, around his breast was
    thrown,
Bare was his head, his sword was red, and from his pom-
    mel strung
Seven turbans green, sore hacked, I ween, before Don
    Garci hung.'

"He was brother to the Perez who was called 'The Pounder' because when he had broken his sword he pulled up an olive tree, and killed a dozen Moors with it. Don Quixote quotes this legend, when he speaks to Sancho Panza of Don Diego Perez de Vargas, and says, 'I intend to tear up the next oak-tree we meet, and with the trunk thereof I hope to perform such deeds as thou wilt esteem thyself happy in having had the honor to behold them!'

"So much for legends and people, and to-morrow for the cathedral, and all the other places of interest with which the city fairly teems."

CHAPTER XIII.

"TOLEDO, BUILT AND WALLED AMONG THE WARS OF WAMBA'S TIME."

T first the cathedral of Toledo is a distinct disappointment.

As Antwerp and Cologne used to be, it is so hedged in by mean houses, that a just idea of its size cannot be gained. Its history is stupendous. The consecration stone, still preserved, says that it was built by King Recared, in 587, and tradition tells of a visit of the Blessed Virgin to St. Ildefonso here, in the seventh century.

The Moors turned it into a mosque, and when King Alfonso V. conquered Toledo, in 1085, he permitted the Moors to worship in it for a time. Later, by the influence of Bishop Bernard, it was made a Christian church again.

All this magnificent building, however, was destroyed by St. Ferdinand, and the present church erected. The exterior is Gothic, massive, with a fine tower, and an insignificant dome, many statues, much carving, and superb bronze doors, especially those at the Puerta de los Leones, so-called from the fine marble lions placed on the pillars.

The Pessimist and I wandered discontentedly around the outside of the huge building, endeavoring to get a good view of it, craning our necks, and giving ourselves cramp in the collar bone, but succeeding only in squinting viciously at the statues, while they leered back at us with mediæval insolence.

"Let us go inside," I said, for I knew the Pessimist was about to make discouraging remarks, and I was too disheartened myself to wish to be compelled to cheer her up.

Fortunately for my spirits, which had sunk far below normal, I was happily disappointed, for the five great naves, four hundred feet long, and bisected by a sixth, were majestic and solemn. There lurked a churchly quiet within their shadowy depths; a glimmer of color filtered through the marvelous stained windows, and the whole church breathed an air of sanctity, loftiness and repose, with none of the gloom so often found in Gothic churches, where there is but a "dim, religious light."

We wandered idly through the many

chapels. Everything was beautiful to rest the eye upon, and one scarcely cared for the mere details of sight-seeing. There are royal tombs, mausoleums of cardinals and bishops, strangely enough without inscriptions or statues.

Perhaps the most wonderful part of the interior is the choir. The pavement is of white marble divided by broad slabs of dark marble inlaid, and over the altar is a an image of the Blessed Virgin in black wood. The Spanish peasant thinks she was undoubtedly Spanish, and would be deeply indignant if you told him she was a Jew. He likes saints and angels represented as dark as possible, "*Moreno pintaron el Cristo !*"

The lower half of the choir stalls is carved into medallions representing the siege and capture of the Moors by Ferdinand and Isabella, while the recesses between the seats in the upper row are divided by jasper pillars.

A curious fact about the choir is that the upper portion represents saints, angels, and patriarchs, while the lower represents warriors, and each row is in a style of carving of a different period.

The Muzarabic chapel was built to preserve the old ritual of the Mass, used by those Goths, who succumbing to Moorish rule, were allowed to retain their own form of worship.

The sacristan told a curious tale of the preservation of this ritual to the Toledan church.

"It differed, señoritas," the old monk said, "from the ritual used at Rome, and the Holy Father desiring to preserve everywhere the unity of the church, which is one of the signs that it is the true church, desired the Toledans to follow the usual rule. They did not like to desert the customs of their ancestors, and determined to make the test by fire, so often used in the Middle Ages. Two huge piles were lighted in the Zocodover; the two missals were placed upon them; one was burned, but a puff of wind blew out the fire under the Toledan missal, and it is used to this day. But only here, in one chapel, in memory of our fathers.

"Have you seen the chapel of Santiago?" asked our kindly guide, and as we answered, "No," he led us to this gem of Gothic work, in the shape of an octagon.

"Here," said the monk, "lies buried Don Alvaro de Luna, Constable of Castile, Grand Master of Santiago. He was the king's favorite, but was executed unjustly at Valladolid, in 1452. He was a man great in peace and in war, and with rare nobility of soul, yet he died an ignominious death.''

We wandered for hours until weary and foot-sore, seeing ever new wonders, until worn out with so much beauty we paused to rest in the quiet cloisters, near the Puerta del Mollete. ''Why is this called '*del Mollete?*' '' asked the Pessimist.

'' '*Mollete*' means loaf,'' I said, ''and loaves of bread were here distributed to the poor. What shall you remember in all the cathedral?''

''The grave of Archbishop Portocarrero,'' said the Pessimist, ''and the inscription, 'Hic jacet pulvis, cinis, nullus.' (Here lies dust, ashes, naught),'' she replied, to my surprise, for she is not given to noticing details.

''I doubt if I shall ever be able to recall anything,'' I said. ''My mind feels like a Nesselrode pudding, cold, and stuffed with all sorts of things; but I 'm certain, I sha 'n't ever forget the impression which the whole thing gives of magnificence and grandeur. Oh for a few mediæval cathedrals in our own nineteenth century!''

''It 's time for some stories,'' said the Pessimist, and I laughed and began.

''When King Alfonso was captured by his brother, Don Sancho, who wished to unite Castile and Leon under his own rule, Donna

Urraca, the sister of both Alfonso and Sancho urged the latter to allow Alfonso to become a monk in the monastery of Sahagun. Don Sancho granted this request, but Alfonso, probably concluding that vows made at the sword's point did not require keeping, promptly ran away from the monastery, and sought refuge with the Moorish king at Toledo.

"Now the Cid had been on the side of Donna Urraca, and so Don Sancho was decidedly displeased with this doughty warrior, who seems to have fought with equal impartiality on any side.   Don Sancho banished him forthwith, and,

> 'The Cid with all his vassals
> Hath left his native land,
> And he has to Toledo gone
> To join Alfonso's band.'

"However, before he got there, Don Sancho evidently thought better of it, and recalled him to court.   During the siege of Toledo, in 1085, Diego, the Cid's only son, was slain, and this city always had mournful associations for the Campeador.

"Alvar Fanez had followed the Cid in all his campaigns, and was made governor of Toledo to represent the Cid, governing wisely and well, and defending the city bravely against the Moors."

"If you do n't mind my saying so," re-marked the Pessimist, "I 'm rather tired of the Cid. Do we have to meet him in every Spanish city?"

"Oh, no," I replied cheerfully. "Not quite. We 're going to bury him in Burgos."

"Allah be praised!" said the Pessimist.

"That 's what the Moors said, when he died," I answered. "Now, we 're going to see some of the churches. Santa Maria la Blanca comes first. It was an old syna-gogue, and was in the Jewish quarter; and the interior is a beautiful collection of polyg-onal columns and horse-shoe arches. The Jews were turned out, and it was made a Christian church, afterward barracks, and is now in a state of repair. El Transito also was a synagogue. It has the motto, 'We who in-habit this land have built this house with a strong and powerful arm.' The Jews abounded in Toledo, and are said to have betrayed it to the Moors.

"The most interesting church in Toledo is Cristo de la Luz, a fine specimen of Moorish architecture.

"It was named from an adventure of our ac-quaintance the Cid. Riding past it one day, the Cid's steed, the famous Bavieca, knelt reverently, and instantly, within a niche ap-peared an image of Our Lord, lighted by the remains of the old Gothic lamps. It is a tiny place, but very perfect as to detail; and here Alfonso VI. went to say his prayers, and hung up his shield to commemorate his victory over the Moors. There it hangs still.''

''What is the legend of El Cristo de la Vega?'' asked the Pessimist.

''That is an interesting church, and what is called *pretoriensis*, the center of a judicial power, and is named from the legend of a Spanish maid, Inez Vargos.

''She was betrothed to Diego Martinez, and he, departing to the war in Flanders, returned a Grandee, and forgot his betrothed.

''She appealed to the governor for justice, and he asked her for a witness. Now, it chanced that Diego's betrothal vow had been made beneath the statue of the Cristo de la Vega, and to this Inez appealed. A vast concourse assembled before the statue, and Don Pedro de Alarcon — the governor — cried, 'Cristo de la Vega, I pray Thee show us a sign, if Thou hast heard Diego Martinez swear to be the husband of Inez Vargos?'

''Fancy the wonder of the great multitude when the arm of the statue suddenly loosened itself from the crucifix, and fell to the side as if to sign assent.''

''What became of Inez? Did she marry the recalcitrant knight?'' asked the Pessimist.

"Of course not. She went into a convent, and he became a Carmelite; but it 's just as well, probably. If I had to get a husband by a miracle, I should n't care for him."

"What is that huge building?" she asked, as we passed a fine structure in the Spanish renaissance style.

"It was built in 1504 by the Catholic queen, and was the Hospital of Santa Cruz, built in the form of a Maltese cross. It is now the Infantry College.

"Next comes San Juan de los Reyes, with walls hung with the chains taken from Christian captives at Granada. Despite all a woman's natural sympathy for the under dog, I think the Moors must have been rather vicious taskmasters, and Ferdinand and Isabella did a good thing when they turned them out. They may have understood the fine arts, but they had down to a fine point the arts of cruelty.

"When Charles V. rewarded the Constable de Bourbon for his treason to Francis I., he presented him with a house here in Toledo; but no one will tell where it is, for it was called the Traitor's House, and the Toledanos conceal its whereabouts as carefully as the people of Marblehead do that of old Floyd Ireson.

"Here is the Alcazar. What a great pile it is! What a shame, it 's falling to pieces, and too, what a perfect color that chalky stone has turned with time!

"The view of the river here is the finest we have had.

"By the time we have seen a few of the private houses we shall be worn out.   In fact I am now, but we must not miss the Talleo del Moro and Las Tornerias, the best examples of the Moorish houses to be found."

"I won't see anything more," said the Pessimist, firmly.   "I shall soon be as mad as a March hare or Don Quixote."

"There are only five thousand lunatics in Spain; please don't make the five thousand and first," I answered.   "But, I daresay, we had better go and digest what we have seen, instead of cramming till we are mentally the size of poor Sancho the Fat, who had to apply to the Moors to reduce his flesh, because his subjects laughed at and would not obey him."

"You talk as if your mind were a mental baloon, and would expand at will," said the Pessimist.

> "'And still the wonder grew,
>   That one small head could carry all she knew,'"

I quoted, and we ceased our sight-seeing, and dreamed where,

"' Rearing their crests amid the cloudless skies
    And darkly clustering in the pale moonlight,
  Toledo's holy towers and spires arise
    As from a trembling lake of silver white.
    Their mingled shadows intercept the sight
  Of the broad burial-ground outstretched below,
    And naught disturbs the silence of the night;
  All sleeps in sullen shade or silver glow,—
  All save the heavy swell of Tejo's ceaseless flow.' "

CHAPTER XIV.

IN OLD MADRID.

"Long years ago, in old Madrid,
Where softly sighs of love the light guitar,"

SANG, vigorously drumming an accompaniment on the window pane, as I looked restlessly into the busy street below.

Fate was proving unkind during our stay in Madrid. We were not to remain many days, and the first one had been rainy and disagreeable. The Pessimist had developed a violent cold, and a wild desire to go home, while I was cross enough to give to her the unpleasant adjectives I had applied to the weather.

At last I remarked:

"I am going out!"

"Not by yourself," said my chaperon, sternly.

"I 'll take the maid with me, then," I replied, ringing for the pretty Madrileña who cared for our room.

200

By means of my small supply of Spanish, some French, and a great many gestures, I managed to convey to her my intense desire for her society, and she ran off to ask the mistress of our Casa de Huespedes (lodging house) if she might play *cicerone*.

In an incredibly short time she brought back a radiant face, surmounted with a black veil, and permission to remain as long as the most gracious lady wished.

The gracious lady was charmed.

"Good-bye, Pessimist," I said; "I 'm sorry you can 't go, but I 'll come home and tell you all about everything, and here 's the 'Diary of an Idle Woman in Spain ' for you to read. It 's the most delightful book about the country that I know."

"You need n't hurry back on my account, for I shall read and sleep," said my friend, with unusual amiability; and Esperanza and I started out.

Everything in Madrid seems to start from the Puerta del Sol, and thither we made our way. What an array of people! What astonishing shops! Gloves, laces, silks, mantillas, and Spanish fans without number; men smoking cigarrillos, laughing, chatting, and devising numberless schemes which prove veritable castles in Spain.

The street railways, *tramvia*, as the Spaniards call them, start from this square, and go in every direction all over the city.

The scene was gay, bright, and Frenchy, but modern, and I turned to Esperanza, begging to be taken somewhere else. That I did not like the city was evident, but what I wanted was beyond her comprehension.

"The Señorita does not like the Puerta del Sol; will she go to the Palace?" she said.

"No; no thank you. I want something old; something different," I answered petulantly.

She knit her brows in perplexity.

"The bull-ring? No? The Town Hall? The Prado? The Congress? No?"

At last with an air of relief she cried:

"Some churches!" and I nodded assent.

Madrid is far from being rich in churches. There is no cathedral worth the name, for the new cathedral, begun in 1885, is not likely to be finished during this century.

Nearly all the churches are of renaissance architecture, with large pillars, insignificant windows, tawdry interiors; and Madrid seems so new, from a historic point of view, that there is little of romance or story connected with the buildings.

"This is San Francisco el Grande," said Esperanza. The church is said to have been founded in the thirteenth century, but the present building replaced the old one in 1760. Here was buried one of the strangest characters of the fifteenth century, Enrique de Villena, a magician, whose books upon the subject of the black arts were burned by order of Henry IV. in the cloisters of St. Domingo el Real. One of these books remains, "Libro de los Trabojos de Hercules," which is still preserved in Madrid by Señor Gayangos.

The books of Villena reminded me of another famous manuscript, and I sallied forth into the Calle General Castaños to see the rare "Chronicle of the Cid."

Esperanza could not understand, but she saw me interested at last, and followed complacently as I sought the famous manuscript, which was written in Castile, in 1207, by a simple monk, called Pedro. The Epic of Spain, it has been called; and it is a fine commentary not only upon the Spanish Bayard, as El Cid is spoken of, but also upon the customs and manners of the times when people went to war as a trade, and courage and cruelty clasped hands.

"Will the Americana see the sacred statue, Nuestra Señora de Atocha?" asked the maid.

"Tell me about it," I said, as we wended our way toward the church of the Buen Suceso, the statue's temporary home.

"It was carved by the Blessed Saint Luke,

and brought to Spain from Antiocha," she said.

Nothing is more pleasing than to hear Spanish peasants tell legends. They do it with such simple reverence and faith that the most incredulous must believe. I always believe in people and things until I am forced to do otherwise. Surely faith is better than doubt.

"At the foot of the figure is the word *Theotokos*. I do not know what it means, señorita, but Fray Pedro says it is the Greek tongue," she continued.

"When the old church of the Atocha was here, every Saturday the king and the queen-regent came to sing the *Salve* at the shrine. Now, the church is being made new, and *Nuestra Señora* is taken to the *Buen Suceso*."

"I am sorry the Atocha is torn down, for all sorts of people were buried there; Mendoza, Charles V.'s confessor; General Palafox, famous in the siege of Zaragosa, and one man in whom I 've always been interested, Bartolomé de las Casas. Do you know about him, Esperanza?"

"No, señorita; will you tell me?" she said, her eyes shining.

"He was a Spanish priest who was very fond of the Indians," I began. "Now, you know, the people who used to live in America in those days were not as I am, white, but copper-colored creatures called Indians; and though they were very kind and gentle, the Spaniards treated them so harshly, and made them work so hard that many of them died.

"Las Casas tried to help them, and wrote books about what the Spanish did, and oh! lots of things," I added, rather vaguely.

Esperanza listened attentively, and of all people in the world, Spaniards are the most delightful listeners.

I thought I had impressed her deeply, both with the fact that I was a wonderfully learned person, and also that Las Casas was a great man.

Whether it was that I overrated the mental calibre of a Spanish girl of seventeen, or that I did not realize the difficulties of history lessons in my somewhat limited vocabulary, —at any rate, all that I received in answer to my lecture was an uplifting of two daintily arched black brows, and

"Is it so much in your country to write about the things our people do? But, of course, the señorita is interested in the Indians, since they are her fathers."

I subsided into silence, and spoke not for several moments, until we entered the church of Santo Domingo.

This is an ordinary looking church, founded

in 1219, by one of the Guzman family, with tombs of all manner of royalties and celebrities.

As I browsed about, over the tesselated pavement, trying to decipher inscriptions with which defacing time had dealt as hardly as with the memories of those beneath, I gave an exclamation of surprise.

"Here he is!" I exclaimed. "My old friend Don Pedro. Let me bid a last farewell to the *Justiciero*. So this is all that 's left of your golden locks and azure eyes and cruel smile. Nothing but dust, and a time-worn monument. No more churches! I want to go and eat luncheon, and rest and think about dear, lovely Seville, the Alcazar, and Don Pedro. Madrid is dull and uninteresting and tiresome."

So we went to a dear little café, "El Suizo," in the Calle de Alcala, and had an excellent *puchero*, and some *valdepeñas*, which soothed my feelings considerably.

A *puchero* is what the French call a *mélange* and is the genuine Spanish national dish. It is to the cuisine what renaissance is to art, a little of everything and not much of anything.

It contains boiled beef, wings of chicken, *chorizo*, herbs, bacon and *garbanzos*. When one has eaten *puchero*, one wishes nothing else, and I enjoyed my lunch, and far more enjoyed seeing Esperanza eat with me.

There is something exquisitely delightful to me about the calm self-respect of the Spaniards.

They respect themselves so keenly that they respect you, too, and the perfect politeness—nay more—courtesy of their demeanor is wonderful. An American chambermaid, taken out for a day, as Esperanza was, would have spent her time in alternate fits of trying to show herself as good as you, and sulking because she felt she was not.

Of all things in Spain, I think the manners of the people strike one as most remarkable. They are never ill-bred, no matter what the class of society in which they live. Their manners vary according to the part of the country in which they are brought up. In Andalucia they are gay; in Aragon, grave; in Castile, deferential; but everywhere, prince or pauper, noble or peasant or beggar, each and all are courteous and thoughtful of the comfort of others.

An English writer tells a charming story of an old crippled beggar, ragged and not too clean, who got into a crowded omnibus. Instantly a young officer in gay uniform rose, and led the beggar by the hand to his seat.

As he was crowded next to two ladies, they smiled, and bowed to him, and he sat there smiling, too, and trying his poor best to occupy as little room as possible.

A pretty story, and one truly illustrative of the Spanish manners. One draws very invidious comparisons between such actions and the ungracious way that seats are sometimes offered in our street-cars, and the almost offensive way in which "miladi" draws her skirts away from the unfortunate by her side.

Esperanza and I sallied forth refreshed and ready to seek "fresh woods and pastures new," and I said, "Now, Esperanza, take me to all the places you like best in Madrid."

The girl's face glowed.

"The señorita is jesting," she exclaimed, but I reassured her. "Then we will go to the Prado," she said; and thither we went, going first, however, as we drove about the gay streets, to see the Bull Ring.

How she delighted in telling me about this huge building!

"It cost eight million reals, señorita, and oh, such glorious courses as we have! Six bulls to die! And oh, the *matador*, and the costumes, and all the people shouting! Ah! you should surely go on Sunday next."

"No, thank you, Esperanza," I said. "I shall content myself with seeing the ring."

The attendants led us into the great sand-covered space with tier after tier of seats rising from it. We saw, too, the long, dark stalls for the bulls, and several ferocious beasts glared at us from behind their bars, arousing in my breast no desire to see them nearer, or to witness a fight.

Esperanza was delighted, and I could with difficulty drag her away. We drove down to the Prado, as the afternoon waned; and many gorgeous carriages were those we saw, as we entered the large meadow, near the Retiro, in the palace of which Philip IV. resided.

The obelisk "Dos de Mayo" stands on the Prado, and this is to commemorate the soldiers who fell on the second of May, 1808, fighting the French.

The fountains in the Prado were playing; and the Fuente de Cibeles is very handsome, with its quaint figures of lions driven by Cibeles.

As we drove out of the shady Prado our carriage drew up at one side of the road, and Esperanza nearly went out of her mind with excitement. She bobbed up and down on the seat until I expected to see her go over the side of the carriage, exclaiming over and over again, *El Rey! El Rey!* "

I thought she had lost her senses, but as I saw our coachman take off his hat, and everybody look expectant, I concluded that something was going to happen.

Something did, and one of the prettiest things I ever saw.

Behind an escort of mounted soldiers came a handsome carriage, drawn by black horses, and upon the cushions a charming boy. Long curls lay on his shoulders, and the black velvet of his suit set off the exquisite hues of his complexion. It was the boy king, with his mother, the queen regent, by his side. The people shouted and cried vociferously:

"*El Rey !*"

He smiled and bowed with such patrician grace as to make him seem kingly indeed, when from the crowd of bystanders came a child's cry. A tiny girl, younger than the small king, was stretching out her fat little hand, full of flowers. Alfonso gave an order to the coachman, and leaned out of the carriage in spite of his mother's detaining hand. At his quick command a guard brought the child to the carriage, and the boy-king took the flowers, pressing a piece of gold into the baby fingers, and smiling at the little one till she smiled through her tears.

Then the shout that went up was deafening, and by a simple, kindly act, such as this, the youthful king won many hearts.

I shall always feel that Alfonso the King, was the most charming sight I saw in Madrid. Esperanza was almost speechless as we drove home, and only remarked, as we passed the church of Caballero de Gracias:

"Jacopo de Grattis died here, one hundred and two years old."

I could have told her that here also was Anthony Ascham murdered, in 1650. He was Cromwell's ambassador, and slain here by English Royalists, because he had voted for the death of poor King Charles I.

We drove past the Town Hall, an oblong building with square towers, and here used to be the Consejo de Madrid, where the *Autos Sacramentales* or sacred plays took place, under the auspices of the *Ayuntamiento*. Calderon wrote seventy-two of these *autos*, but many of them were stolen or lost. Lope de Vega's are even finer than Calderon's.

Near by was the house of Ximenes, and from the balcony on the Calle del Sacramento, the great cardinal stood, when he made his memorable answer to the nobles.

They asked the haughty churchman by what charter he had power over them; and pointing to the troops and cannon in the valley of the Manzanares below, the great statesman replied, "These are the powers by which I govern the kingdom, and I will continue to do so until the king, your master and mine, comes to relieve me.''

The Torre de los Lujanes next caught my eye, and I had only time to glance at its noble outlines before hurrying home to tell its story to my friend, for it grew late.

''Well, what have you seen?'' asked the Pessimist, as I burst in upon her. ''And what do you like best?''

''I like the little king, and the tower of Francis I. Oh! I want you to see that tower. It is so interesting.''

''What Francis I.?'' she asked.

''Why the Francis I. of France,'' I exclaimed.

''How did he get there; by aerial navigation?'' she demanded.

''Oh! don't you remember? I always liked that story.

''Well, in 1520 both Charles V. of Austria and Spain, and Francis d'Angoulême were rivals for the throne of France, and gay handsome, joyous, brilliant, courteous Francis was far more pleasing to the French than the great Charles, stern and cold as he was. Francis said, when the rivalry began, 'We are but two gallants courting the same mistress, and he who fails will have no excuse for ill-temper,' but they came to blows about it finally.

''Then came the episode of the Constable

du Bourbon, whose life Louise of Savoy ruined, because he would not marry her.

"He turned to the Spanish, and it was to him the dying Chevalier Bayard said, on the field of battle, 'Pity not me; I die as an honest man. I rather pity *you*, in arms against your king, your country and your oath.'

"Upon this disaster, at which all France mourned (for everybody adored The Good Knight, as Bayard was called), followed closely the capture of Francis at the Battle of Pavia. Hemmed in by the enemy on all sides, his chosen knights dying around him, twice thrown from his horse, twice wounded, his magnificent coat-of-mail stained deep with blood, the gallant king was at last forced to yield his sword.

"Charles was exultant. The royal prisoner was brought to Madrid, and imprisoned in that very tower I saw to-day, that of Los Lu-janes. Here he is supposed to have written the line to his mother, 'All is lost save honor,' and here he languished; although the author of the 'Stories of the Kings of Navarre' tells us he could hear the singing and merry-making at his capture in the valley below.

"Then he was taken to the palace, and kept close prisoner in a manner scarce befitting his rank and name. After remaining a year, he signed the Treaty of Madrid, relinquishing to Charles, Burgundy and Italy, and giving up his two sons as hostages. Hurrying from the gloomy prison, Francis passed the Bidasoa, and crying, 'I am King again!' hastened to Bayonne. Then followed more wars, Charles swearing he would make, 'the King of France as poor as any gentleman in his dominions;' and it was not until 1544 that the Treaty of Crespy settled the wars which had lasted a quarter of a century.

"There 's a sword which belonged to Francis down in the Armory, and we must go there to-morrow and see it and the famous pictures in the Gallery, but I do n't believe there 's much else you 'll care for, Pessimist."

"I would care for some pleasant weather more than anything," she remarked, rather grimly, as we prepared for table d'hôte.

PICTURES OLD AND NEW.

HE next day deigned to smile, and the Pessimist awoke more cheerfully inclined than was her wont, so we hurried out to see our pictures while the spirit moved, reaching the famous gallery when the light was fine.

The building is large and low, and was used as a barracks during the time of the French occupation. Is there any place the poor French are not accused of desecrating? From the church of Santa Maria della Grazie, in Milan, where the Percheron horses defaced with their vandal hoofs da Vinci's 'Last Supper,' to every city in Spain, cries are heard about the French.

Such an array of pictures! We first looked at those of the foreign schools, feasting our eyes upon the works of Raphael, Titian, Guido Reni, Paul Veronese, Tintoretto, Domenichino, Andrea del Sarto, Claude Lorraine, Poussin, Rembrandt, Rubens, Van Dyke, Correggio, Watteau, Wouvermans, and Teniers.

Then we gasped and sat down.

"What do you remember?" asked the Pessimist, at last.

"Only two: Raphael's 'La Perla,' and Titian's 'Charles V.'

"Of the first Philip II. said it was the pearl of all his pictures, but many think it was called 'La Perla' from the tiny oyster among our Lord's playthings. It cost ten thousand dollars, and was bought from the short-sighted Puritans when they sold the crown effects of poor Charles I. of England.

"It was painted by Raphael for the Duke Federigo Gonzaga of Mantua, and is one of the master's finest works.

"Titian's 'Charles V.' I shall never forget. Somebody says it is the finest equestrian picture in the world.

"The great emperor is represented on horseback as he appeared at the battle of Muhlberg, and the armor he wore is in the Armeria now. Titian was sent for several times at Augsburg to paint the emperor's portrait; and he seems to have had a clear conception of the character of that wonderful man, for perfect comprehension of his subject shows in every stroke of the artist's brush.

"I like this picture far better than 'La Gloria,' though that is considered Titian's masterpiece."

"It seems to me that Charles V. never did anything but fight," said the Pessimist.

"He did one pretty thing, if he never did anything else. Do you remember Longfellow's poem about him? He was encamped before a beleagured Flemish city, and a swallow built its nest at the top of the royal tent.

"The courtiers started to dislodge it, but the emperor stayed the daring hand.

> "'Let no hand the bird molest,'
>   Said he solemnly, ' Nor hurt her!'
> Adding then by way of jest,
> 'Golondrina is my guest,
>   'T is the wife of some deserter.'

"He left the tent standing there, not only until the siege was over, but even when he returned to Spain.

> "' So it stood there all alone,
>   Loosely flapping, torn and tattered,
>   Till the brood was fledged and flown,
>   Singing o'er those walls of stone
>   Which the cannon shot had shattered.'

"It 's nice to think of that stern old emperor, whom everybody feared, being so gentle to the wee birds."

"We 're all 'building nests in Fame's great temple, as in spouts the swallow builds,' " quoted the Pessimist. "We do n't always have such pleasant things to hear of great people."

"Now we must go and see the Spanish pictures," I said.

"First Murillo; I suppose the 'Conceptions' are his best. The greatest is said to be the one in the Louvre, but I love them all; the misty, vaporoso style, the great, soft, dark-eyed Madonnas, the floating Titian hair, the blue robes and darling babies, bodiless, and floating around airily on wings.

"Then there is the 'Annunciation,' and the lily is fairly pick-able while 'St. John the Baptist' is the dearest little fellow I ever saw."

"Where is the 'St. Elizabeth?'" asked the Pessimist.

"Over in the Academia de San Fernando, and there are also the paintings of the dream of the Roman noble who founded the church of Santa Maria Maggiore at Rome.

"One *admires* other painters; one *loves* Murillo, and seems to be closely in touch with his tender heart.

"Now comes the famous portrait of Murillo by Tobar. He was Murillo's best pupil, and that he loved his master well shows in the care with which he has painted this beautiful portrait. Velazquez's 'Surrender of Breda,' is said to be his finest work. There it is. Look at the splendid soldiers, and the fine background, with Breda in the distance. General Spinola is accepting the surrender of the heavy Flemish leader with perfect courtesy, and his fine, high-bred face is marvelously well-done.

"Vulcan's forge is another famous Velasquez, but I do n't fancy it, though one cannot help admiring the masterly handling of the subject.

"The Velasquez which I like the best is that of Philip IV. on horseback. The horse seems about to step out and prance down the room, arching his neck and neighing, and the king seems alive, as he sits there against that cool blue and green background. To see Velasquez's pictures is always to remember his figures, and to have them live in one's mind forever.

"Now comes Ribera, who was called 'Lo Spagnoletto.' Ugh! his pictures give me cold shivers. Sombre, fierce, and powerful, some of his work reminds me of a dissecting room. Do n't let 's look at his pictures, though 'Jacob's Ladder' is fine in its strange way.

"De Amicis says, 'Ribera never loved,' and yet he draws the eyes to his work with a sort of artistic hypnotism. His 'St. Anthony' is exquisite.

"Goya comes next, Spanish to the finger tips, painter of bulls and brigands; an Aragonese, haughty, fiery, full of genius, painting with a ferocious energy in each stroke of the brush. His finest work is the huge canvas representing the French soldiers shooting down the Spaniards on the fateful second of May. The whole picture breathes the spirit of fiery patriotism. He seems to have a gory head on the very end of his brush, so vivid is the painting, but it is superbly handled in every detail. Zurbaran is the only one left of the great Spaniards, though Alonzo Cano, our acquaintance from Granada, Pacheco,—Murillo's friend—Herrera, Juan de Juanes, and many others are represented.

"Zurbaran's 'St. Peter Nolasco Asleep' is an exquisite visionary thing, and has earned for the artist the title of The Spanish Caravaggio."

"Oh! do let us go. I cannot even think of any more," cried the Pessimist, and we hastily sought the open air, and went over to the garden of the Buen Retiro, to rest our tired eyes before driving to the Armory.

The Buen Retiro is one of the finest parks in Europe, but we saw only the small and pretty garden at the corner of the Alcala, and the Salon del Prado, where Philip II. had a hunting box called El Cuarto, to which he added towers and galleries, making it similar to a villa in which he had lived with Queen Mary when he was in England.

We glanced at the Botanical Garden, but found it not to be compared to many others, so hastened to the Armeria, the finest armory in the world.

"We can see only the exterior of the Royal Palace, as the king and queen are occupying their apartments, and strangers are not admitted; so we shall have to content ourselves with a glance at the great pile," I said, and we entered the Armory.

The first impression is that one has suddenly plunged into the Middle Ages. Shields hung upon the walls above, and burnished as bright as mirrors, reflected the swords and hauberks and daggers until it seemed as if there were millions of the ferocious weapons.

"Oh! Pessimist," I cried; "there is Pelayo's sword. Only think of it. He was one of the heroes of the ages. When all Spain was at the feet of its Moorish conqueror, he, with his brave band of only thirty, retired to the Pyrenees, and there fought and defeated every alien who came to do him battle. Once in a difficult pass of the mountains, he overthrew a hundred thousand Moors; but that was by the aid of Santiago, who appeared upon a snow-white charger and fought for Pelayo."

"Saint James had a way of turning up at the right moment, had he not?" asked my auditor.

"Oh, yes," I answered. "Tradition says St. James's body was found in Galicia by Bishop Theodemir, and because a star stood over the place where the grave was, they made a shrine, and called it *Campus Stellæ*, and the saint is called St. Iago de Compostella.

"Another time when St. Iago made himself prominent was at the battle of Clavijo, in which King Ramiro, successor of Alfonso the Chaste, distinguished himself. The verse says:

"'A cry went thro' the mountains when the proud Moor drew near,
And trooping to Ramiro came every Christian spear,
The Blessed Santiago they called upon his name,—
That day began our freedom and wiped away our shame.'

"I believe the particular cause of dispute just then, was the yearly tribute of Christian girls to the Moorish harem."

"There 's your favorite's sword," said the Pessimist, pointing to a large and very ancient sword, inscribed 'Gonzalo de Cordova.'

"Is n't it a splendid one? There is a weapon which belonged to Bernardo del Carpio. How the schoolboys would thrill if they could see that. I do n't suppose the boy lives who has n't recited, 'Bernardo del Carpio' in his palmy days, with a suspicious moisture in his eyes.

"That Valencian sword belonged to Queen Isabella. Look at the motto: '*Nunco veo paz Comigo.*' That one was Pizarro's, and there Cortez's, and here 's the very identical sword that the Great Captain had given him by King Ferdinand. On that sword, once pregnant with magnificent deeds, the oath of allegiance to the Princes of Asturias is taken. See, there is an inscription on the gold pommel, '*Facta Italiæ pace,*' etc. Gonzalo, do n't I wish we were back in your own Cordova!"

"There, that will do," said the Pessimist sternly. "Whose sword is that with the Perrillo mark?"

"That 's of a famous make, and this one belonged to Garcilaso de la Vega. It 's said to be the very blade with which he beheaded the Moor in the Vega. I hate seeing these; it makes me homesick for Andalucia."

"Speaking of Granada," said the Pessimist, "it seems to me this says something that will interest you," pointing to a magnificent suit of armor, marked, 'Boabdil El Chico, El Rey de Granada.' "

I gasped, and speechless with interest, looked at Columbus' armor; thirty-six suits of Charles V., including that which he wore when painted by Titian; Francis the First's helmet and shield (Pavian relics), and swords, daggers and helmets belonging to nearly every important historical character in Spain.

Then came the baby armor, figures of the Infantes in full armor, and last of all we saw the votive crowns of the Goths. One with the motto, "Svinthilanos Rex offeret," was enormously heavy, with gold and precious gems. Svinthilic was the twenty-third Visigothic King; he reigned in 620 A.D.

"There is a curious circumstance connected with these crowns," I said. "They were worn once, on some grand occasion, and then presented to a church as a pious offering. Conde says that Moussa ordered four hundred royal hostages to accompany him to Syria, and these wore upon their heads diadems of gold.

"When Tarik was confined in the Alcazar at Toledo in a secluded room of the royal palace, he found twenty-five gold crowns inlaid with hyacinths and other precious stones, for it was the custom that after the death of a king, his crown, with his name, age, and the length of his reign engraved upon it, should be laid aside there.

"See those jousting spears and banners, and think of tourney and feast and combat; see how the sunlight caresses those silken broideries, captured from some Turkish pasha at Lepanto; look at the jewels in that helmet, gleaming no brighter than the renown of its heroic wearer!''

Soon after this the Pessimist and I had a vigorous discussion.

''Are you going to a bull-fight?'' I asked. She turned on me her glittering eye, and regarded me with stern displeasure. I bore up under it as best I could. At last she spoke. ''I have frequently remarked that your trip to Spain seemed to have demagnetized your morals, but now, I must say, I am completely astonished.''

''Why?'' I asked, very meekly.

''Do you mean to say that you are so lost to all womanly dignity as not to realize that you have said anything?''

The Pessimist is a dear, but she was not built for dignity.

The fitness of features is one of my hobbies. Majesty goes with Roman noses and tall figures; and calm eyes and dignity go together. But the combination of a precious pug nose an undeniably stout figure, and peppery temper does not harmonize with statuesque dignity. The sight of the Pessimist on the high horse convulsed me with laughter, and I fairly shook as she continued her lecture.

"I am at a loss for words; utterly at a loss," she said sternly. ("You do n't seem to be," I hazarded, *sotto voce.*)

"To think," she went on, "that I have harbored in my bosom a viper—a blood-thirsty creature who would enjoy seeing dumb creatures tortured! You 're the kind of girl who would go to a foot-ball game, I suppose."

"I would n't," I answered rather nettled, "but I must say if a lot of silly men with hair like feather dusters want to get themselves killed, I have n't the least objection."

"Oh! very well. Go to your bull-fight, but I 'm disappointed in you," she said, a little red spot on each pale cheek, and her usually pale eyes blazing like coals.

"But—" I remarked.

"But nothing," she interrupted. "I can 't conceive of your wanting to go."

"Neither can I," I said composedly.

The Pessimist stared.

"But you asked me—" she began.

"Oh, yes," I said, smiling in the serene consciousness of victory," I did ask you, of course, but only because I wanted to tell you that if you went, it would have to be alone. I would n't go if Adonis invited me, and gave me a ten-pound box of Huyler's to take."

It was the first time on record that she had

been angry with me because I agreed with her.

People who have lived in Madrid are full of enthusiasm over the charms of the pleasant city and the many delightful bits of interest stored away in unfrequented quarters. Unfortunately, travelers see but little of the real life of the city, and we were disappointed in the Spanish capital after the delights of Andalucia.

"After all, the modern Spaniard has his advantages," I said to the Pessimist, as we were leaving Madrid. "He may be ready to quarrel if the tail of his dignity is trodden upon, but when one is courteous to him he is incomparably agreeable. We have been in Spain many weeks, and have traveled entirely alone, yet we have never had an unpleasant word said to us. We 've not seen a drunken man in all this vast city, and noble and peasant are alike polite and charitable.

"If we do n't care for Madrid we must do the people justice; if the Madrileñas *will* wear French bonnets instead of picturesque mantillas, let us forgive them these peccadillos, and say in their own pretty way, 'Madrileños, *vayan Ustedes con Dios !* '"

CHAPTER XVI

FROM ARANJUEZ TO SEGOVIA

HERE Joseph Bonaparte held court," I exclaimed, as we drove through Aranjuez, "until the crash came, which bereft him of the toy his good elder brother had lent him. Kingdoms were mere baubles to Napoleon, who was a second edition, bound in gilt, of the French monarch, whose lesson read: 'Je suis l' etat.'"

"Please don't moralize, but tell me the history of this place," said the history-loving Pessimist.

"The Order of Santiago had estates on the river Tagus, and the finest of these was called Aranzuel; and here trees and flowers were planted, olives raised, and a villa built for the Maestro of the Order. Later, this Maestranza was ceded to the crown, and Queen Isabella made Aranjuez one of her favorite residences.

"Charles V. and Philip II. improved it, but fires destroyed a large part, and Philip V. rebuilt it, and made this Spanish palace a veritable Fontainebleau.

"Since the court has left Aranjuez in favor of La Granja, so far as any social life is concerned, it 's as dead as a summer resort in winter."

"What a queer little village," said the Pessimist, "It seems out of place in Spain."

"It 's Dutch," I answered. "The Marquis Grimaldi, when he returned from his embassy to the Hague, built it like the cities he had seen in Holland.

"How queer the straight, wide, treeless streets; and the houses, two-storied, with small windows and low roofs!

"The Marquis of Salamanca, the man who built the first Spanish railway (that of Aranjuez), lives in a beautiful villa near here."

"Where are we going first?" asked my companion.

"To see the palace. That is it, and how beautifully situated it is! The avenues of elms and sycamores are superb, and those two rivers, which meet and form such charming little islands, and have such dashing waterfalls, are the Tagus and Jarama. Do you remember Schiller talks in Don Carlos about '*Die schönen Tage in Aranjuez?*' "

"I do n't know Schiller," said the Pessimist.

"Neither do I," I answered with exemplary frankness; "I read that in the guide-book. The palace is built of brick, and seems more like a fortress than a royal dwelling.

"We must hurry and see the interior, because the gardens will take almost all of our time.

"The porcelain room is the chief sight. There! Is not that magnificent? The whole wall is lined with the finest Capo di Monti porcelain in high relief.

"Then come two rooms like our beloved Alhambra, and in the chapel Titian's magnificent 'Annunciation,' presented by him to Charles V. There 's another palace, the Casa del Labrador, with a balustrade containing fifteen thousand dollars worth of gold, doors which unlock with silver keys, and a score of costly novelties useless and extravagant. Now, for the gardens, said to be as fine as any in the world, though those of La Granja are finer."

The scenery is varied, for there is a fine park, large in extent, and superb in beauty. Avenues of trees, with their branches forming arcades; shrubs, flowers, and the Tagus flowing along, its torrent now confined to form a lake, now bubbling over masked cataracts;

vases, statues, fountains and wonderful flowers, and vines from all parts of the world.

Then there is the landscape gardening in the Italian style; and stiff as this usually is, the natural grace of the Spaniard shows itself in the arrangement of the wonderful flower beds. These are masses of harmonizing hues, with small yew trees trimmed into green balls like Noah's Ark trees, myrtle hedges, and carefully cut borders.

These are interspersed with fountains, of which one notices that of Hercules, with its famous columns of Calpe and Abyla (Gibraltar and Ceuta), and the fountain of Bacchus.

In the middle of the garden, about the Casa del Labrador, the trees are especially fine; there are gigantic Lebanon cedars, elms as large as those at the Alhambra; kiosks, grottoes, and labyrinths abound, and in every direction the eye rests upon something new or strange or beautiful.

The crown paddocks on the banks of the Tagus are filled with horses of the famous Aranjuez breed, splendid cream-colored creatures.

Around the gardens are vineyards; but the wine made here is not especially good, although the great Bodegas made by Charles III., in 1788, were erected on a magnificent scale.

Wandering through walks and groves, heavy with flower scents and vocal with the music of the bird orchestras, one makes invidious comparisons between these gardens and those of Calderon at Granada or the Alcazar at Seville, where nature is left to wander at her own sweet will, aided, but not coerced by the skillful hand of man.

One thinks also of all the historical personages who have wandered here; of Charles V., dreaming perhaps of that labyrinth at Seville which he was to order to be made. When his head gardener said he would plant it with myrtle, and 't would take five years to grow, the sickly emperor exclaimed fretfully, "*Dios!* Man, five years is a life-time!"

Here in the Parc des Cerfs, tradition says that another Charles shut up his family, and made them learn *Paters* and *Aves* for a pastime.

Here wandered Philip the Fifth, dreaming of gay France, and the golden age of Louis Quatorze; and he tried to turn the Spanish gardens into French ones, *à la* Versailles. He could not do it any more than he could move the haughty Dons over whom he had come to rule, and turn them into French dandies, gay and licentious.

The Pessimist and I very much enjoyed Aranjuez. Some one says, "A friend is one to whom one likes to say, "Do you remember?" and my friend and I stored up many things over which to talk in future days.

After Aranjuez one naturally thinks of La Granja; and thither we turned our steps, eager to compare the two places, rivals in many ways.

La Granja is on the Segovian railway, and lies among the mountains, snow-capped and filled with splendid gorges; and a visit there is a treat, as the scenery is marvelously beautiful.

It is called also San Ildefonso; and here Philip V. conceived the idea of building a palace which should surpass Versailles, and he employed many celebrated architects to model the structure; he died, however, soon after it was completed. The court comes out to the palace every year for the months of July, August, and September. The palace itself is not remarkable; the apartments are light, airy and modern, while on the lower floor is a collection of statues and antiquities made by Queen Christina of Sweden.

The gardens are what every one comes to see, and the Pessimist and I grew very enthusiastic over them. As we wandered about, our eyes were fairly dazzled by the fountains, twenty-six in number, and I exclaimed with wonder over the remarkable Cascade Cenador, which is a huge sheet of water glistening in the sunshine, and sparkling like a mass of brilliants in a silver setting.

"Look, Pessimist!" I exclaimed, "there is the *Fuente de las Ranas* (of the frogs); and see how curiously the creatures have adapted themselves to the idea of the sculptor!

"The next is *El Canastillo* an immense basket of fruit and flowers from which start forty water jets, rising seventy-five feet into the air. It is very wonderful, but I like my fountain of Lindaraja better."

"Oh, you're determined not to like anything better than Andalucia," said the Pessimist. "As for me, I think this garden is the most superb in the world. Which is Philip the Fifth's fountain?"

"He made several of them, but the Baños de Diana is the one he liked best. When it was all finished, and playing for the first time, he stopped to see it, and said: 'It has cost me three millions, but for three minutes I have been amused!'

"Only fancy having to pay a million a minute for your amusement. At that rate, I should be amused for about one-fortieth of a minute in all my lifetime."

"He ought to have had you with him," said the Pessimist grimly.

"Thank you, Pessimist," I answered, "I

suppose you mean that for a compliment, but I 'm not ready for cap and bells yet, nor do I pose as Mark Twain's monkey.

"There 's something that ought to make your patriotic breast beat with joy. Look! Among those superb statues of Daphne, Apollo, and Lucretia, is one of America."

"I 'm having too nice a time to be patriotic," said the Pessimist.

"What! the Pessimist enjoying herself! *Mirabile dictu!* Hurrah for La Granja!" I exclaimed wildly.

"Be quiet, the guard is looking at you, and you 'll be arrested for a Cuban sympathizer," said my friend sternly. "Where did La Granja get its name?"

"It means grange or farm-house, and was little more than that when Philip V. bought it from the monks of El Paral.

"Now, it 's time we went to get lunch, at that nice, clean fonda, for I 'm hungry enough to eat my words."

"It 's lucky there 's a prospect of luncheon," said the Pessimist, "for I 'd not like to be near when you were forced to do such a thing."

"Now, for Segovia," I cried, as, refreshed with a dainty *déjeuner*, we hurried to the train. "It is but five miles away, and as different from what we have seen as Goth from Moor.   Yet, it has a charm of its own; and who do you think built it?"

"Have n't an idea," said the Pessimist.

"First it was a Roman villa, but no less a person than Satan himself is said to have assisted at the beautifying of stern Segovia."

"What is that huge thing looming up in the distance?" asked my friend.

"That is the great Segovian aqueduct, said to have been made by Trajan.   It carries water into the city from the Sierra Fonfria, nine miles away.   It 's like a giant's bridge,— sixty-nine and one-half miles long, made of huge blocks of gray granite, joined without cement.   See what beautiful vistas and pictures are formed through the archways, one hundred and two feet high.   Ordinary people say it was built by one Licinus, a Roman, but you and I know better, for here is the *true* story.

"One fine day Monsieur le Diable saw a fair Segoviana drawing water from the river, and knowing she was as indolent as fair, he whispered, 'What wilt thou give to the man who brings thy river to thee, fairest maid?'

" 'Myself,' she answered, and laughed, thinking the king's fool had come to jest with her.   Imagine her dismay, next day when she awoke, to find the aqueduct built in a single night, and a stream of purest water running into her kitchen.

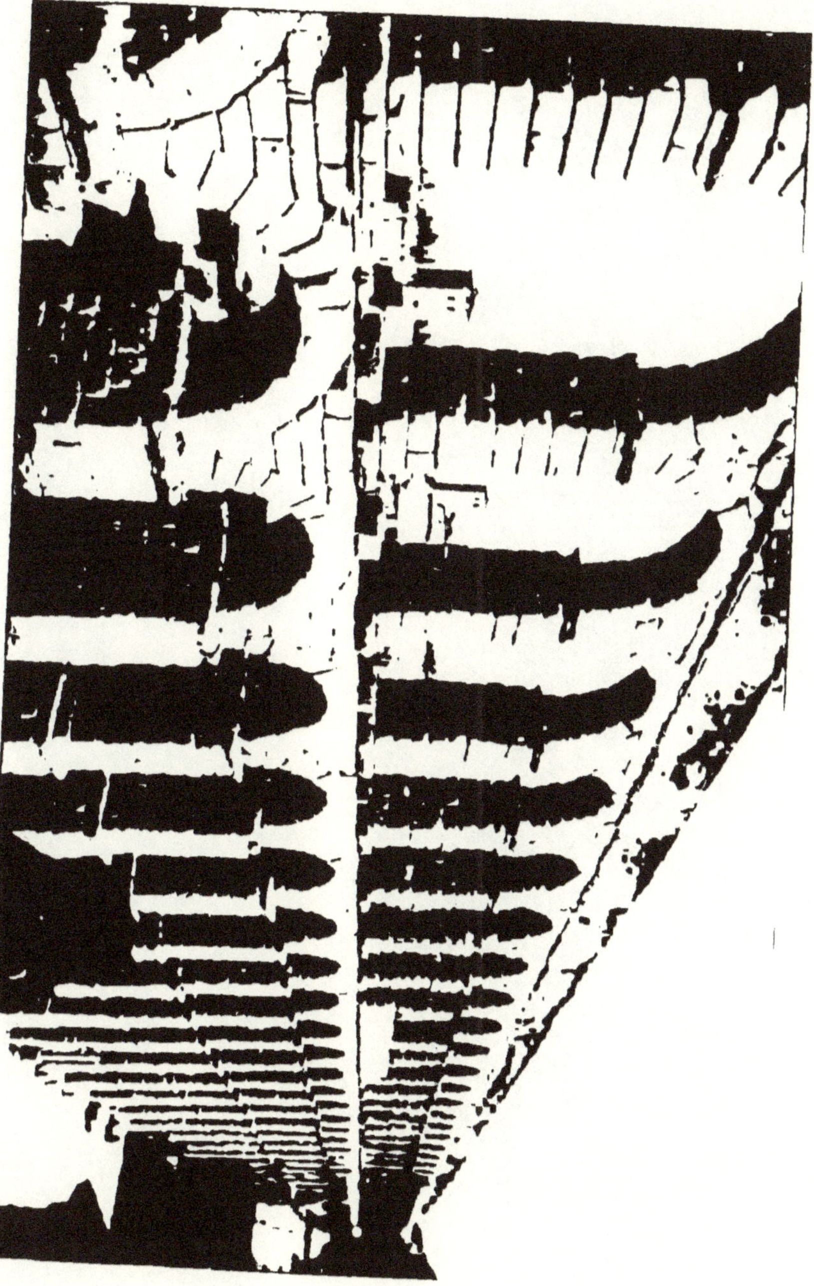

"The devil, while he does not always keep his promises as well as in this case, expects us to keep ours, and the Segovian maiden sold her soul to his Satanic Majesty for the great aqueduct."

"There 's more sense in that than in many of your tales," said the Pessimist, "for this is such a wonderful piece of engineering, I do n't wonder the simple peasants thought it took a superhuman agency to manage it."

"I like Segovia already. I can 't wait to find a hotel. Let 's give our luggage to the first porter we see, and begin to go about at once. The hotels are sure to be poor, and the sights are not."

For once the Pessimist acquiesced, without a grumble, in what I said, and we wandered about the city, until the stars came and drove us to seek other shelter than the soft Castilian night.

Segovia is beautiful. It is impossible to picture anything quainter than its stern walls, narrow streets, tiled roofs, churches, convents, granite houses with iron balconies, and little dabs of trees, trying hard to grow, though evidently much oppressed by the spirit of the past, which breathing upon them, deadens the air in which they live.

Some one compares Segovia, aptly, to a noble Don, poverty-stricken, yet haughtily drawing about him like a cloak, the tattered remnants of his past glories.

The city lies upon a hill-side, and is outlined against the noble arches of the aqueduct, beyond which lie green slopes, crowned with hills, and the snowy Sierra de Guadarrama in the background.

"The Alcazar is one of the most perfect specimens of the fortress-castle, which I have ever seen," I said to the Pessimist, as we stood upon the slope which leads to the castellated towers, with tiny turrets like pepper-pots, perching around the top.

"It was built by Alfonso the Learned, in the eleventh century, and here he wrote several of his books. All manner of royalty has lived here—even Charles I. of England, when he visited Spain, in 1623.

"Gil Blas was confined in the dungeons, which are fearfully deep and dark. Is not the castle striking? See how its proud towers reach aloft, while the base, firmly seated on a rocky promontory seeks the ravine watered by the Eresma. Let us go in and see the Moorish-Gothic rooms," and we entered under the fine gateway.

"Look at the shields of Castile with Moorish characters emblazoned on them," said the Pessimist. "It looks odd enough, and there are stalactite ceilings like those in the Hall of Justice in the Alhambra."

"It 's beautiful," I answered. "Here is the Pieza del Cordon, so-called because King Alfonso used to study here; and one day, while he was conjecturing as to whether the sun really did move around the earth or not, there came a blinding flash of lightning. It made the king feel that the heavens disapproved of his scientific research, and he had the cord of St. Francis carved in stone around the room."

"Then Galileo was not the originator of his theory, after all," said my friend. "What else happened in the Alcazar?"

"Here, in the Sala de los Reyes, in 1326, a young court lady let the Infante Don Pedro fall out of the window into the river. She was promptly beheaded; and there 's a slab in the Alcazar chapel, representing the baby prince with a sword in his hand."

"Carelessness was a crime in those days," said the Pessimist, "and if people made the excuse, 'I forgot,' I fancy they were not likely to have a chance to say it a second time."

"Another person who was held in durance vile in the castle was the prime minister of Philip V.," I said. "He was the Duke de Riperda, a Hollander, and became a naturalized Spaniard. Escaping from the Alcazar, he turned Protestant, then Mussulman, was made a Bashaw and Generalissimo by the King of Morocco, and finally died in abject poverty near Tangier.''

''Are we to go to the cathedral now?'' asked my friend, and as I responded in the affirmative we soon reached the quaint building, erected in 1525, by the same architects who built the Salamanca cathedral.

How curiously the buttresses flank the rounded end of the building, and the carved pinnacles fairly spring aloft. It is Gothic, but a sturdier style than the Milan cathedral, less delicate, more massive, and far more suitable to the stone of which it is built.

The interior is plain, light and simple, with beautiful stained glass and a superb *retablo* by Juan de Juni.

''Who said there were no sculptors in Spain!'' I exclaimed. ''This 'Descent from the Cross ' is one of the most superb things I have ever seen. Our Lord looks divine, and yet how the dear human body has suffered! The Blessed Virgin's heart seems utterly rent with grief, and all the figures are expressive, yet nowhere is the realistic side brought out too painfully.''

Fairest of all the Segovian churches is lovely San Esteban, close by the cathedral, upon the Plaza de San Esteban.

Never shall I forget that perfect tower, dating from the thirteenth century, and rising in five arcaded tiers, its slender arches, pointed and rounded, giving a glimpse of heaven's blue, and the quaint steeple, with its tiny dormer windows peering out like eyes. It is unique and most charming.

Below the tower is a *corredor* or open cloister running along the south side, and its slender shafts are graceful beyond description.

There are curious tombs, too, and the Pessimist and I wandered long among them, wondering at the sculptured faces, so calm and peaceful now, yet of those whose lives had been turbulent enough.

> " His bones are dust,
> And his good sword rust.
> His soul is with the saints, we trust,"

I quoted, as we left San Esteban, and slowly wandered on our way through the deepening twilight to our hotel.

"Pessimist, how do you like Segovia?"

"Did you notice the peasant before the big crucifix in San Esteban?" she asked, not replying to my question.

"What of her?" I queried.

"She was the most beautiful creature I ever saw," said my friend with unwonted enthusiasm. The Pessimist was scarcely given to admiring other women. "She was dressed so strangely. A short skirt showed her little feet, an apron of striped goods in soft colors covered the front of her dress, a kerchief was about her throat, and over her dark hair, which curled down over her ears, was a heavy black hood which lay upon her shoulders. She was saying her rosary, and the light from the altar lamp fell upon her face. It was the most perfect Spanish face I'd seen since we landed at Cadiz."

"The women here are nearly always beautiful, and are grave and sweet, and little like their impetuous southern sisters," I said. "I wish I had seen your beauty. I admire the dignified northern type of Old Castile far more than the sensuous Madrid *chula*, the languorous Valenciana or gay Sevilliana.

"Women are a great study everywhere, but I don't see how you can think of petticoats in the midst of the architecture of Segovia, Gothic, pure, massive, splendid! This Gothic poetry in stone raises my mind heavenward, and fills me with lofty thoughts.

> Like forest's interlacing boughs
>   The columns arch toward Heaven,
> And with aspiring pinnacles,
>   The sky's pure blue is riven:
> My soul mounts up these stony steps
>   Reaching a loftier height,
> Searching through carven traceries
>   The Heaven's perfect light,—

I murmured, but the Pessimist answered:
  "I am hungry."

CHAPTER XVII.

THE ESCORIAL AND AVILA.

OME one says, 'To understand the Escorial one must have studied deeply the character of its founder,' " I said as we bumped along in the omnibus which carried us from the station to the village of Escorial.

"Who was the founder, and why must one know his character?" asked the Pessimist.

"Philip II. built it in 1565, but the idea was conceived long before. The Spaniards of that day were peculiarly religious, almost morbid in their devotion. The mind of Juana la Loca, daughter of Ferdinand and Isabella, was unbalanced, if she was not altogether insane, and, as was natural from her temperament and race, her unhinged mental faculties brooded over religion. Charles V., her son, great emperor as he was, inherited much of her enthusiasm, which showed itself chiefly in his never failing desire to retire into a monastery.

"An English writer says, 'Spain must be judged by the east, never by the north;' and the indolence of the eastern sultans has often obtruded itself into the nature of the Spanish sovereign.

"In the quiet of the royal palace the emperor dreamed dreams, and saw visions of the more perfect seclusion of the cloisters, and his natural trend toward piety often led him to seek the aid of the church when the cares of the state became too great.

"Before his death the emperor expressed a wish to his son Philip to have a burial place for himself and his descendants, and in accordance with his father's desire, which tallied so well with his own ideas, Philip built the Escorial.

"There was yet another motive. Philip's patron was St. Lawrence, to whose intervention he ascribed the victory of San Quintin, which occurred on the feast of St. Lawrence, 1557. He gives his reasons at length in his own words, which"—But here the omnibus, drawn by mules, bumped so violently that conversation was impossible, and I was compelled to look at the wild scenery in silence.

The Guadarramas, rocky, and clad with pines, sloped down to the plain, which stretched far away to meet the sky.

Juan Bautista de Toledo was the architect

of the great palace of the Escorial, but Philip was the leading spirit in the enterprise. He often came from Madrid to watch the progress of the building which is wonderfully simple, grand and massive. It was twenty-one years in building, and cost six million ducats.

Built in the form of a parallelogram, it is divided into many courts, the convent and offices, the rooms of the royal household, the cloisters and the church. All about the building cluster low houses, perfectly white, with red-tiled roofs, over which the soft green of the trees casts swaying shadows.

We went first to see the church whose huge cupola rises among its towers, a fine specimen of Græco-Roman architecture.

"Tell me about it," said the Pessimist, as we entered the nave and looked about us at Doric columns and arcades.

"Oh! I can 't," I said; "it 's too big to talk about. There are numberless pictures by everybody, of saints and holy people, but they 're mostly people I 'm not acquainted with. In that little chapel is the tomb of the late Queen Mercedes, but we really have n't time to see it all. It would take weeks. Here is the Capella Mayor. The altar is superb, of marble and inlaid jasper, and the altar-piece is one whole piece of jasper.

"The doors leading into the *Sagrario* are

solid mahogany, and the *relicario* is one of the finest in Spain. General Houssaye and his troops stole most of the valuable things, but those still remaining are very wonderful.

"On either side the altar are the oratorios of dark marble, for the use of the royal family when at Mass. Those figures on the right-hand side of the altar are effigies of the kings and queens. Charles V. is kneeling on a cushion, his hands raised in prayer, his thin face looking sad, yet with a rapt expression. Beside him is Isabella his wife, and behind are his daughter Maria and his sisters Eleonora and Maria.

"Under the high altar was built the Pantheon, in fulfilment of the wish of Philip II., that Mass might be said over the bodies of the kings. Come, let us go down and see the tombs and have it over."

"You may go; I will wait here," said the Pessimist. "It makes me uncomfortable to see such things."

No amount of urging could shake her decision, so I went alone down the marble steps. Cold, darkness and oppressive silence met me, and my eyes could scarce penetrate the gloom to distinguish the royal tombs. Indeed, one could hardly call them tombs. On the eight-sided room are placed in rows of niches the marble caskets for kings and mothers of kings only. All are neatly labeled like specimens in a scientific exhibit, and the effect is grewsome rather than solemn.

After a hasty glance at the *Panteon de los Infantes*, a new room in black and white marble, pure and cold, where are buried the lesser princes, I hurried back to the Pessimist, glad to be above ground again.

"How did you like it?" asked my friend.

"Not at all. Let's see something cheerful," I answered. "What did you see while I was gone?"

"The room where Philip II. died," she said. "A little bit of a stuffy place it is, and the one he lived in is not much better."

"He had the simplest tastes imaginable," I said. "Let's go to the choir now."

We went through the sacristy, and stopped to glance at the pictures,—Zurbaran's Ribera's, Guido Reni's, and the great "Santa Forma" (Holy Wafer), a strange painting, sketched by Rizzi, and finished by Claudio Coello. The subject is the ceremony which took place in this very spot when Charles II. was here.

The figures are portraits: Charles, his courtiers, the Dukes of Medinaceli and Pastrana, and many other notables. The procession was in honor of the holy wafer kept upon the altar, which wafer is said to have shed real drops of blood when rudely trampled upon by Zwinglians at Gorcum in Holland, and to have been preserved and given by the Emperor Rudolph II. to Philip II. The picture is set in superb carved marble pillars, the workmanship of which is beautiful beyond description. In the sacristy were fine specimens of embroidery so delicate as even to illustrate in silk scenes from the Bible. Embroidery was a fine art in Spain, especially in Ciudad-Rodrigo, and some of the robes and vestments cost two hundred thousand dollars.

By the time we reached the choir every faculty was fatigued beyond endurance, yet our nerves were at tension, and we felt we must see all the glories which unfolded before our wondering gaze.

Here were the plain, dark choir stalls, two rows, each stall perfect in its simplicity, made of ebony, cedar or box-wood. In a small stall knelt Philip II. at prayer when a messenger brought him the glorious news of the victory of Lepanto. The king's face did not even change in expression; he went right on with his prayers.

In one of the frescoes of the ceiling the artist painted his own head, and a witty contemporary, Siguenzo, said that he was glad to see the painter had put himself in Paradise, now, for he was not likely to get there in reality, since he was too much given to the love of money.

The crystal chandelier—injured by the French—was made in Milan, and is still a fine example of Italian glass.

The reading desk is a great golden eagle, carrying upon its back the gridiron of Saint Lawrence, after whom the Escorial was named.

"Convent next, then palace," I said, with renewed energy. "Come, Pessimist, you can rest to-night."

"I 'm sorry to miss it, and to be always resting, but I really think you 'll have to leave me here, and go on with the guide. When I get rested I 'll see what I can, but I do n't want to keep you," and she sat down determinedly. I was sorry for her fatigue, yet glad to feel I could wander at will, and neither talk nor explain.

I started off to see the convent, which one enters from the church through the *Sala de Secretos* (Hall of Secrets).

"What whispers have been heard here," I said to myself as I slowly wandered through the room, in any part of which the least sound can be heard, owing to the form of the ceiling. I fell to idly speculating as to whether one really could hear, and as to what quaint tales of love or vengeance might have been thwarted through the listening walls.

Noticing two Spaniards at the far end of the room. who were talking in low tones, I thoughtlessly paused a moment to see if I could hear them speak.

Alas! the old proverb about listeners proved true, for one man said to the other, in Spanish:

"What 's the señorita by the door. English or American?"

"An American." said the companion. "They go about alone; the English never."

"But why? Is it because they have no husbands?" asked his friend.

The second one shrugged his shoulders.

"It is said." he replied. "that their husbands stay at home and work. and the señoras fly from one thing to another, like bees. Some of them are so pretty it is dangerous, though they never seem to see a man. This one is not half bad. but there are prettier," with a glance which took me in from head to foot.

I retired from the scene with what equanimity I could muster. and felt convinced that one could hear in the chamber of secrets.

Through the Doric cloister and the Patio de los Evangelistos I passed into the Sala de Capitulos (Chapter House). and dallied over the paintings which line the walls. There are scores of pictures. among them Titian's somber "Martyrdom of San Lorenzo," though the light in the chapel where this hangs is so poor that one can have no adequate idea of its artistic merit.

The library of the Escorial had long been the goal of my ambition, and when I stood within that magnificent room, beneath the vaulted ceiling, painted with subjects personifying the arts and sciences; when I saw the ebony, cedar and orange-wood cases, the marble pavement, the jasper reading tables, and then, books, books, books, like Dominie Sampson, I could but cry, "Prodigious!" and words could not tell the longing which arose within me to stay right there forever and a day, and study everything.

Philip's ambition to have the handsomest convent, the handsomest church, and the handsomest palace in the world, may or may not have been gratified, for other places compare favorably with his efforts in those lines. But, as to the library, it is beyond praise. There are about sixty thousand volumes, bound in black or purple leather, in nearly every known tongue. Strange as it may appear, of all the fine collections that of Arab literature is the poorest, whether from neglect or Spanish prejudice against the Moors, I cannot say. Among the rarest books is the "Codice Aureo," containing the gospels of

Matthew, Mark, Luke and John, in solid gold letters.   It was begun by order of Conrad II., the German emperor, and not completed until the eleventh century, and the illuminating is the finest in the world.

Here were the Spanish chronicles from the earliest days, when they were the only history or literature written, and they present to the reader a perfect and most interesting picture of the times.

The palace is at the northeastern angle of the building, and at the present date the interior is very different from that which what its founder originally intended.

"I wish but for a cell in the palace I have built for God," said Philip, and the fitting up of the royal dwelling was plain to a fault.

Since his demise, his successors have not agreed with his severe tastes, and the walls are magnificently hung in tapestry from designs of Goya, Teniers, and Bayeu.   The subjects chosen are suitable, and neither frying saints nor stewing martyrs adorn the walls, as is often the case with Spanish art.

Philip's room remains as he left it; with a few pieces of plain furniture and the chair in which he sat where he could see the chapel, and hear the monks at matins or at even song. His religion gave him the strength to endure his sufferings with superhuman patience, and the stern, morose man, after months of torture, died calmly and quietly, his father's crucifix in his hand.

I found little else of especial interest in the palace save in the Sala de las Batallas (Hall of Battles), the paintings of war scenes by Granello and Fabricio. These are absorbing to one who studies old costumes and armor, and I could have spent hours in enjoying each detail.

There arose before my eyes a pitiful picture of the patient Pessimist, awaiting my return, and I hastened back to find her talking to a custodian, who had whiled away her time with legends galore.

"What do you think of the Escorial?" she asked.

"I have heard it talked of all my life, and everybody calls it something different. The commonest synonym is 'the Leviathan of Architecture,' but why it is compared to Job's crocodile I can't tell. Some one else says it is 'the grandest and gloomiest failure of modern times;' another speaks of it as 'no building at all, but the reflex of Philip's brooding, gloomy mind.' De Amicis says one should be grateful every day that one does not have to live in the Escorial. I am at a loss what to think of it, now that I have seen it; far more so than before I had been there at all.

"Philip said to Herrera, when telling him how to continue Bautista de Toledo's work, that he wished him to make it, 'simple in form, severe in style, noble without arrogance, majestic without ostentation, having always present that the edifice is to be built for the glory of God, and of our holy Catholic faith, and to be a temple, a cloister, and a tomb.'

"The more I think of it, the more I seem to see into Philip's mind. Morbid, melancholy and stern, he was thoroughly just, and his idea of God was of His justice and grandeur; and the Escorial, gloomy, somber, rising in stern simplicity toward heaven, as the thoughts of its founder rose, is an exponent of the soul of the strange king, who kept not only his own subjects, but half of Europe writhing in anxiety, as to what he would indulge in next."

"What about Don Carlos?" asked the Pessimist.

"Nobody will ever really know how he died," I answered; "whether he pined away for love of his stepmother, lovely Elizabeth of Valois, or of a fever from over-eating (for he was a fearful glutton), or in a prison, or whether his father killed him. Poems and plays have been written about him and his character, but the manner of his death will always be one of the things on which to speculate.

"They do say that if one opened his casket in the Pantheon, his body would be found beheaded, but whether because of treason to his father, or because that half-crazed man posed as Abraham sacrificing Isaac, *quien sabe?* After all, what difference does it make how we die?"

"The dark corridors haunt me," said my friend, "and the Escorial is like a ghost-story to a child in the dark; she would n't miss it for anything, and it is delightfully awful, but it makes her shiver ever afterward to think of it."

"Them 's my sentiments!" I replied slangily. "I 'm glad we 're going to Avila."

The train sped swiftly along, into tunnels, and over the mountains until we reached the picturesque town which seemed like a castle upon a rock, for its Gothic walls and towers rise upon an isolated hill from crags scarcely less bold in outline. It is one of the most persistently old cities in the world, and refuses to grow young.

Granada is in its second childhood, and Garzon, the photographer there, has even a modern telephone; but Avila, Gallio-like, careth for none of those things.

"All sorts of fables exist about the origin of

this rugged city," I said to my friend as we rambled about the streets.

"Somebody says that one of the many Herculeses, who was a King of Spain, married Abula, an African princess, and their son founded Avila. However, Count Don Ramon, son-in-law of Alfonso VI., repeopled it in 1088, and the fine walls are a good sample of the military defenses of the eleventh century."

"It 's almost as gloomy as the Escorial," said the Pessimist.

"That 's because everything is made of dark granite," I replied.

"Come, let us hurry and see the cathedral, for we 've no time to waste here, but must hasten."

The cathedral is as massive as a fortress, and a part of the apse absolutely forms a portion of the city walls. It was begun in 1091, and was many years in building. The interior is a very pure Gothic, though spoiled by some so-called restorations.

There are fine carved portals in granite, the saints represented as watching over the footsteps of those entering. The carving in stone is one of the best examples in Spain, especially that over the north door-way, representing the coronation of the Blessed Virgin.

The stained glass is in the soft hues, which

seem to have been so easily attained in the Middle Ages, and which are almost unattainable now, those tints which make the modern artificer green with envy to think that the secret of their production is lost.

"It does not seem like a church," I said, as we wandered about the lofty aisles. "It is so like the keep of a castle that one wants to cry, 'What, ho! Warder!' and expects to see shields and hauberks, rather than beads and missals."

"I do n't like it," said the Pessimist. "Let 's go somewhere else."

Obediently I led her away, and next we saw the church of Santo Tomas, a mile out of the city, where lies buried little Prince Juan.

"He was the only son of Ferdinand and Isabella," I said, "and only think how many hopes are buried here. What a beautiful tomb! He was so young, so good, so fair, if the old chronicles can be believed. His marble effigy shows these traits in his expression.

"His boyish face wears a look of knightly resolve and earnestness. He had been knighted for prowess on the field of battle, as the iron gauntlets show, since none but knights could wear them. How calm and sweet he looks! The Infantes' circle scarcely touches that brow o'er which the cares of life had passed but lightly.

"It nearly broke his mother's heart, and too, his stern father's, for Juan was their idol, and all their hopes centered in him, since the Infanta Juana was insane. One seems to feel the keenness of their loss at this tomb. I wonder if any one sorrowed over Isabella's tomb as she sorrowed here? Not Ferdinand, surely, for he was not even constant to her memory. Ah! the mother love *is* the most wonderful thing on earth, after all."

The Pessimist looked sad, too, and we both moved away from the beautiful tomb in the silence which a wave of sentiment enforces.

The chief reason for visiting Avila is to see the Santa Casa, the birthplace of Saint Teresa, and the Pessimist and I went to the southwest gate outside the walls where the convent stands. She was a strange character, "Teresa of Jesus," as she is called,—strange yet noble, with the nobility a great devotion always gives an unselfish nature.

Where the Guadarramas separate the Doero and Tagus in the south of Old Castile, Saint Teresa was born, in the rock-girt city of Avila, called in early days, "de los Caballeros," from the knights who gathered here to fight for king and religion against the Moors.

In later days the city has borne another name, "Avila Cantos y Santos," (stones and saints); and this strange nomenclature arises from the Toros de Guisando, huge granite blocks existing in the country round, bearing some resemblance to bulls (hence toros,, and connected in some strange way known only to the intricacies of the peasant's mind, with the saints for whom Avila is famous.

"Near the Dominican monastery, early in the sixteenth century, there stood in the rugged street of Avila the house of Don Alonzo Sanchez de Cepeda," I said to the Pessimist. "He was a Castilian knight of high lineage, his arms, still over the door, bearing the lion surrounded by eight crosses of Saint Andrew, granted to a noble Sanchez in memory of the capture of Balza from the Moors on St. Andrew's Day, 1227. In this quaint, mediæval house on the twenty-eighth of March, 1515, was born Teresa, and here she grew to womanhood, bright, graceful, playful, modest, and noted for her great good sense. She gives in her own words a beautiful picture of her home life, simple and natural as it was.

" 'I had a father and a mother who feared God,' she says, 'and my father was much given to the reading of good books, and had them in Spanish so that his children might read them. He would not keep slaves, and said he could not endure the pain of seeing that they were not free.'

"A fair picture of the times, and a noble family. The brothers, all save one, who entered religion the same day as his sister, served in the wars, loyal to their country and king, brave and noble. Teresa, at seven, desired to go to Morocco to convert the Moors, but found a difficulty in her way in the shape of her parents. She and her brother stole away by the Adaja Gate, toward Salamanca, intent on being martyrs, or as Teresa expressed it:

" 'I desired quickly to *see* God, and thought the way to do so soonest was to die.'

"Alas for youthful fervor! She was brought back again ignominiously to lessons; and occupied her spare time in building play-convents, and wanting to be a nun, 'though not so much as I had longed to be a martyr,' she says.

"After her mother's death, when she was still a child, Teresa began to be worldly, to care for dress and romances, to gossip with young people, and led a frivolous, although innocent life. Finally, her determination to seek the cloister being fixed, she entered the convent of the Incarnation in Avila.

"Her conventual life was by no means an easy one. Sensitive souls the devil delights in torturing, and Teresa was tormented by doubts and distractions, and by physical ill-health, until a confessor was sent to her who greatly helped her. She became holy and pious, was the friend of St. Francis Borgia and St. Peter of Alcantara, and had those ecstasies which have made her the subject of so much controversy. She reformed her order, founded convents, and wherever she went sowed seeds in the fertile soil of Spanish piety, which seemed to spring into life; and not only in Spain, but all over the world, the Carmelites bear witness to the strength, earnestness and piety of Teresa de Ahumada.

"A visionary she has been called, but so has nearly every unworldly soul who forgot self for the best good of others. When she died, all Spain mourned, and Avila, her early home, is remembered to-day, not for the mediæval greatness of its knights, but for a woman who ruled not by might nor by force of arms, but by her own determined belief in the power of prayer to conquer all.

"A writer says of her, 'The memorials of one who, in a ceaseless fight of forty-seven years, conquered self, suffering, persecution and time, would alone call for a visit to Avila, even if the city itself were not a place of deep interest and useful study.'

"Devotion, unselfishness, sweetness and strength,—these were the traits of that most wonderful woman of her time, 'Saint Teresa of Jesus.'"

CHAPTER XVIII

"OLD TOWNS WHOSE HISTORY LIES HID IN MONKISH CHRONICLE AND RHYME."

LMA mater de virtudes, ciencas y artes,' " I quoted to the Pessimist, as we sat in the Fonda del Comercio, the best hotel in Salamanca.

"This is a university town, and nearly all the great writers of Spain have studied here."

"Tell me about the University," she demanded.

"It was founded in the thirteenth century, and was one of the earliest in Europe, and was given grants by Alfonso IX. and Ferdinand III. It ranked before Oxford, and had ten thousand students.

"The system of Copernicus (which at first was believed by many to be arrant nonsense) was taught here, and yet when Columbus expounded his theories before the professors he was met with derision. Let's go and see it

all, now," and we went through the quaint
streets.

The façade of the University dates from the
time of Ferdinand and Isabella, whose arms
and escutcheon are seen over the portal, and
it is a fine sample of Gothic-plateresque, with
gargoyles, busts and medallions. The renaissance staircase is superb, and leads to a library
of eighty thousand volumes.

In the chapel are the ashes of Fray Luis de
Leon, a lovely soul. I said to the Pessimist:
"He was so clever that he entered the University when only fourteen, and afterwards
went into a monastery.

"His enemies denounced him to the Inquisition, for private spite, accusing him of
having a Jewish taint in his blood. Of course
they, knew that nothing would so enrage the
Spaniards as to call him a Jew. The Inquisition carefully examined into the charges,
and kept him in honorable captivity to keep
him away from his enemies. So careful were
they that witnesses were examined from every
part of Spain; and to all charges he said
merely that he was in the hands of his su-
periors, and desired ever 'to be a loyal son of
Mother Church.'

"At last the Grand Council at Madrid acquitted him, to the great discomfiture of his
enemies and the joy of the common people,

whose idol he was.   As soon as he was discharged, he returned to Salamanca; and in 1576, he rose to preach to a crowded audience, saying after his five years absence, danger and imprisonment, as if he had been away merely a day, ' My children, as we remarked when we last met—'

"Dear, natural, beautiful old man, he died almost sainted in the eyes of all who knew him.   He wrote in Spanish instead of in Latin, a thing very unusual in the writers of the day; and his name is linked indissolubly with the University of Salamanca.

"Now, we 'll see the cathedral, built in 1513, and fine Gothic, superb beyond words. The tower over the portal is by Churriguera."

"Who was he?   I 've heard nothing but 'Churrigueresque' since we left the Moors," said the Pessimist.

"José Churriguera, born at Salamanca, was an architect, who was to his profession what Gongora was to poetry—rococo, in other words.   It 's just as suitable as stays and crinoline on the Venus de Milo.   The artists of his school put gilding on wood, marble and bronze tortured into grotesque shapes.

"It 's nearly as bad as landscape gardening, for nothing artificial can ever be artistic. However, the Salamanca cathedral is the finest specimen in Spain, and is almost one of the wonders of the world, with its lace traceries in stone.''

''The interior of the cathedral does not seem much, after some we have seen,'' said the Pessimist, as we looked at the Gothic roof, renaissance gallery, and fine statues. The roof is supported by marvelously graceful arches, delicately colored.

''There's nothing anywhere like Seville, and Cordova, Granada and Toledo; but here in the oratory is a delightful relic,'' I answered.

''There it is, the Crucifijo de las Batallas (Battle Crucifix) the very one which our old friend the Cid always carried to battle.''

''I thought it was about time to hear of him again. He turns up with clock-like regularity,'' said my friend.

''Possess your soul in patience. He shall be interred with military honors in Burgos,'' I said, laughing.

''Oh, I know him!'' she replied dubiously. ''He won't stay put. What else do we see?''

''One of the finest specimens of Byzantine in all Spain, the old cathedral,'' I answered, as we went up the steps of the beautiful building, which dates from the twelfth century.

The superb carved stalls, the old organ with its carved and gilded front, the antique cloisters, and fine dome, all claimed our time, and nowhere are there more beautiful tombs than those of the Anaya family, before the high altar.

"Now," I said, "we go to the convent of San Esteban, where Columbus lived safe from the storm his enemies were raising for him, for Salamanca has the honor of having protected him, and Deza believed in his schemes when no one else did.

"I can see the discoverer's wise, kind face as he sat here beneath these medallions and bas-reliefs, so calm, so deeply furrowed with thought, so determined in resolution, and stamped with that belief in himself without which no one can accomplish anything.

"Here is the Casa de las Conchas, in a small street near the University. The shells, emblems of the Mendozas, are encrusted all over the outside of the large, square-looking tower, and the quaint windows look at one inquiringly. The pavement reminds me of the fairy story where the girl had to walk on razors.

"Here lived Bernardo del Carpio. Do n't you remember him in the readers in your early youth? It was to Salamanca he came, when the king promised his father's release. Here he knelt to kiss his father's hand, but found it stiff and cold.

"The Leonese king had kept his oath to release the count, by murdering him in prison;

he then dressed the dead body in costly robes, and mounting it on a horse, led it out to the impatient son.

"'Father!' Bernardo murmured low, and wept like
  childhood then—
Talk not of grief till thou hast seen the tears of warlike
  men!—
He thought on all his glorious hopes, and all his young
  renown,
He flung the falchion from his side and in the dust sate
  down."

"This one house is perfectly mediæval," said the Pessimist. "I 'm glad we came to Salamanca if only to see it. What next?"

"Pessimist," I exclaimed, "it strikes me you 've got to have a new name. You 're growing interested in everything. What does this mean?"

"It means that I think Salamanca is the nicest place we 've been in since Granada," she answered.

"Hurrah for Salamanca then! Let 's go and see the Palacio del Conde Monterey. Monterey was so rich after he was viceroy of Naples, that beggars give one as a blessing, 'May you have as much gold as Monterey,' and Philip IV. made a great favorite of him.

"Here 's the place he lived in; and did you ever see such lace-like stone carving? The turrets and windows and balconies are just the place for gay ladies and handsome *cabal-*

leros.   Oh! the mediæval days were those of chivalry and romance, and far better in some respects than our prosaic, money-getting age.''

''It seems to me you 're the Pessimist now,'' said my friend. ''Of what sort of stone are all these edifices built? It 's of the most beautiful creamy hue, and so rich.''

''It 's native stone, and is so easy to work that it 's no wonder everything is perfect in detail,'' I replied.

Salamanca is the only place of its kind in the world. Quiet, deserted, almost dead as to any life of the present day, it lives forever, fairly teeming with vigorous memories of those who are no more.

''Was n't there a battle here?'' asked my friend.

''The Battle of Salamanca was in Wellington's time, and ended in complete rout of Marmont's men. The French nearly ruined Salamanca, pulling down 'thirteen out of twenty-five convents, and twenty out of twenty-five colleges,' said Wellington in his dispatches.

''The battlefield was two miles from the city, near the river Tormes, and where there are two small hills called the Arapiles. Of these Wellington took possession, and with his sixty thousand English soldiers, swooped down upon the hundred thousand French, and in forty-five minutes he had reduced his enemies to a pulp. 'I never,' he said, 'saw an army receive such a beating in all my life, and if we 'd had an hour more of daylight, the whole army would have been in my hands.'

"Thiers said of the battle: 'That frightful and involuntary battle of Salamanca had unforeseen consequences for the English army, for it gave her victory instead of inevitable defeat, and began the ruin of our affairs in Spain.' "

"I 'm glad of it," said the Pessimist, viciously. "I like to have the French beaten when they do such inartistic things. It 's bad enough to have them steal Murillos and spoil architecture, but it 's almost as bad to have their absurd, perky little bonnets supersede the graceful mantilla."

"Pessimist, my dear, it 's a good thing we are leaving, for if you stayed here much longer I should have you claiming Salamanca as your own. Would you prefer being called a '*Roma pequeña*' after the old name of the city, or will Salamanquiña content you?"

"American will do nicely," she replied calmly, and I subsided.

Then Salamanca was left behind with its glories of architecture, its dead grandeur, its Puerta de San Pablo, where hundreds of statued saints keep watch over the quaint old houses.

We mournfully bade "*adios*" to each nook and corner where lurked the picturesque and romantic, and were jogged along through a parched, scorched-looking country, northward toward Valladolid.

"Cantalapiedra!" I said, as we lingered at a small station. "What a name! But are not the oaks and that pine wood a delightful change from the arid plains through which we have come?

"Now we are nearing El Carpio. There are ruins here, and a crypt; which last was the vault of the Carpio family. That ruined Moorish tower has many a legend about it, and the Carpio palace is still standing."

"To what place are we coming?" asked the Pessimist, who had resumed her pessimism at leaving her beloved Salamanca, and was shrouded in unutterable gloom.

"This is Medina del Campo, quite a celebrated place," I replied. "That fine old castle, whose red towers contrast so well with the fields of corn, is the Castello de la Mota, where Isabella the Catholic died, November 26th, 1504. She was a wonderful woman, a strange combination of the womanly virtues of constancy, tenderness and purity with strength, power and cleverness. Her death put Spain into a fine uproar between the ambitious designs of her husband and her son-in-law.''

''What else is there here that 's interesting?'' asked my friend, as we lunched from our capacious basket,—a necessity in Spain where station restaurants are few and far between.

''Zamora is only three hours away; but we can 't go there and reach Valladolid to-night, so we 'll have to 'play go and see,' as the children say. Do you know the ballad of how Doña Urraca gained Zamora?''

''Tell it to me,'' said the Pessimist, as she sat with olives in one hand and a flask of Valdepeñas in the other.

''King Ferdinand I., of Castile, when dying, apportions his domain amongst his sons, but makes no provision for his daughter Urraca, who speaks out in meeting, vigorously:

> '' 'To good Don Sancho comes Castile,
> Castile the fair and gay,
> To Don Alfonso, proud Leon,
> Don Garcia has Biscay,'

and she complains most bitterly that she has nothing, and cries:

> '' 'I may wander through these lands
> A lonely maid, or die !'

''At this her fond papa repents him of his partiality, and remarks:

> " 'In old Castile there stands a tower,
>   Thou may'st hereafter claim,
> A tower well peopled and well walled,
>   Zamora is its name.
> On this side runs the Dauro round,
>   On that bold rocks do frown,
> The Moorish land is all about,
>   In truth a noble town.
> Who dares to take it from thy hand
>   My curse be on his head!'
> They all replied, " Amen! Amen!"
>   Don Sancho nothing said!'

"His silence proved pregnant with meaning; for no sooner was his father dead, and Urraca peacefully settled in her town, than Don Sancho sent an army to besiege it.

"The Cid was at the head of the host, but when the fair chatelaine appeared on the walls and fought him with that keen weapon, the tongue, he retired in dismay, and refused to wage war upon a woman.

"For this he was banished to Toledo, but Don Sancho recalled him to fight the Moors, and finally everything was peaceably settled with Doña Urraca."

"Such a fuss over nothing!" said the Pessimist, scornfully. "It seems to me they always did such things. It's a pity they could n't stop fighting before they began."

There 's a strain of Hibernian in the Pessimist which is peculiarly alluring to me, and I smiled as I continued:

"Zamora was named from the Arabic *Sa-morah*—a turquoise; and the Moors, under Al-Mansoùr (who was a second Attila) besieged it so long that, though they conquered it at last, the saying 'À Zamora no se ganó en una hora' has become a proverb among the Spaniards. It is often used when some 'faint heart' finds it very difficult to win his 'fair lady.'"

"To what are we coming now?" asked my friend, as we neared a small place upon the Duero.

"Tordesillas; and there is the nunnery of Santa Clara, whither Juana the Mad went to die, watching over the coffin of the wretched Philip the Fair, whom she had always so adored that his neglect unhinged her reason."

"It seems to have been a regular cult with royal Spaniards to enter the cloister. How many did so besides Juana and Charles V.?" said my friend.

"Philip II., several Alfonsos and Bermudos, and most of them needed a little season of prayer, for their lives were scarcely fit preparations for heaven, poor things! But how fast we are getting on! Here is Simancas, where all the archives are kept. Among them are the original deeds of the surrender of Granada, the Grand Captain's accounts of the wars in Italy, and any number of valuable state documents. When you write a history of Spain, this is where you 'll have to come and live," I said.

"When I write a history, it will be that of a less bloody country than Spain," said the Pessimist, loftily.

"All history is bloody. One gets used to it in time," I replied calmly; but we did not discuss the point further, for I quoted (knowing that the beauty of sentiment and rhythm would charm the poetical Pessimist),

> "'My heart was happy when I turned
> From Burgos to Valladolid,
> My heart that day was light and gay,
> It bounded like a kid!'"

"I presume that 's original; it sounds very like your poetry," said my friend.

"You flatter me," I cried. "That 's from one of the oldest Spanish ballads. I see you cannot appreciate the antique. But here we are at our destination, the Belad Walid (Land of Walid) of the Moors; Valle de Lid (Land of Conflict) or the Pincia of Ptolemy. There is so much to see here we shall never get away."

Valladolid is delightful, but its hotels are not the best, and the Fonda de Francia, the best, only tolerable. However, the Pessimist and I were so tired that we slept well and awoke ready for the fray, and started out early to see all that was to be seen.

"Every imaginable thing has happened here," I said, in reply to her demand for history.

"The court was here for years; here the Cortes refused to set aside Juana and acknowledge Ferdinand; here, after his haughty letter to Cardinal Ximenes (which broke the poor man's heart), Charles V. entered to meet the Cortes of Castile upon his accession to the throne. Here, in this little house in the Plazuela del Rastro, Cervantes lived. His house is No. 11,— there, near that small wooden bridge over the Pisuerga.

"Cervantes was commanded to write a description of the fêtes when Philip III.'s son was christened, and all Valladolid was in an uproar of joy and festivity. No. 2 Calle Ancha de la Magdalena is the unpretentious house where Columbus died, May 20th, 1506. His body was placed in the convent of San Francisco, but removed to Seville, whence it was taken to Cuba."

Leaving this we came to the Plaza Major, a wide, pleasant square surrounded by a granite arcade, thronged with people, and three-story houses with airy balconies and arched doorways.

In the Plaza de San Pablo, the royal palace, a gloomy pile, saddens one, so lifeless does it appear. The interior has a fine patio with busts of the Roman emperors, a splendid stairway and balconies on the second story.

"Here Philip II. was born," I said to the Pessimist. "He did much for Valladolid, and is held in great remembrance here. He fairly pervades the whole town, and sometimes with vivid memories, for I recall the Auto-da-fé which he celebrated in the Plaza Major, and at which thirteen persons were burned."

"They stab in the south and burn in the north; Spaniards are pleasant people!" the Pessimist said grimly.

"Come, come; treason! You shan't talk so about my Spaniards. You know you're as charmed with them as I am. You merely choose to air your pessimism; is it not so?"

"Is there anything nice in Valladolid?" She ignored my question.

"San Pablo is delightful. It's one of the most perfect Gothic monuments in Spain, and with the College of San Gregorio (built for poor students who could not pay) is absolutely paralyzing in its entrancing beauty.

"By the way, this is the place where our old friend Don Pedro el Cruel repudiated Blanche de Bourbon.

"Hither Wellington came, after the battle of Salamanca, and made a grand entry through the Puerta de Santa Clara to the delight of all the inhabitants.''

''Is there a picture gallery?'' asked my friend.

''I regret to say there is, and we 're going to it now. It was the College of Santa Cruz, founded by Cardinal Mendoza, and there are some good paintings by Antonio Pereda, a native of Valladolid. His best work is a 'Spanish Noble,' in the Munich gallery.

''There are some curious pictures painted on mother-of-pearl, four and twenty in number, all of the 'Passion of Our Lord,' and some fine examples of Berruguete's work. He was the Spanish Leonardo da Vinci, and was carver, sculptor, and artist, living in Valladolid nearly all his life, near San Benito el Real. Hernandez's 'St. Teresa' is a masterpiece, and some of Juan de Juni's are remarkable for their breadth and vigor, but when one has seen the Seville and Madrid galleries, other Spanish museums seem little in comparison.''

We next went to the cathedral, a granite edifice, designed by Herrara, and left unfinished when the architect was called to Madrid to build the Escorial. It is simple and effective, but cold. Within is buried Pedro Ansurez, the founder of Valladolid, who did much for the city, and yet has no statue to his honor in the place he so fondly loved. We went to see the Casa de las Argollas where the constable, Alvaro de Luna, was confined before his execution, and the house is named from the iron links in the chains worn there by the great prisoner.

"In the Calle de San Martin lived Alonzo Cano, our Granada artist who was tortured for killing his wife. Do you know he did n't do it after all, for somebody says her dead hand was found holding a handful of auburn hair, and his was black!" I said.

"Calderon lived at 22 Calle de Teresa Gil, in that quaint house.

"Valladolid is a revelation to me. I feel like dancing for joy to think I have seen it. Such places are enshrined in one's memory like a pet saint, to remember and think over ever 'after. Not for its streets, for they 're narrow and ill-paved, sometimes even ill-smelling; nor for its people, who are not, my dear, gay Andalusians; but because it 's such a perfect remembrancer of the glorious architecture of those days when every man seemed to hold a cathedral in his brain,— the days when lofty thoughts sprang upward till they reached the turret roofs of college and church, convent and university. Such things always make me want to be better and do lofty work in the world. Yes, Valladolid silently preaches 'Sermons in stones.' "

CHAPTER XIX

"BURGOS, THE BIRTHPLACE OF THE CID."

IEZ meses de invierno y dos de infierno" (Ten months of winter and two of hades). "Yes, indeed!" exclaimed the Pessimist. "Traveling in Spain has its drawbacks. One gets up at five in the morning, jogs along at a snail's pace all the forenoon, in order to arrive at midday in a place hot enough to broil a baby."

"Now, that is pure pessimism!" I replied. "Or is it because it is the fashion for travelers to run down Spain? This is the very first morning on which we have had to arise and shine with the sun. It's our own fault, because we dawdled till we missed the night train, and it's no hotter than plenty of May days at home. Come, come; remember where you are—in the famous birthplace of the Cid."

"Bother the Cid!" she said irreverently.

"Be careful!" I exclaimed. "You know the fate of those who show disrespect to his memory. Remember the Jew!"

"What Jew?" she asked scornfully.

"Do you mean to say you have forgotten about the Jew who dared to touch the body of the Cid?" I cried. " 'T was when all Spain mourned the death of El Cid, 'The Beauteous Beard.' His corpse lay in state in the church of San Pedro de Cardeña, five miles from here, nestling among the hills of Old Castile. A Jew entered the sanctuary to look at the dead hero's body. There he lay, all in his armor dressed, the hilt of his good sword 'Tizona,' a double-hilted weapon, in his hand, and upon the worn and rugged face the perfect calm which comes once only to such restless natures as his. 'There thou liest,' said the dog of an unbeliever, as those of the race of Isaac were called. 'Thou art the great Cid. Thou hast made my brethren groan at lending their good golden pistoles, and all Spain to tremble at thy sword. Thy great black beard was thy pride; of it thou saidst, "God be praised, I thus keep it for my pleasure, and never hand of Moor nor Jew hath dared to touch it!" Thou hast classed God's chosen people with the dark-skinned Moor in thine arrogance. Oh, haughty one, thy beard is thin and gray! Thou liest at my feet. See *now* the hand of the Jew dares touch thee,' and Isaac reached forth his hand to pull the Cid's beard.

"Then, what a sound was heard! The Jew fell down upon the hard stone floor in a fit. The attendant priests came hurrying in, and there they saw that the dead hand of the Cid had grasped his sword, and drawn it forth full a foot from the scabbard. Ah! Pessimist, how dare you in the face of such a story frivol over the memory of that doughty hero? Beware, minion!' I hear him cry. 'Beware, lest my vengeance smite thee. I am Ruy Dias de Bivar, the Cid Campeador!'"

"Fiddlesticks!" replied my friend. "Do you think you could forget the Cid (who seems to have been a cross between a brigand and a mercenary, from the way he plundered on his own account, and fought for whichever side had not happened to banish him) long enough to take me to see just a few of the sights of this up-hill-and-down-dale city, since you were determined to bring me here?"

"I 'll take you everywhere," I replied cheerfully, "but do n't think you can get away from El Cid. He pervades Burgos, as Sozodont or Pear's Soap advertisements do the Hudson. We 'll go to the Cathedral first."

"I 'm so tired of cathedrals," grumbled the Pessimist.

"I can 't help that. Burgos Cathedral is

one of the largest and most beautiful in the world. You 'll never forgive me if I. let you miss it. When you get back home, and are over being tired, you 'll hate me for not making you see it. Some one will say: 'Of course you saw Burgos Cathedral?' and when you humbly reply, 'No,' they 'll put on a pitying look and say, 'Oh, that 's the finest thing in Spain!' and you 'll go down to your grave disgraced forever, branded as one who has lost her opportunities.''

"You say I 'll hate you then, if you do n't take me to see it, and I say I shall hate you now if you do,'' she grumbled.

"Oh, hate away; I 'm callous,'' I answered; and to the Cathedral we went, through those delightful streets.

Burgos straggles along the bank of the Arlanzon, with utter disregard for propriety as to the matter of the straight path, though eminently scriptural in the narrowness of its ways. The streets go anywhere, wind about uncertainly, stop when they 're tired, begin again farther on, and are thoroughly Spanish, hence delightful.

The old houses nearly all date from before the seventeenth century, and have tiny balconies enclosed in glass, like mummy cases. Everything is painted in all the colors of the rainbow — houses, doors, roofs; and it is fairly startling after white Cadiz, the cool streets of Andalucia, or the dark and frowning battlements of Old Castile.

"De Amicis says, 'If there were at Burgos an asylum for mad painters, one would say the city had been painted one day when its doors had been broken open,' " I said to the Pessimist, as we gazed upon the kaleidoscopic scene. "He always says the right thing. Nobody else should ever write a book on Spain, for he has said everything, and in the most charming way it could be said. We are nearing the Cathedral which—"

I ceased abruptly, to find out what was the matter with the Pessimist. She had stopped, and was standing stock still in the middle of the street, looking over the roofs of some houses, absolutely spellbound. As my eye followed hers I did not wonder at her absorption. There they were, those two beautiful spires, as wonderful as Cologne and Antwerp, though not so well known.

Oh, for Shakespeare's pen to write to them a sonnet, or the brush of Michael Angelo to paint that picture! The day was warm and fair; the sky that clear, cloudless blue which is deeper than the warmest hues of summer days. Against the sapphire background stood out the twin spires, three hundred feet in height, like Mexican filigree, their traceries and carvings shining in the sun, delicate in finish, perfect in outline, faultless in detail.

By day the sun gleams through the carving, and the blue sky peers between the soft-hued stones like a caressing glance from azure eyes veiled by white eyelids. By night the myriad stars glisten midst the traceries of stone, like gems set in a wondrous carven coronet.

"What is that?" the Pessimist asked at length.

"Nothing to speak of. Nothing worth seeing," I replied as disagreeably as I knew how; and that 's really saying a great deal! "Only a part of the Cathedral of Burgos, which you would not see because you had seen 'so many cathedrals!'"

"You may crow if you like," said the Pessimist, "but how was I to know that angels built these towers? No man could ever have devised that heavenly thing. I succumb. Take me there. I shall henceforth be like the Puritan named 'Obadiah-bind-them-in-chains!' I am converted to cathedrals."

Having my enemy at my feet, I could afford to be generous, and I led her in complete silence round the low-roofed houses which block the way to the Cathedral.

We seemed not to care to know that it was thirteenth century Gothic, pure in style, and founded by Saint Ferdinand in 1221, in honor of his marriage with Doña Beatrice, daughter of the Duke of Suabia. We could scarcely force ourselves to enter, but sat upon the steps of a house opposite, in utter silence. There were the spires, or belfry towers; the square lantern with its points and pinnacles so carved that the eye wavers and falls in trying to trace the matchless designs. There were the statues,—saints, angels, and virtues,—all under stone canopies as delicate as cramoisie or velours; there were statuettes of kings and prophets around the transept, and the wonderful façade of the Puerta del Perdon; three portals with pointed arches surmounted with the sculptures of the Coronation and the Immaculate Conception of the Virgin, and the fine statues of Ferdinand and King Alfonso the Sixth. Rose windows, trefoils, open-work balustrades, ogival windows, arches, pillars, ajimez windows with superb glass, soft in hue, delicate in design; and everywhere, in every niche and corner and crevice, statues, statues, statues, angels, saints, prophets, priests and kings, cherubs and seraphs, with crosses, candles, harps and lyres. This was Burgos Cathedral.

We sat until a sympathizing crowd of small children had appeared from the cracks of the stone pavement—or so it almost seemed, so suddenly did they swarm about us. They

thought us ill, and offered everything imaginable. As one child at last darted away to
bring his mother. I managed to gather together enough remnants of Spanish from the
scrap-bag I call my brain. to assure them that
we were only tired: and as we went inside the
portal we left them smiling pityingly at the
mad Americanas. Only one, a tiny crippled
lad. with a wizened brown face, followed, and
timidly plucked my arm.

"It is the Cathedral. señorita." he whispered. "It is because you like it so well?"

I wondered at the penetration of this child
of the people. and said:

"Why do you think the Cathedral would
make one ill? And what is your name. *chico*
(little one)?"

"My name is Alegrio. and I know it is our
cathedral which makes you so still, for I come
here at times. and here one can forget all—
even when one cannot run like other *niños*,
and one must always be in pain."

I lingered in the lovely portal over which
the carven saints looked down so sweetly upon
this descendant of their makers and upon the
alien.

The little lad was strangely sweet. He was
of the darkest Spanish style, the midnight
type in which lurked such fire and pride, the
hair as if a raven drooped her wings to protect

the childish head, the skin of pale olive, upon which the carmine flush shows so plainly the rich blood coursing in the haughty, grave Castilian. The quaintness of his being called Alegrio—mirth. What irony of fate chanced to give this afflicted little creature so gay a name?

"How came you by your name?" I asked. "I never heard it before."

The boy smiled a smile which flashed over his face as the moon bursts from behind a dark cloud.

"My name was Jacobo, for Santiago and for my father, Jacobo Vastelejo, a *sereno*. My mother being dead" (here the child blessed himself solemnly, a pretty way the Spanish have of honoring their dead), "I lived with him in the Calle de la Calera; and then it came that my father died, and I was left alone. Fray Luis, at the monastery there, took me to go to school.

"One day as I went to mass, there came a call, and some one cried that a boy was in the Arlanzon, and I quickly ran to see if I might help. He was a *niño*, much smaller than I, señorita, and I pulled him out. I got quite wet myself, and running, lest I miss the mass, I soon was very hot, for it was summer and the sun was high. Then I had the fever, and when I came to myself again, I was as now—"

he touched the shortened leg with his little crutch.

"It was confirmation time, and my name was to be Jorge, for brave San Jorge who fought the dragon, but I said a lame boy could not fight, and San Jorge would not want me for his knight. Then there came Fray Luis, and he spoke to me so beautifully that I wept.

"He said the *buen Dios* perhaps had taken joy from me because he wished me to think more to give it to others. Would I not like to take Our Lady's name, Alegria, for she is called 'Our Lady of Joyfulness.' He said it would remind me always that the good God wished me to make others joyful. So I was confirmed at Pentecostes, and they called me Alegrio.

"Will you come to see my chapel?" he asked earnestly.

My eyes had filled with tears at the simple story told so naïvely, and I nodded assent as the lad led us through the magnificent choir and transept, formed by four large piers, like beautiful towers sculptured in the rich creamy hue of the Ontorio marble.

We reached the Puerta Alta with its ogival portal and concentric arches, fantastically decorated. Here, on the right was a railed chapel, and on the shrine the beautiful figure of

Nuestra Señora de Alegria (Our Lady of Joy).

"There 's her altar," whispered Alegrio, "I come here every day. She was like that, Fray Luis says; not just her mouth and nose perhaps, for it 's so long ago that she was here we cannot be sure how she was; but I think she looked like that in her eyes," and the boy's worn face seemed to take the same uplifted look as he gazed around the solemn aisles.

We made him happy with kindly words, and (although he had not asked alms) a golden coin, the like of which he had never seen before, and as he bade us "*Adios*," and "God bless you," and the tap of his little crutch reverberated down the stone pavement, I said to the Pessimist:

"The best sermon ever preached in the great Cathedral of Burgos was preached this morning by that little ragged atom who calls himself Alegrio."

The Pessimist did not answer, and her eyes were full of tears.

"More Cid!" I exclaimed, as we reached the cloisters, and passed into the little chapel where lies buried Juan Cuchiller, servant to Henry the Third, a rare domestic who sold his cloak to buy his master's supper.

The effigy of Cuchiller is of the finest alabaster; a dog, the emblem of faithfulness, crouched at his feet.

"Here is the famous coffer; and now for a story which will delight your soul, O Cid-hater, since it doth not redound to the credit of my doughty hero of renown!" I exclaimed. "Know then, O Pessimist, that El Cid was often hard put to it to find the money wherewith to continue his various campaigns, and this was especially the case when he waged a certain war against Valencia. Now, to despoil Jews. was, in those merry days, a right Christian thing to do, and El Cid sent word to two Jewish merchants of Burgos that he must have money.

"The Burgalese Jews had, mayhap, heard some such remarks before, and also there had been cases where the Cid had forgotten his promises to pay, so Rachel and Vidas remarked that they would like some security.

"The Cid's trusty messenger sped back to his master, and returned to the Jews bearing two magnificent coffers, hasped with iron, and under strong lock. These, he said, contained the master's jewels and plate, and were his surety for the loan of six hundred marks.

"The Jews accepted with pleasure, no doubt spending the greater part of their spare time praying that God would smite the ungodly

Cid, enemy of their race, in which case they
would get his jewels.

"Meantime the Cid conquered Valencia in
the most approved fashion, spoiled the city,
and sent for his coffers Alvar Fañez and Martin Antolinez, who repaid the six hundred
marks.

"What do you suppose the clever Jews
thought when they heard the truth? The Cid
had filled his chests with sand! So much for
the chest story and the Cid as a man of business. He ought to have been on the Stock
Exchange."

"Humph!" said the Pessimist. "What
else are we to see in the Cathedral?"

"Oh! all sorts of chapels, and things," I
answered. There are superb bas-reliefs of the
Passion of Our Lord in the Transagrario; the
choir has one hundred and three carved walnut
stalls, inlaid and traced with medallions and
canopies; where the baptistry now is, was the
old chapel of Santiago. The Escalera of the
Puerta Alta was carved by Diego Siloc, and
nobody in all the world carved such foliage,
grapes, and draperies, as he did. We can 't
see them all, but we must not miss the 'Cristo
de Burgos.'

"It 's in the Chapel del Santisimo 'Christo
de la Agonia,' and is an image of Our Lord,
crowned with thorns. It was said to have

been carved by Nicodemus after he and Joseph of Arimathea buried Our Lord, and was discovered in a box floating about the sea. It is peculiarly realistic, for the hair, beard, and eyelashes are real.''

''I do n't like it,'' said my friend. ''It 's too lifelike.''

''The Cathedral has one hundred and twelve windows, one hundred and forty-four pictures, sixty tombs, seven organs, forty-four altars, one hundred statues, and—''

''If that is the case would you mind taking me away? I did n't come to make a pilgrimage, and as I can 't see it all I 've seen enough,'' interrupted my companion, and I reluctantly led her away.

''What is that green gateway?'' she asked, as we meandered about the streets. ''It looks as if things had happened there.''

''Things have,'' I replied. ''That 's the Arco de Santa Maria, built by the Burgalese after the rebellion of the Comunero, when Charles the Fifth came to visit the city. Do you see those figures? They are to represent the Spanish heroes, the Cid, Layn Calvo and Fernan Gonzalo, with Cæsar in the center and the Blessed Virgin above them all. Look at the turrets and battlements, and close by are the bastions of the former walls.

''What splendid cavalcades have passed under that arch! After Charles the Fifth abdicated in the Netherlands, in 1556, he stopped at Burgos on his way to his chosen monastery at Yuste in Estremadura. Great were the festivities. Bells were rung, the streets hung with tapestries and velvets, the town illuminated, and all was rejoicing until the former Emperor left to become a mere private citizen, leaving the country in the hands of his son, the grave, stern, wholly Spanish Philip the Second.''

''What happened in the castle?'' asked the Pessimist.

''Pedro was born there, and the Cid was married.

"Within his hall of Burgos the king prepares the feast,
He makes his preparations there for many a noble guest.
It is a joyful city, it is a gallant day,
'T is the Campeador's wedding, and who will bide away?

Layn Calvo, the Lord Bishop, he first comes forth the
    gate,
Behind him comes Ruy Diaz in all his bridal state;
The crowd makes way before them as up the street
    they go,
For the multitude of people their steps must needs be
    slow.

Then comes the bride Ximena ; the King he holds her
    hand,
And the Queen, and all in fur and pall, the nobles of the
    land.
But when the fair Ximena stood forth to plight her hand,
Rodrigo gazing on her, his face could not command.

He stood and blushed before her—then at the last said
   he:
'I slew thy sire, Ximena, but not in villainy.
In no disguise I slew him—man against man, I stood;
There was some wrong between us, and I did shed his
   blood.
I slew a man, I *owe* a man; fair lady, by God's grace,
An honored husband thou shalt have in thy dead father's
   place.'"

"Such was the Cid's bridal, here in quaint old Burgos; and very different was the castle in those days. Now, it's almost a ruin, for it was the scene of bloody conflict with the French when Wellington and Soult were at swords' points along the banks of the Arlanzon.

"Now we are going to drive out to Las Huelgas, the famous convent. It was founded in 1180 by Alfonso the Eighth, and is one of the most beautiful spots in Spain. The order is Cistercian, very strict, and only women are allowed to see the nuns, who belong to the nobility, and must bring a dowry. This is rather unusual, for most orders do not require an entrance fee.

"Many great nobles have been among the sisters: Berenguela, daughter of St. Ferdinand, and Maria of Aragon, aunt of Charles V. One of the most curious things to see is the chapel of Santiago. Here the esquires, ready for knighthood, used to '*velar las armas*' (watch the arms) or keep their vigil before they were

to be knighted. All night long the candidate for knighthood watched, his sword and spurs on the altar; he vowed to lead a life of chastity, to succor the weak, and serve the lady of his choice, and when the morning broke, he received the accolade in a curious manner.

"Saint James was a warrior-saint; and in this chapel is preserved an image of him in which the arms are moved by springs. A sword was fastened to the right hand of the statue, and the spring was touched, and the sword fell gently upon the shoulder of the aspirant for knighthood. This saved the Castilian's pride, for it was deemed beneath his dignity to receive the accolade from a man. In Las Huelgas is also preserved the banner of Alfonso the Eighth, which he carried at Las Navas de Tolosa, and Alfonso the Seventh and Alfonso the Eighth are buried here. The church has been called the 'Escorial of the North'; and many spectacles of history were held there in the days when Burgos was the chief city and Madrid a mere town."

"Is this where your beloved Cid was buried?" asked the Pessimist, as we wandered slowly through the dim aisles.

"No, San Pedro de Cardeña was his chosen burial place. We won't go there, for it's a dreary drive across windy, rocky wastes, and only the chrysalis is there; for the Cid's bones and those of Ximena, his devoted wife, were removed to the Town Hall in Burgos, where they are kept in a walnut urn, and are shown to curious visitors by *permiso* from the Ayuntamiento."

"Where do we go now?" asked my friend.

"To see La Cartuja, one of the sights of Burgos," I answered, and we drove rapidly thither.

The convent was once very wealthy, but since the religious communities were suppressed in Spain, it has degenerated, and now only four or five poor, lonely Carthusians inhabit its walls. The exterior of the church is Gothic, with fine flying buttresses, pinnacles and pointed-arched windows, and the principal façade has the arms of Castile and Leon. The interior is divided into three portions, each railed in, one for the monks, one for the lay brothers, and the third for the people. The famous altar, designed by Gil de Siloe, was finished in 1499 by order of Queen Isabella, and gilded with gold brought from America by Columbus.

"See, Pessimist," I said. "the tombs here are said to be the finest in all Europe! Those two in the centre are of Juan the Second and Queen Isabella of Portugal. Look at the sides, crowned with wonderful statuettes, under filagree canopies, with open work leaves, vines, fruits, birds, and the *tout ensemble* so finely and delicately executed that one can scarcely follow the intricate work.''

''Who erected the tombs?'' asked my friend.

''Queen Isabella, in 1489; they were designed by her favorite, Gil de Siloe, and cost six hundred thousand maravedis. Look at that crucifix. Is it not a wonderful work of art? The allegorical scene over it is that curious old symbol of the Pelican wounding her breast—an early Christian type of Our Lord.

''' The Pelican, brooding in agony
    Because her young are starving 'neath her eyes,
Pecks at her breast until her life's blood flows
    To nourish them, and in the desert dies.'

''This burial ground is the saddest I ever saw. Think of it! Four hundred and fifteen Carthusians buried, here, forgotten, their graves neglected, overgrown with moss and weeds, the tall cypresses rising over them as stately as Gothic spires rise to heaven. No tears are shed for them, unless the water, trickling from the deserted fountain, weeps, or the dew casts a tear upon the flowers which lie above their quiet breasts. Forgotten in death, were their lives wasted? *Dios sabe !* ''

''Well, since you can't possibly find out, would you mind coming back to Burgos?'' said the Pessimist. ''I never could see any sense in waxing sentimental over a musty old grave-yard, filled with people whose very names you do not know."

> " ' E'en such is time, which takes on trust
>   Our youth, our joys, our all we have,
> And pays us but with earth and dust,
>   Which in the dark and silent grave,
> When we have wandered all our ways,
> Shuts up the story of our days,'

said old Sir Walter Raleigh," I answered, and we drove slowly back toward the city.

There was yet one more pilgrimage to be made in Burgos, and we hurried to the church of Santa Agueda. It is a simple building, pure in style, with an ogival nave, and it is chiefly interesting from its close connection with the legends of the Cid.

"It was one of the *iglesias juraras*, or a church where those suspected of villainy could be purged by oath," I told the Pessimist, "and the story is as follows:

"Don Sancho, brother to King Alfonso the Sixth, had been foully murdered in Zamora, and the king was suspected of having had a hand in his brother's death. The 'Romancero' says that the scene was as follows: 'In Santa Agueda, at Burgos, where knights are wont to take their oaths, the oath of Alfonso was also taken after his brother's death. The gallant Cid, who held a crucifix, made him swear the truth upon an iron lock, a crossbow, and the Gospels. The words he speaks are so awful that the king shudders at them.

"'If thou should'st not speak the truth on what is asked thee, namely, if thou hadst any part in the murder of thy brother, may knaves kill thee,—knaves from Asturias and not from Castile; may they kill thee with iron-pointed bludgeons and not with lances or shafts, with horn-handled knives and not with gilt poniards. May those who do so wear clogs and not laced shoes; may they wear rustics' cloaks and not the courtray cloaks or those of curled silk; canvas shirts and not Hollands embroidered; may each of them be mounted on an ass and not on a mule or a horse; may they make use of rope bridles and not of leathern ones, well-tanned; may they kill thee in the fields and not in a city or a village; and may they tear thy heart, all panting, from thy breast!'

"The oath was so awful that the king did not venture to take it, but a knight said to him, 'Swear, and fear naught, brave king; never was a king perjured nor a Pope excommunicated.' The gallant king then took the oath, and swore that he had had no hand in his brother's assassination; but even then he was filled with anger and indignation. 'Thou wast wrong, O Cid, to make me take that oath, for later thou wilt have to kiss my hand!' he said.

" 'To kiss a king's hand is no honor to me?' said the Beauteous Beard.

" 'Get thee hence from my land, thou Cid, false knight, and come not back till a year has elapsed,' cried Alfonso. Thus ends the 'Romancero,' and the curious story of the oath of Santa Agueda.''

"What does the oath mean, and why was it so awful?'' asked the Pessimist.

"Each clause meant a particularly degrading kind of death. He was to be killed by *Asturians*, because a Castilian deemed it a deadly disgrace to be killed by any provincial; by a bludgeon, because only peasants carried them; by a knife, because knights carried gilt poniards; by those who wore clogs and canvas shirts, because nobles wore laced shoes, embroidered Hollands, and courtray cloaks; and in the fields, instead of a city or village, because there would be no priest to give him the sacrament, and he would die unshrived.''

"What a queer lot they were,'' said the Pessimist. "It makes little difference, now, whether they were slain by prince or pauper.''

"Nothing makes any difference unless one thinks it does, and then it makes all the difference in the world,'' I said, philosophically.

We wandered around the streets of Burgos,

re-visiting our favorite haunts, sorry to say good-bye, and thinking resentfully of the morrow, when we must leave. I could have looked forever at the Cathedral towers. How wonderful they looked against the pink glow of the sunset! How pure was their perfect outline! How lofty and aspiring were their pinnacles! My last glimpse of those never-to-be-forgotten towers, as the night shadows began to fall about us, was as the last gleams of daylight enwrapped their Gothic traceries and lacy frost-work, and made of each a veritable *torre del oro*, fairer far than that one which gleams beside the rippling Guadalquivir in gay Seville.

CHAPTER XX

ALL THE WAY TO ZARAGOZA.

EN hours to Zaragoza!" I exclaimed, as we steamed out of the Station Puerta de Atocha at Madrid. "We 've a long day in which to study history. The first place of any account is Alcala de Henares. I wish we could have stopped there, for it 's very interesting. It was an old Roman city, spoken of by Pliny, and vases and coins which belong to the Roman period are often found. Don Bernardo, Archbishop of Toledo, conquered Alcala from the Moors, in 1118, and Alonzo VI. gave the city to him and his successors. Raimundo, who followed him, became absolute sovereign, and gave the people their *fueros*, or charter. This was full of the queerest rules, for instance: 'The man who will pull another by the beard is to be fined four *maravedis*, and have his own beard cut away; and if he should have none, let him have an inch deep of flesh cut into his own chin.'

"The people of Alcala were kind and tolerant to the Jews, but hated the Moors. Here, the martyrs, Saints Justo and Pastor, mere boys, were killed in the reign of Dacian; and here in later years was born Cervantes, the star of Spain, who from this simple town shed the beams of his genius over all the world, and whose radiance never dims. He reminds me of another jester who wrote mock heroics, one of which, upon the 'Death, Burial and Honors of Chrispina Maranzmona,' the cat of Juan Chrespo, was published in Paris, in 1604. Cintio Merctisso was the writer's *nom de plume*, and no one has ever been able to discover exactly who he was. Here is his best example of the subtle Spanish wit:

'Up in the concave of the tiles, and near
    That firm-set wall, the north wind whistles by,
Close to the spot the cricket chose last year,
    In a blind corner far from every eye,
Beneath a brick that hides the treasure dear
    Five choice sardines in secret darkness lie;
These, brethren-like, I charge you take by shares
And also all the rest to which you may be heirs.
Moreover you will find in heaps piled fair—
    Proofs of successful toil to build a name—
A thousand wings and legs of birds pecked bare
    And cloaks of quadrupeds both wild and tame;
All which your father had collected there,
    To serve as trophies of an honest fame;
These keep and count them better than all prey,
Nor give them, e'en for ease or sleep or life, away.'"

"Is Alcala popular, now?" asked my friend.

"No; it's as dead as the traditional doornail," I answered. "In 1836 the great university was removed to Madrid, and this proved the death-blow to Alcala de Henares. It used to be thronged with *estudiantes*—merry fellows, who, gay and lazy, sang and danced and studied (when perforce compelled), in rags and picturesque cloaks, strumming their guitars under the balconies. Cardinal Ximenes, minister of Ferdinand and Isabella, studied in Alcala, and founded the university. Here it was that he spent the last years of his life. His famous polyglot Bible, in six volumes, was published in the year 1522. This comprises Hebrew, Septuagint, Greek, Chaldaic, and Vulgate versions, and is a wonderful work. In Alcala also are kept the Alfonsine Tables, drawn up by Alfonso X. in the thirteenth century.

"In the church of Santa Maria, Cervantes was christened, in 1547, and there is a record of his baptism by Bachiller Serrano. From Alcala upon the plains which line the bank of the muddy Henares, where the stately elms shade the wind-blown place, we come to Guadalajara on the Henares and not far from the Tagus."

"Is that the same river we saw at Aranjuez?" asked my friend.

"Yes, it rises over to the east of Guadalajara. The city is the capital of the province of the same name. Francis I. was confined here on his way from Pavia to Madrid, and here he was fêted with bull-fights and festas and tourneys, by the Duke del Infantado. Francis, wily as he was brave, challenged the gouty old duke to single combat, but upon Infantado's applying to Charles V. for permission to fight, royal sanction for the unequal combat was refused.

"There's a fine palace here, belonging to the great Mendoza family, and a curious inscription over the patio, where the stone griffins and lions keep watch. The inscription gives in detail all the names and titles of the founder, as if to glorify him as much as possible, then ends with, ' *Todo es vanidad*,' quoting Solomon with would-be humility."

"Is there any history or legend about this country?" asked the Pessimist, somewhat restive under all these statistics.

"You're getting to be a perfect cormorant for stories," I said. "Don't you think you could lay aside your desire to fill your mind, and eat your dinner? It's a less elegant but quite as necessary an occupation. We are going to stop twenty minutes at Guadalajara, and nobody can tell when we shall have another chance to eat, for you know in what vagaries Spanish railway trains indulge."

We had *pollo con arroz* for dinner, or as it is sometimes called, "arrozà la Valenciana," because it 's the great dish of the Valencianets, as the people of Valencia dub themselves. It is a delicious concoction, a savory stew with chicken, rice, sausages, and pimientos, or sweet Spanish peppers. It reminds one of the saying, "La bête se nourrit. L'homme mange. L'homme d'esprit seul soit diner;" and the Pessimist and I dined vigorously, finishing with fruit and a draught of wine just as the train's whistle lazily remarked that it was time to go.

Nothing in Spain shows the national characteristic more plainly than the various whistles. A boy goes whistling along the sunny road. His tone has none of the alert cheeriness of a Yankee farm-lad's pipe, the insolent pert shrillness of a Chicago Arab's. It sounds sedate and lazy. The factory whistles are loud and prolonged, and yet they never cry in shrill discontent, "Make haste, make haste, cigarette girls, or you 'll lose your wages!" They politely suggest—for even whistles are polite in Spain—that if it so pleases, you may resume again those labors which you are gracious enough to engage in entirely for the good of your employers, not to mention your own peseta a day.

Even the railroad whistles are reserved,

well-behaved affairs, gently reminding the most gracious passenger that if it so pleases him the train will start between the time of whistling and the morrow, *perhaps*. Not at all that there is any hurry. "To—ot! To—ot!" slowly and civilly it says, but only that you, the stranger and guest, for whose sole benefit the train was run on that particular day, that you may reach your destination in good time, before the evening dews fall too heavily, and endanger the health of the most estimable Americana.

Ah! Spanish whistles—cousins very far removed from your shrieking, demoniacal, strident, American relatives—dear Spanish whistles, I sing your praises loud and long!

"Is not this a charming country?" I said to the Pessimist as our train wended its leisurely way through fields and meadows full of flowers.

"Castles and towns in due proportion each,
As by some skillful artist's hand portrayed;
Here, crossed by many a wild sierra's shade,
And boundless plains that tire the traveler's eye;
There, rich with vineyard and with olive glade,
Or deep-embrowned by forests huge and high,
Or washed by mighty streams that slowly murmured by."

"See," I cried, as we stopped at a village, "there is some excitement here. Look at those men, resplendent in costumes of black velvet and gold. I wonder what they can be."

I leaned far out of the window, watching the assembled peasants greeting the two men, and asked a guard what it all meant.

"Bull-fighters, señorita," he said. "They have been to Madrid to the fights, and are come home for the wedding of Miguel. The tall one is Miguel Valdez, one of the best *matadors* in all Spain, and he marries Dolores Sanchez, sister of the other *matador*, José. They are celebrated people, and all the village is joyous when they come home."

They were superb fellows; tall, finely-built, every muscle developed and brought into play, their faces strong and yet not brutal; they gave me a tinge of surprise that a sport so fierce and cruel should not leave ignoble traces upon the faces of its devotees. Much is said of the cruelty of the Spaniard, and it seems to be due to one thing. As a race, Spaniards are physically brave. They do not fear to suffer themselves; they suffer without a groan, and they can scarcely realize that others cannot so readily endure pain. They were originally hardy and vigorous warriors, used to giving and taking and to a rough and ready life. Since civilization has done away with much of this in the modern Don, it has failed utterly to make him gentle or mild.

The proverbial cruelty of the Spanish, as a nation, will always be a mystery to those who, knowing individual Spaniards, feel the warmth of their friendship, the charm of their courtesy, the beauty of their family-life, and the genuine goodness of their hearts toward all whom they love. It almost seems as if this cruelty of theirs might be an inherent quality which they themselves did not realize—a sort of Berseker rage—unpremeditated and unintentional.

We were nearing Siguenza, which is built on a knoll whose green slopes touch the Henares.

"The city has massive walls and strong gates, and seems a veritable feudal stronghold," I said. "How the castle towers above it all! That is a fitting symbol of the power of the nobles in those old days when cities were almost unknown, and all the life, save that of the mere children of the plow, was clustered about the castle gates."

"What is there at Siguenza?" asked the Pessimist. "I 'd like to hear something interesting."

"I 'll make up something, if you do n't stop demanding wonders," I replied. "I firmly believe you are thirsting for horrors. Do you see that curious castellated building with flying buttresses ending in balls, and which has a balustraded parapet crowning the façade? That 's a wonderful old church, dating from the twelfth century, and the interior is said to be one of the most striking in all Spain.

"Many strange things have happened in this old Cathedral of Siguenza, and within its dim aisles and shadowy archways lurk memories strange and wonderful. 'T was in some such minster as this that King Pedro forced homage to Inez de Castro. Do you remember the story? One of the numerous Infantes had married, without his parents' consent, Doña Inez, a daughter of the De Castros, and his stern father had refused to have her acknowledged as Infanta. The Infante Pedro remained faithful to her; but she fell ill, and died before he came to the throne.

"At last his father died, and Pedro succeeded to the kingdom. His first act was to have his wife's body exhumed from the convent where it had lain embalmed for months. He assembled in the great cathedral a vast multitude of knights, squires, princes, and lords, and, crowning the inanimate form of his still beautiful queen, he commanded every one to do her homage. There she sat in state, in her costly robes of gold and pearls, a diadem upon her ebon locks above the brow so regal, yet so pale and

> " Beside her stood in silence
> One with a brow as pale
> And white lips rigidly compressed
> Lest the strong heart should fail,

> King Pedro with a jealous eye
>   Watching the homage done,
> By the land's flower and chivalry
>   To her, his martyred one.
>
> There is music on the midnight—
>   A requiem sad and slow,
> As the mourners through the solem aisles
>   In dark procession go;
> And the ring of state and the starry crown
>   And all the rich array
> Are borne to the house of silence down,
>   With her, that queen of clay.
>
> And tearlessly and firmly
>   King Pedro led the train,
> But his face was wrapped in his folding robe
>   When they lowered the dust again.
> 'T is hushed at last the tomb above—
>   Hymns die, and steps depart.—
> Who called thee strong as Death, O Love?
>   Mightier thou wast, and art!"

"That is very fine," said the Pessimist, "but it seems rather unlike the ancient idea that 'a live dog is better than a dead lion.' There was little of such constancy, methinks."

"Far more than one imagines," I answered. "I am more struck with that trait among Spaniards, than anything else. They seem to love but once, whatever the exigencies of Fate or Fortune. No matter how many times they may have to marry for reasons of state or any other cause, their hearts seem 'true to Poll' in very many cases. Charles the Fifth never loved any but his Isabel of Portugal; Ferdinand, though he married Germaine de Foix, never cared for her; and remember Juana de Loca's devotion to that wretched, worthless Philippe le Bel. Do n't you recall Mrs. Hemans' verses about Queen Juana?

"The night wind shook the tapestry round an ancient
    palace room,
And torches, as it rose and fell, waved through the
    deepening gloom,
And o'er a shadowy regal couch threw fitful gleams
    and red,
Where a woman with long raven hair sat watching by
    the dead.

'They told me this was death, yet well I knew it could
    not be;
Fairest and stateliest of the earth, who spoke of death
    for *thee?*
They would have wrapped the funeral shroud thy gal-
    lant form around,
But I forbade, and there thou art a monarch robed and
    crowned!

'Ah! when thou wak'st, my Prince, my Lord! and hear'st
    how I have kept
A lonely vigil by thy side and o'er thee prayed and wept;
How in one long, deep dream of thee my nights and
    days have passed,
Surely, my humble, patient love must win thee back at
    last!'

In the still chamber of the dead thus poured forth day
    by day,
The passion of that loving dream, from a troubled soul
    found sway,
Until the shadows of the grave have swept o'er every
    grace
Left, 'midst the awfulness of death, on the princely form
    and face.

And slowly sank the fearful truth within the watcher's
    breast,
As they bore away the royal dead with requiem to his
    rest,
With banners and with knightly plumes all waving in the
    wind,—
But a woman's broken heart was left in its lone despair
    behind!"

"You seem to have an attack of poetry," said the Pessimist.

"I have, and I have it badly," I answered serenely. "My mind is a literary scrap-bag; and just now I'm making a crazy quilt, so it comes in very handy. We're approaching a tunnel two thousand nine hundred and twenty-three feet long. I wonder why it is that anything which sounds especially fascinating in the guide-book is sure to have disappeared before one reaches .the place, while a 'tunnel,' or 'Fonda poor' or 'palace closed for repairs' always turns up with monotonous regularity."

"Who's pessimistic now?" demanded my friend; and I welcomed the two thousand nine hundred and twenty-three feet of tunnel at that moment, for it saved me a reply.

"Do you see those hills? They are called Santa del Solorio, and are a spur of the Sierra del Guadarrama. We are coming to Calatayud. It was called Kalàt-Ayub, or Castle of Ayub, and is one of the most important cities of Aragon," I said. "Martial was born there, and it was a veritable stamping ground for Moors and Christians.

"There are perfectly delightful *mazmorras*, or gypsy caves, cut out of the rock as they were at Granada, and the inhabitants are picturesque and generally interesting. Calatayud was captured by our friend Alfonso el Batallador, in 1120.

"Wake, wake! the old soil where thy children repose,
Sounds hollow and deep to the trampling of foes.
The voices are mighty that swell from the past,
With Aragon's cry on the shrill mountain blast;
The ancient Sierras give strength to our tread,
Their pines murmur song where bright blood hath been
    shed."

"More poetry," sighed the Pessimist. "What river is that?"

"The Jalon; but before long begins the Ebro.

"'Fair land! of chivalry the old domain;
    Land of the vine and olive, lovely Spain!
    No sound of battle swells on Douro's shore,
    And banners wave on Ebro's banks no more.
    How oft these rocks have echoed to the tale
    Of knights who fell in Roncesvalles' vale.
    Of him renowned in old heroic lore,
    First of the brave, the gallant Cid Campeador,
    Of—'"

I stopped suddenly, for the Pessimist had cast upon me an awful look.

"You promised me solemnly that we would inter the Cid in Burgos, and I refuse positively to hear even his name again. 'Let sleeping dogs lie,'" she said severely.

"I beg your pardon. It was n't I; 't was Mrs. Hemans who mentioned him then," I said meekly. "We are nearing Zaragoza— and I will try not to poetize any more, for some time at least. You won't mind my humming 'Trovatore,' will you? In the dungeon of La Torreto, Leonora's lover was confined and sang —

"'Ah! I have sighed to rest me!'

"The Aljaferia at Zaragoza is one of the most delightful sights in Spain. It was a Moorish palace, but afterwards became the residence of the Aragonese kings. It is used for barracks now, but has many interesting things about it. There is the salon of Santa Isabel where the Queen of Portugal was born in 1271. She was named for her aunt, Saint Elizabeth of Hungary (Isabel and Elizabeth are the same names), was daughter of Pedro III. of Aragon, and was famous for her sweetness and wisdom. The ceiling of the Aljaferia was gilded with the first gold Columbus brought from America.

"There are all sorts of lovely old houses, dating from 1500, in Zaragoza, and it was a favorite residence with the nobles and *caballeros*. I wish we could have been here on the twelfth of October, for that is the day of the great feast in honor of the Virgin del Pilar, and forty thousand pilgrims come here every year. The town is then beautifully decorated and lighted."

"We saw enough of *fiestas* in Seville," said the Pessimist. "Oh! what is that?"

"The dome of Our Lady of the Pillar. Is it not wonderful? See the sunset glow on the blue and gold Moorish tiles of the great dome. How beautifully the Ebro winds about under that dark bridge, with its arches overgrown in moss and vines. Quaint old Zaragoza, we have reached you at last; famous in song and story, favorite city of the Kings of Aragon, beloved by Saint Iago, and visited by the Blessed Virgin, so says tradition and legend, with which your narrow streets and shadowy corners are rife. Delightful Zaragoza—"

I ceased, for during my rhapsody the Pessimist had been reading the guide-book, and interrupted with "Zaragoza, also famous for pneumonia and intermittent fevers, changeable climate, the *cierzo* (cold west wind) and *bochorno* (hot east wind); for brackish water, hence the saying, 'Mas comemos de lo qué hebemos' ('We eat more than we drink'); for—" but I interrupted in my turn.

"You 're only trying to be pessimistic now. The east wind and west wind do n't blow both at once. Every climate is changeable;

and as for the brackish water we will break off a piece now and then, as they say they do in Saint Louis. Or else we will drink Cariñena wine, which is famous everywhere.

"One has to drink wine sometimes in Spain, or live to wish she had. Come, come Pessimist; here we are in the nice railway station. We 're going to like old Cæsaria Augusta which the Moors called Zaragoza. We 'll have dinner, and meantime here is some poetry for you, and a nice legend:

> "' At Sansuena, in a tower,
>   Fair Melisendra lies;
> Her heart is far away in France
>   And tears are in her eyes.
> The twilight shade is thickening laid
>   On Sansuena's plain,
> Yet wistfully the lady dear
>   Her weary eyes doth strain,' "

I quoted. "Sansuena was the old name for Zaragoza, and Melisendra had been conquered by Moors. Gayferos, her gallant husband, hunted all over Spain, but obtained no glimpse of his wife, and she thought he had deserted her. Seven years she was captive; and one day she leaned from out her turret window, and a horseman came across the plain. She talked with him long, bemoaning her lot. At last he revealed himself, and she let herself down from the tower, and eloped with her own husband.

> "'And he hath kissed her pale, pale cheeks,
>   And lifted her up behind.
>   St. Denis speed their milk-white steed,
>   No Moor their path shall find.'

"So they got away safe into France. This is the very Sansueña; and so picturesque is it that I feel as if a gay knight lurked within each shadow, and that the balconies were full of lovely maidens."

We reached Zaragoza late in the afternoon, and were very tired, but an excellent table d'hote at the Hotel de las Cuatro Naciones revived us, and we started out to see the old Aragonese city which lies so beautifully upon the *vega* between the Ebro and Gallego.

It was cool and pleasant; a soft breeze came from the olive-covered hills where snowy villas gleamed in the summer moonlight, seeming like white birds, with their wings folded in rest.

Zaragoza is quaint beyond description, and the effect of its narrow streets, tall dark houses, and plain architecture gives something almost war-like to the very air one breathes, and its fortress-like towers and turrets stand out like sentinels against the sky.

The city has been the scene of the most terrific conflicts. It was always a mooted point with the Moors, and torn by inward dissensions. During the Peninsular War its record is extraordinary.

General Lefévre-Desnouettes besieged the place, and said he would soon conquer it, *"malgré les trente mille idiots que s'y opposeraient;"* but he had to fall back, as the self-same "idiots" did not in the least know when they were beaten, and refused to yield.

It was during the second siege that Palafox distinguished himself. He was a young *hijo* of Zaragoza, as bold as a lion, the idol of the people, and he led them on where they would follow no organized authority.

"Guerra al cuchillo!" was the cry, and the Aragonese, as brave as they were haughty, held out against cannon, onslaught and famine. Men and women fought like heroes, and here it was that Augustina, the Maid of Zaragoza, distinguished herself. When her lover fell, she mounted his gun and fired it for him; and, as Byron said, the French were "foiled by a woman's hand before a battered wall."

When the surrender at last had to be made, it was upon the most honorable terms, and the siege of Zaragoza has gone down to history as famous, with Saguntum, Numantia and Troy.

> "Ah, Zaragoza—blighted be the tongue
>   That names thy name without the honor due.
> For never hath the harp of minstrel rung
>   Of faith so felly proved, so firmly true.

> Mine, sap, and bomb thy shattered ruin knew;
>   Each art of war's extremity had room;
> Twice from thy half-sacked streets the foe withdrew;
>   And if at length, stern fate decreed thy doom,
> They won not Zaragoza, but her children's bloody tomb."

The Pessimist and I went as soon as we could to see the Leaning Tower* one of the wonders of Spain. It was built in 1504, and is an octagonal clock tower of beautiful workmanship, leaning ten feet, owing to a faulty foundation. There it stood in the Plaza de San Felipe, and we came toward it slowly, our guide talking of the streets through which we passed. This, was the Calle de Jaime First; that, the street of Palafox, heaped with dead and dying once, when the beautiful Ebro seemed a river of blood.

He was a wonderful creature, that guide; tall and stalwart, for the hardy northern Spaniards are larger and more sturdy than the Andalucians, if not so graceful. His hair was the soft, cloudy black which lies so lightly above the brow; his skin the pale, clear olive, with no color to mar the perfect hues of brow and cheek; his lips carmine under his slight black moustache. His eyes were large and dark and liquid beneath their long lashes, and he wore a cloak thrown gracefully over one shoulder, and on his head

* In 1894, this was destroyed owing to its unsafe condition.

The Leaning Tower at Zaragoza

a dark *berret*, pulled to one side over his temple with that unconscious picturesqueness which is a Spaniard's birthright, as are his pride and his loyalty.

He took us to the cathedral, La Seo as it is called, which existed in 290 A.D., when Saint Valerio was bishop. A mosque, a church, and a cathedral, it has grown by degrees, built little by little, and is a strange mixture as to architecture.

Pillars, statues and towers, Corinthian, Græco-Roman, and plateresque, all are mingled in its construction with better result and more grace and harmony than one would deem possible. This church has been to Aragon what that of Rheims was to France, for the kings were crowned here, and here many magnificent rites and ceremonies have been performed.

> " A dim and mighty minster of old time,
> A temple shadowy with remembrances
> Of the majestic past; the very light
> Streams with a coloring of heroic days
> In every ray which leads through arch and aisle
> A path of dreamy lustre; the rich fretted roof;
> And the wrought coronals of summer leaves,
> Ivy and vine and many a sculptured rose,
> The tenderest image of mortality,
> Binding the slender columns whose light shafts
> Cluster like stems in corn sheaves."

"In the Trascora, señoritas," said the guide, "was where the Blessed Virgin appeared to Canon Fuenes, and spoke to him.

And she spoke, of course, Aragonese-Spanish, with the old Limousin pronunciation. Some, indeed, there are who say she spoke Castilian, and that *that* is the purest Spanish, but we Aragonese know better, señoritas. Now you must see El Pilar, for we have two cathedrals here in Zaragoza, you know. When Santiago came to Spain, of course he came to Zaragoza; and in a dream Our Blessed Mother came to him, and she stood upon a pillar and told him she desired a chapel built in her honor, and on that very spot. When Santiago awoke, he at once started to build, and from that came Nuestra Señora del Pilar. The great bell of the cathedral always tolls without any human hand at the rope, before the death of a king of Spain.''

''I remember that story,'' I said.

" Heard you last night the sound of Santiago's bell?
   How sullenly from the great tower it pealed
      Ay, and 't is said,
   No mortal hand was near, when so it seemed
   To shake the midnight street,
      Too well we know
   The sound of coming Fate. 'T is ever thus
   When Death is on his way to make it night
   In the Cid's ancient house."

The cathedral of El Pilar is a great contrast to La Seo, a huge edifice, looking rather unfinished and with many colored domes and a magnificent view across the Ebro, upon whose banks it lies.

The interior contains the jasper pillar upon which the Blessed Virgin stood, when she appeared to Saint James and asked him to build a chapel for her, and the Virgin's treasures, which were plundered by the French to the extent of one hundred and forty thousand dollars.

As we stood in the dark street, suddenly a lantern flashed upon us, and a voice spoke to the guide. Such a mediæval figure! We saw a tall man, wrapped in a heavy cloak, which, flung aside, showed a dagger in his belt; a soft hat was on one side his head, and in one hand a bunch of keys, while from the wrought-iron Moresque lantern in the other there flashed a strong light.

It made ghostly shadows creep from the moonlit crevices, and we asked eagerly, "What is he?"

"*El sereno*, señoritas," said Felipe; "every night he comes to watch the street. If thieves break in, one raises a window and cries, 'Sereno! Sereno!' If one is ill, the sereno calls a doctor. If one comes home very late by chance, and feels not quite as in the morning, and cannot perhaps find the keyhole, the sereno comes and lights him home, and with his huge key opens the house door. So, too, perhaps, if one must have a wife who owns a tongue, the good sereno saves him from a

scolding at coming in so late.   Ah! the sereno
is a good fellow, and one without whom the
night would be a terror here in Spain."

"Has he keys to all the doors?" I asked.

"Each one; that is, all those within his own
square.   *Adios*, Señor Sereno," he cried as
the man, satisfied that we were not molesters
of the peace, went down a dark street.

"I shall sleep better, now I know we 're
done up in cotton wool by *el sereno*," said
the Pessimist.

I laughed, for one of her eccentricities is to
sleep, peacefully, all night, and assure one
in the morning that she has n't closed her
eyes.

"The university is fine.   Will the señoritas
see it, or go to a *café chantant* and see some
dances?" asked Felipe.

"Oh, dances by all means!" we cried.
"We have universities at home."   And we hurried away to the Caso, a fine street and broad,
with shops and lights and a merry crowd.

I had a guilty conscience.   I was neglecting
the university, where many famous men had
been educated, and which claims the honor of
having had Goya ("Francisco Goya y Lu-
cientes, Pintor Español," as he signed himself) among its pupils.   I do not like Goya,
and there are artistic souls who accuse me of
not doing justice to his genius.   I do not deny

his power, and it may be a case of "I do not like thee, Doctor Fell," but to me, much of his work is grotesque and weird, if not grewsome.

However, when one has a guilty conscience, it is always a good thing to stir up some one else and have company, and I felt it my duty also to improve the Pessimist's mind, so I said:

"I am astonished at you. You should long for the seat of learning where Goya disported himself. Do n't you know that he is considered one of the greatest of Spanish painters? He was a artist, soldier, bull-fighter, and nearly everything else, and led a roving life, blessed, however, with a wife who forgave him everything, and that meant much, *sabe Dios!* His subjects portrayed every type from prince to beggar, and the student of *costumbres* could study him forever. When he died at Bordeaux in 1828 he left many remarkable examples of his marked but eccentric genius, and perhaps the best known of his works is the painting of our friends Saints Justina and Rufina, of Sevillian fame. Shame upon you, Pessimist, that you 're not interested in him."

"He 's not here, or I might be," she replied, unmoved. "As it is, I prefer our guide."

The *café chantant* was an odd affair. We

entered a large room, so filled with smoke it seemed that one could cut it with a knife; but soon we grew used to it, and saw a dais upon which sat the musicians, with a piano, bass-viol, two violins, flute, and clarionet. The men played well, with much spirit, and the dancing was marvellous.

> " When for the light *bolero* ready stands
>   The *mozo* blithe, with gay *muchacha* met,
>   He conscious of his broidered cap and bands,
>   She of her netted locks and light corsette,
> Each, tiptoe perched, to spring and shake the castanet."

Not so seductive as the Sevillian, the Zota, or true Aragonese dance, is more spirited, and quite as graceful. The men, especially, were charming in their curious costumes. They wore red kerchiefs around their heads, black corduroy knee-breeches, a loose upper gar-ment of gay stripes belted at the waist, and white hose, with high-heeled shoes.

"Andalucia for fair women, and Aragon for brave men," I whispered to the Pessimist. "Are n't they splendid?"

"Yes, indeed!" she answered, "I never saw finer;" and we sipped our coffee from the huge iron-stone china cups contentedly. Each cup had a little tin sugar-saucer which fitted the top of it, and no cream was provided. The people sat at small tables, chatting and laughing, and though the furniture of the place was most primitive, and the people evidently of the *hoi polloi*, every one was gay, happy and courteous. We wandered home, charmed with our visit to Zaragoza by moonlight.

"Pessimist," I asked, "what do you think of Felipe?" as we stood on our balcony and watched his graceful figure in picturesque cloak as he went down the street and whistled a few bars from the Marcha Real:

"He 's out of a story-book," she said. "He looks like Linnæus or Dante, or somebody I 've seen pictures of, and is as perfect a type as was Diego at Granada, mediæval and not *fin de siècle*," I said. "He might be a noble or Don, Infante or prince.

Oh! Spanish guide, with dusky eyes
 Aglow with thought and passion,
I wonder oft, if in thee lies,
 In some strange guise or fashion,
The spirit of Don Rodrigo,
 Or Moor or old Castilian
Who, where the Ebro's waters flow,
 Has danced with cheeks vermillion,
And played his graceful mandolin
 To many Spanish ladies,
Or with the war-cry fierce, 'To Win!'
 Has drawn his sword at Cadiz.

CHAPTER XXI

A MOUNTAIN MONASTERY.

O the west the grand peaks of the Sierra de Alcubierre, and around us an uninteresting country; few trees except olives, here and there, like soft gray-green balls; villages few and far between; and some vine-clad hills. The Pessimist and I were nearing Monzon, where the Cinca river divides Aragon from Cataluña.

"On the height above the town is a very old castle, repaired by the Templars in 1143, and given to them by the famous Count Ramon Berenguer," I said. "Those old ruins on the second height are Roman. We are soon to reach Lerida, on the Segre, over which is a fine bridge. Lerida is the capital of a province, and has twenty-three thousand inhabitants. It was Roman, Gothic, Moorish, and now is merely a ruin; but the old cathedral is one of the most interesting in

Spain. In the new cathedral are kept our Lord's swaddling clothes, said to have been sent to the King of Tunis by the Sultan Saladin, in 1238, and stolen thence by a slave.

The great plains are called Llanos de Urgel, and stretch for miles toward the Pyrenees where the Urgel prince-bishops hold sway.

The Pessimist could not keep awake to hear me prose about Lerida and Cervera, and the little towns through which we passed. Even Manresa did not awaken her, picturesque as it is on the Cardona's banks.

Near here is the great salt mine at Cardona, a regular salt mountain, five hundred feet in height, and belonging to the Duke of Medinaceli. It was not until the guard called "Monistrol" that she awoke, and we gathered together our wraps and hurried from the car. There was a neat station, filled with pilgrims, and an obliging porter helped us into the little funicular, a small tram, a cross between street and railway cars.

In a very few moments we were steaming up the side of Montserrat over a strange circuitous route, now tunneling the dark mountain, now peering into a deep gorge, now surmounting crags and peaks, then shooting around curves, sharp enough to make one dizzy as, looking directly below, one saw the very track one had traversed a moment before.

Above us towered the mountains, their granite rocks crowned with peaks and points of curious formations. Serrated and jagged, they stood out grimly against the sunset sky, like the huge teeth of some Titan's saw. Below were pines and wooded hills, and through the distant valley, which stretched in green loveliness, wound the slender ribbon of the river—the Llobregat.

Beyond, far beyond, rose-hued and fair, against the blue sky gleamed the snows of the Pyrenees, tinged with the rays of the setting sun, which shed abroad such loveliness as to bathe his death-bed in regal splendor. We were

> " In sight
> Of the snow-crowned Sierras freely sweeping,
> With many an eagle's eyrie on the height,
> And hunter's cabin by a torrent peeping,
> Far off; and vales between and vineyards lay
> With sound and gleam of waters on their way,
> And chestnut woods that girt the happy, sleeping
> In many a peasant home."

Up and up our car climbed, until after two hours, we reached the monastery gates.

"This is a strange place," said I to my friend, as we asked admission at the porter's lodge. "There is no regular charge and no hotel, only a café, where one can get meals, though many pilgrims bring a sack of bread and potatoes over their shoulders, and roast the pota-

toes at a little fire, eating nothing but their own provender while they remain here. We get a key from the porter, are assigned to a cell, and when we leave we give him exactly what remuneration we please.''

A young monk brought us a huge iron key, and bade us follow him; and out of the dingy office we went, up a steep flight of stone steps, dark as Erebus, through gloomy halls, down a long corridor with doors on each side. One of these iron-barred portals our guide unlocked, and, handing us the key, disappeared. Such a room! A veritable monk's cell, though in a part of the monastery now unused by the brothers themselves, and kept for hospitality to those strangers or pilgrims whom chance, curiosity, or piety brings hither.

The furniture, if such it could be called, was plain, almost rude. Two curtained iron beds contained rough mattresses, coarse sheets, and a blanket, all scrupulously clean. There was a small iron stand, holding a basin and mug, while a huge old-fashioned ewer stood upon the floor of dark flags, while the ceiling of wooden rafters was painted in alternate stripes of dull red and blue. The walls were roughly whitewashed, and upon them hung a small hand-glass and a wooden crucifix. Two wooden chairs completed the furniture of the cell.

I stepped to the window to look out. What a wonderful scene! The window opened upon a tiny balcony, which overhung the square court of the monastery. To the left were the huge old buildings, rising dark and grim against the sky. To the right the mountains towered above us, while in front the hills sloped down to the beautiful valleys. The moon was rising, and seemed to rest tenderly upon the old, gray church, and to invest the gnarled tree trunks with romance and grace as though some knightly spirit lived within them.

"It is a wonderful place," I said to my companion. "I do not wonder that one of the greatest minds of his age was impressed with Montserrat, and found it his Sinai. There is something truly inspiring in the majestic solitude of such a spot. Great thoughts come to one, and great deeds grow from great thoughts. Loyola must, indeed, have formed his plan of life while on his vigil in that beautiful old church over there."

"What had he to do with Montserrat?" said the Pessimist. "Tell me about him," settling herself to listen.

"Ignatius Loyola was the youngest son of a Spanish Don, and was born in 1491, in Guipuzcoa. Even as a boy he showed rare virtues, and his father placed him at the court as page to King Ferdinand of Castile. Loyal, brave, chivalrous, with charming and graceful manners, he was soon a court favorite, but his vigorous nature preferred rather the stirring life of the camp. Here he was the idol of his soldiers, but being wounded at Pampeluna he was captured by the French. Such had been the prodigies of valor which Loyola had performed, that the French sent him to his own home to have his wound healed. During the time of his convalescence the inaction tried his gallant spirit, and one day he chanced—as men call it—upon a volume of the 'Lives of the Saints.' The courage and patience of those whose lives he read appealed to him, and he determined to endeavor to lead such a life.

"Upon his recovery he set out in secret for the Monastery of Montserrat. The monks of this monastery, Benedictines, received Ignatius gladly, and his first act was to exchange his fine garments with a poor pilgrim, taking the beggar's plain penitential robe in place of his knightly robes; his next was to make the vigil of arms in the church.

" Down the moonlit aisles he paced alone
    With a free and stately tread,
And the floor gave back a muffled tone
    From the couches of the dead.
The silent ones that round him lay,
    Not crowned and helmed they were,
Nor haughty chiefs of war array
    Each in his sepulchre.

But the sword of many a field was there,
    With its cross for the hour of need,
When the knights' bold war-cry sunk in prayer,
    And the spear was a broken reed.

Hush! did a breeze through the armor sigh?
    Did the fold of the banner shake?
Not so; from the tomb's dark mystery
    There seemed a voice to break;
And it said, 'The sword hath conquered kings
    And the spear through realms hath passed;
But the cross alone of all these things
    Might aid me at the last.'"

"As did the esquires of old, on the eve of their knighthood, so Ignatius Loyola watched all night before the famous altar of Nuestra Señora de Montserrat. Laying his knightly sword on the altar, he knelt in prayer, offering his life to God, and when the morning broke he set forth upon his pilgrimage, little thinking that for centuries the place of his vigil would be shown to strangers from strange lands, and his name be revered for generations.

"Upon leaving Montserrat, Loyola was accosted by an officer of justice, who said to him, 'Sir Pilgrim, is it true that thou hast given thy suit of fine raiment to a poor beggar? In the valley below there lies in the prison one who swears thou hast given him thy robes, taking his in exchange, and we hold him there to know if he speaks truth.'

" 'It is true. I beg of you release the man,' cried Ignatius, much chagrined that his first act of charity should have done ill rather than good. 'The cloak was of scarlet velvet, marked out in gold and fur, and the small clothes were of green.'

"After seeing the beggar released, Loyola continued his journey to Manresa. There he worked in the hospital, tending the most loathsome cases, practising severities upon himself, but always gentle and tender to others. His broad, high forehead was furrowed deep with care; his dark eyes had a far-away look; his large firm mouth was kindly and sweet; and he combined strength with gentleness in an unusual degree. The promise of his youth was fulfilled, for there has seldom been a more remarkable character. Noble by birth, he humbled himself to lowly service; proud, he became humble; a soldier, he became a monk; and through all his career of toil, privation, danger and ill-health, he preserved his clear mind and wonderful judgment.

"One of the greatest societies ever formed was founded by him, and his followers go from ocean to ocean, and almost from pole to pole; and even those who do not believe in nor sympathize with his aims cannot fail to admire the heroism of his followers, and the character of Saint Ignatius Loyola, founder of the Society of Jesus."

"Who founded Montserrat, and why was it so famous?" asked the Pessimist, as I ceased talking.

"Cristobal de Virues, the poet, who lived in the sixteenth century, and was one of the greatest Spanish poets, wrote a dramatic epic called the 'Montserrat,' " I said; "and he tells the story of the founding of the monastery.

"Garin, the hermit, living within the rocks and fastnesses hereabouts, committed a horrible murder, but was seized with remorse, and went to Rome to beg absolution. This he received, but only with severe penance, being forced to grovel as a beast, and not look up to heaven for months, because his crime had been one of such unusual magnitude, a murder, cruel beyond words. However, his penitence was so sincere that the Blessed Virgin appeared to him in a vision and restored life to the one he had murdered. In gratitude to her, and in her honor, Garin founded a monastery in the very place where his crime had been committed, and from that has grown Montserrat.

"It is extraordinary how strong a hold the idea of reparation and penance has upon the Spanish mind. Spaniards seem to have a genuine feeling that they must offer up their lives to atone for their crimes. It is absolutely astonishing how many Spanish nobles are in monasteries even at the present day, serving patiently, often as lay-brothers, giving up the world and all they hold dear, in expiation for some youthful faults.''

The next day we set forth to discover the beauties of the ''jagged mountains,'' and our first visit was to the church where Loyola made his famous vigil. It is a beautiful structure, though the old portion is nearly destroyed, with only a Byzantine portal and a section of the lovely Gothic cloisters remaining.

''It 's all very well for you to descant upon reverence,'' said the Pessimist, ''but I cannot understand how anybody can have the least feeling of sentiment for that queer, little black doll they call, 'Our Lady of Montserrat.' ''

''To understand one thing a person generally has to comprehend a dozen others,'' I answered. ''First of all the Spaniards like dark people; then, think from what rude ages that statue has come down, and remember the Spanish bump of reverence for anything their fathers have had. There is little use in reasoning over what people believe, for while of course they should have 'a reason for the faith that is in them,' they cannot help their beliefs (in a certain sense), any more than they can help their affections. Then you must recall the story of the discovery of this statue. In the year 880, Bishop Gondemar, hearing shepherds say that lights were seen, and strange noises heard upon the 'jagged mountain,' went there to discover what were the causes.

"In a cave he found this small statue of the Blessed Virgin, said to have been carved by Saint Luke. Concealed by the Bishop of Barcelona when the Moors invaded Cataluña, it was left in the cave at Montserrat.

"Bishop Gondemar tried to carry the statue away to Manresa, but it grew heavier at every step, and at last the bearers concluded that it wished to remain at Montserrat. A shrine was made, and a church built, and to this day it has been one of the greatest places of pilgrimage ever known."

"The scenery is certainly worth a visit," said my companion, as we climbed the mountain sides together. The narrow path was steep and rocky, yet bordered with shrubs and a rich variety of flowers — hepaticas, jonquils, daisies, holly, and ivy vines running wild and tangling everything. Tiny chapels were scattered along the route, consisting of small rooms inclosed with iron railings, each having at the end an unpretending shrine, and on the floors of these were votive offerings of money, anything from a copper penny to a golden ducat.

The valley below, with its white villages, churches, and green fields, was even more beautiful in the light of the morning sun than it had been the evening before. We hated leaving the wonderful prospect even long enough to see the caves, yet did not wish to miss them, since they are among the wonders of Spain. It takes six hours to see them all, so we contented ourselves with a glimpse at two or three.

The *Gruta de la Esperanza* is a large grotto with a stalactite roof, leading to another cave called *El Camarin*. Beyond is the Boudoir of the Sylphs, and still farther on the Devil's Well, twenty yards deep. The interiors of these caves and grottoes are most unusual. They have stalactite roofs, many of them boasting stalagmites as well, and the walls are incrusted with calcareous shapes. The stalactites have in places formed huge pillars, which gleam as if powdered with diamond dust and are tinged with rainbow hues. We reached the light of day, gasping for breath, muddy and tired, for it was a serious undertaking, but even the Pessimist enthusiastically declared that she "would n't have missed it for anything."

The chain of which Montserrat is a part is

a spur of the Pyrences. It is thirty-three hundred and ninety feet above the level of the sea, and worn by wind and weather into the "*aiguilles*" which form so strange an adjunct to the varied scenes.

"We leave for Barcelona in a few minutes," I said, "and I must go and pay our dues. Our meals at the Fonda have not cost much, and have been excellent, and as for our cell here in the Hospederia we pay what we choose, though the guide-book says a dollar a day is the usual price. Is it worth it, Pessimist?"

She made no reply for a moment. She looked out of the window once more at the magnificent sweep of grandeur from sky to valley, and then she said thoughtfully, as she turned away to prepare for our journey,

"I think even I could be good up here. It's the nearest heaven we have been in all Spain."

"Literally or metaphorically?" I asked, as usual most flippant when most deeply moved.

The Pessimist answered laconically:

"Both!"

CHAPTER XXII.

THE SPANISH GENOA.

ROM Monistrol to Barcelona is only a two hours' ride, and the Pessimist and I reached the great seaport town early in the evening.

"The nicest thing we have seen on this trip was the flag dog," said she as we neared Barcelona.

"It was the cleverest thing, the way he took the flag from the train-man there on the peak of the mountain, and, holding it in his mouth, waved it to signal all was well."

"The scenery was superb," I said, "but one is almost glad to descend to the ordinary plane of existence again. I liked seeing the peasants there at Montserrat. They seemed simple and devoted, quite unlike those noisy French pilgrims who pervaded the whole place and made everything smell of garlic. They chattered continually, and the Spaniards were so quiet. Well, we are getting nearer France every day, and somebody calls Barcelona the Spanish Paris. We are to stay at the Fonda Oriente, which is a Spanish hotel; most of them here are French or Italian."

"What a beautiful street!" cried the Pessimist, who, with her usual perversity, seemed determined to like Barcelona, principally because she saw I did not.

"That's the Rambla, a sort of miniature Champs Élysées," I said. It was a fine street, with handsome buildings and large trees bordering a park which ran through the middle of the street. The lights were brilliant, the crowds of people gay, the scene bright, but wholly French. There were little tables at the sides of the street, people drinking, laughing, chatting, and everywhere was mirth and jollity, all the abandon with which the French take their pleasures, and none of the Spanish grace and dignity.

"Alas! I feel as if we were leaving Spain to-night, for this is as truly 'un petit Paris' as Brussels, and as much of an anachronism as a *sereno* would be on the Bois de Boulogne," I cried.

Next day it was even worse to one so afflicted with Spanish fever as was I. Barcelona is a fine city. Everything has been showered upon it of wealth and beauty of situation to make it delightful. Mountains form a background for its plains, fine trees thrive in its balmy breezes, flowers blossom in its many parks; indeed, nowhere since Andalucia had we seen such a wealth of flowers of every variety as those which perfumed the soft June air.

The harbor stretching along the Paseo de las Acacias from the Barceloneta to the fort of Atarazanas, is one of the finest on the Mediterranean coast, and it is a beautiful sight as one looks down upon it from the Castle of Monjuich. This is the largest of the many fortifications of Barcelona, and is south of the town, on a high hill. Its name comes from Mons Jovis, and it has often been the object of the fiercest attacks, since to possess it was to command the town.

The view is a beautiful one, yet, in spite of its unrivaled situation, its splendid dower of churches and monuments, its energetic manufactories, its affable people, its unsurpassed harbor, thronged with shipping, Barcelona is a city of trade, of seaport activity, of French life, modern and agreeable, yet nowhere and in no way Spanish nor romantic.

"We are leaving romance and the Middle Ages," I said to the Pessimist. "Historically, Barcelona is interesting, for Hamilcar, the Carthaginian, founded it in 237 B.C., and Cæsar made it '*colonia*,' calling it Julia Augusta. Ataulfo, first Gothic king, brought his court hither, and made it the capital of Hispania-Gothia. Abdul-Aziz conquered the city, but the Moors did not long retain it, for Charlemagne came, saw, and coveted. 'God free me from my friends who come to aid me with my enemies' is an old Spanish proverb, ever since Charlemagne came to help the Christians drive out the Moors, and quietly annexed Barcelona to his duchy of Aquitaine.

"The city was governed by counts, and was prosperous with a great Levantine trade, rivaling Genoa and Venice. Barcelona has always been revolutionary, and her people seem to possess the turbulence and vivacity of the French and little of the sturdy loyalty of the Spaniards. The Barcelonettas were so jealous of Castile that no account can be found in the annals of the city of Columbus' magnificent entry into the harbor, when he had given a new world to the Spanish sovereign.

"Laces, silks, and all sorts of beautiful things are to be bought here—" I stopped in dismay. A slow, pleased smile had spread itself over the face of my companion, and I knew in an instant that my rash speech had precluded any sight-seeing for the nonce.

Some people take to shopping as naturally

as a duck to water. The Pessimist loved it, not buying things she needed or really wanted or had the money for—any woman likes that. There 's something radically wrong about a woman who does not like buying pretty things wherewith to adorn her home or help to make herself lovely in the eyes of those she loves. But *shopping* is quite different. Shopping means looking for hours at things you do n't want and can 't afford, and buying a few because you 're "ashamed not to buy anything," and because things are "such bargains," and you "*may* want them some day."

"Let 's go shopping," said my friend; and as I had not the strength to combat her evident determination, nor the heart to disturb her open delight, I weak-kneedly agreed, and we went. My advice to another is "*Don't !*" As sure as crops fail in Kansas, the result will be bankruptcy. We paraded the Rambla, and bought lace which was like frost spun on cobwebs; we haunted the Calle de la Plateria, and squandered our substance on silver fili-gree. Not only everything exquisite and deli-cate of modern ware, but rare bits of antique, such as made one's mouth water, so to speak. Of course we bought a pair of the earrings which the *payesas* wear, though what we were to do with them neither of us knew. Then came fans, not so fascinating as those at Seville and Madrid, but tempting enough—gay, lacy, French affairs, and ivory carvings of every kind, and silks without number at almost a song for cheapness. The Pessimist was incorrigible. Nothing stopped her.

"There 's a picture gallery in the Paseo Pejares," I hazarded. "Fine libraries, a museum of natural history, some of the best theatres in Spain, hospitals—"

"Just look at this mantilla. It 's only six dollars, almost a shawl, and of such a beautiful design. I shall know what 'real Spanish ' means hereafter when applied to laces," was her reply.

"The university is near the Plaza de Cataluña. It 's a fine pile of buildings, founded in 1873, and is the best of all the Spanish universities. There are twenty-five hundred students—"

"They 're the ones who burned our flag," said the shopper. "I 'm going to get a dozen pairs of gloves; they 're perfect beauties."

"You 'll have to pay duty on them, going into France," I said, disagreeably. "Oh, won't you come and see the cathedral at least? It is Catalonian Gothic of the fifteenth century, and beautiful with a calm simplicity, though lacking the minuteness of detail which marks fourteenth century Gothic."

"If you 'll keep still while I try on six pairs

of gloves," said the Pessimist, graciously, "I 'll go to the cathedral with you."

I resigned myself to my fate, and waited, making meditations upon the utter selfishness of womankind.

The Pessimist was a monster to prefer gloves when I wanted naves and transepts. One uncomfortable idea popped into my head, that she might possibly be putting the boot on the other foot, and regarding me as equally inhuman for not preferring her pet amusements.

Such a thought being untranquillizing—to coin a word—I quickly put it aside, and took to wondering what had made her give in. Usually she shopped for hours at a time. Could it be that her pocket was empty? I was ashamed of myself for imagining such a thing, and felt very guilty when she turned around with her most engaging smile, and remarked:

"I 'm ready. We 'll go to the cathedral now, and anywhere else you like."

"Let 's have lunch first," I said, guiltily conscious that I had wronged her. "I saw a charming café on the Rambla quite near here. I want to treat you to a Spanish ice."

"Thank you," she said, and as amicably as two turtle doves we ate our ices, and started to the cathedral.

Down the Calle Puerta Ferrisa to the Plaza Nueva we went, and stood before the cathedral, which is really beautiful. The belfry towers are very lofty, and the bell, the oldest in Barcelona, tolled forth the mid-day Angelus as we paused before the great flight of steps which leads up to the building. Over the door is a strange bas-relief of the contest of Vilardel and the Dragon, a legendary story of Barcelona.

The Moors—always blamed for everything —let loose their Dragon over the country-side when Vilardel was forced to give up to his swarthy enemies his castle of Vales. God tried him in many ways to see if he was worthy to kill the fearful beast, and at last, being satisfied of his piety, presented him with a miraculous sword, which would bisect the thickest trees, and cut chasms in rocks. Vilardel met the dragon, and killed him, crying, "Well done, mighty sword, and still more mighty arm of Vilardel!" Alas, for his pride! At the instant he spoke, a single drop of the dragon's blood fell dripping from the sword upon his arm. The blood was the deadliest poison, and the boaster instantly dropped dead, punished because he had not said, "Not unto us, O Lord! but unto Thee be the glory."

"Come," I said, "let us enter the church.

The interior is arranged in the French way, with an aisle and chapels around the apse. In the crypt is kept the body of Saint Eulalia. Do you want to go down?''

''No, thank you. I 've had all the crypts I want, and am tired. You can go where you like. I mean to sit by this beautiful pillar and reflect upon my sins;'' and my friend seated herself calmly.

''Principally those of extravagance,'' I added, laughingly, as I turned away.

I like the Pessimist. She 's like good wine, and improves with age. Her idiosyncrasies are so uncertain that she seldom bores one. But one of my favorite pastimes is wandering at will over some historic spot, without having to listen to a prosy guide droning out facts jumbled into an *olla podrida*. Neither do I like to do the droning and ''personally conduct'' my party, *à la* Cook's tourists-guide. I enjoyed Barcelona Cathedral as much as anything in Spain, but I have no neatly labeled facts about it, only a pleasant memory of dim aisles, and splendid tombs and dreams of days when the vast naves resounded to martial tread in the times of stately pageant and romantic story—times when, if manners were ruder and punishments hastier, and hearts perhaps harder, the life was simpler, the purpose stronger, and duty the loadstar.

> "To them was life a simple art
>   Of duties to be done,
> A game where each man took his part,
>   A race where all must run,
> A battle whose great scheme and scope
>   They little cared to know,
> Content as men-at-arms to cope
>   Each with his fronting foe."

Heedless of passing moments I wandered through the lovely cloisters, when some one at my elbow remarked, acidly, "When you have quite finished inspecting the remotest pinnacle of the roof, and the deepest depths of the lowest crypt, I am ready to return to the hotel. Not that I want to hurry you, but it is past the time for *déjeûner à la fourchette*, and I dare say even you will want some if you can 't get it."

I started guiltily. I had utterly forgotten the Pessimist, and I went with her meekly, afraid to mention that I wanted to see the church of Santa Maria del Pino, named from an image of the Virgin found in a pine tree, and upon the steeple of which a blessed pine is always placed on Palm Sunday.

I also intended going to San Pedro de las Puellas, where the nuns once cut off their noses to prevent being taken by Al-Mansûr's soldiers. Such a conquest of feminine vanity ought to be kept in remembrance, especially as Spanish noses are so pretty.

We passed the Lonja or Exchange, a fine building dating from 1832, and the Casa de la Disputacion with the famous chapel of Saint George, where the most delightfully ugly gargoyles peer down from the roof. The Gothic façade is one of the best in Spain; but I could not stop even to glance down the Calle del Obispo, for the Pessimist led me sternly on until we reached the pleasant dining-room of the Oriente.

Seated at a table, with luncheon in progress, she thawed perceptibly, and at last I ventured a question on a subject over which I had been pondering for some time.

"Pessimist," I said suddenly—for the way to get information from her is to attack her before she has time to think—"why did you leave the Rambla and go to the Cathedral?"

"I had n't another '*real*,'" she said thoughtlessly.

"I knew it!" I cried, exultingly and viciously. "And now vengeance! You shall have no more, you spendthrift, since I keep the purse, until we 've seen all that we ought to see in Barcelona. To-morrow we leave, and this afternoon we shall drive out to Barceloneta, the sailors' quarter, and Gracia, a lovely suburb, and after you 've been good all

the afternoon you may wind up on the Ram
bla, and buy yourself poor again."

"Humph!" said the Pessimist. "Evi
dently you think might is right."

"No, but 'possession is nine-tenths;' an
you 've spent your tenth, you see."

CHAPTER XXIII.

"ADIOS ESPAÑA!"

E must go," I said, as our train steamed out of the large station on the Paseo de Industria. "This is our last day in Spain, and we must make the most of it. I never ex-pected to grieve at leaving Barcelona, but even the waiter at our Fonda I regarded tenderly, because he was Spanish. I 'm glad we chose the route along the sea-coast, for the breeze is delightful. There is the bull-ring. The *Corridas* are not good here, for the people are too Frenchy to care for them. Allah be praised! there 's the last glimpse of Barcelona. Charles the Fifth said he would rather be Count of Barcelona than king of the Romans, but I would rather be an Andalucian peasant than either."

"I do n't see how I ever got you out of Andalucia," said my friend.

"Moral suasion," I answered. "Then I 'll

admit that I thought if the beginning of our journey was so agreeable, the end might be better. If I had known as much as I know now I 'd be on the Torre de la Vela listening to Diego's guitar at the present moment.

"Badalona is our first stop. It was the Betulo of the Romans, and was and is famous for gardens and orange groves.

"Next comes the Cartuja of Montalegre; and there 's a nice tale about the foundations. Two school boys were going home from the university of Barcelona, and stopped there to rest one day long ago.

"'If I am ever Pope,' said one. 'I shall build a convent here.'

"'Very well; when you do,' replied the other, 'I will come and live in it.'

"Years passed by, when one day a friar went to Rome, sent thither to see the Holy Father. What was his surprise to see in Pope Nicholas V. his old schoolmate, and the promised convent at Montalegre was built, and Fray Juan de Neo given charge of it.

"It was nearly destroyed during the war of 1835, but has been repaired. After Montalegre we come to Mongat, and here is the castle where the people made such a wonderful defense in 1808. They stood out four days against all of Secchi's division, and when the place was captured at last, by means of light guns and many soldiers, not one of the garrison lived to be taken captive."

"They were brave fellows, as all Spanish seem to be, peasant as well as prince," said the Pessimist.

"The peasants are often the bravest," I said.

"' Iberia! oft thy crestless peasantry
  Have seen the plumed Hidalgo quit thy side;
  Have seen, yet dauntless stood, 'gainst fortune fought
    and died!'

"Now we 're approaching Gerona. See how beautifully the river winds about. It 's a fine city, absolutely defunct as to any activity, but full of tradition and romance, and thoroughly Spanish. Every year they have what is called the 'Profaso de la Tramontana,' a pilgrimage to the church of Nuestra Señora de Requenasens, and the many pilgrims go thither to pray fervently that the north wind may be tempered to the shorn lamb of Gerona."

"Where is Figueras?" asked the Pessimist, a trifle sleepily, for she took frequent naps when traveling—a delightful habit of hers which enabled me to get thoroughly read up in the guide-book between times, and then pour my information upon her.

"Figueras is not far away, and has the most important citadel in Cataluña. It is almost impregnable. The castle crowning a rock is shaped like an irregular pentagon, and the fortifications are wonderful. The cisterns are inexhaustible. There are bomb-proof arsenals, stabling for five hundred horses, and barracks for twenty thousand soldiers. The fortress cost one million four hundred and twenty-five thousand dollars, and is the key of the whole frontier.

"We are nearing the Pyrenees now, and what a superb chain they are! From Biscay and Biarritz to Cérbére and the Mediterranean the mountains are full of interest for scenery and fact and legend."   .

"Tell me all about everything," said my companion, and she settled herself comfortably to listen.

"Some day we 'll go to Biarritz, and take a trip through the whole Pyrenees. It 's quite delightful over at the opposite end from where we are now. Some one says of this part, ''T is little known, save by the smuggler, the flying Carlist, and the buck or izard.' I 'm not well acquainted with the last three varieties, but people seem to be able to be smugglers with perfect ease."

"They are n't," said my companion guiltily. "That Barcelona lace is eating a hole in my pocket at the present moment. If you think I am smuggling 'with ease' you 're very much mistaken. It 's far worse than the Spartan boy and the fox."

I laughed maliciously. I had not been sure the shoe would fit the Pessimist, but had strongly suspected as much. "If you mean to smuggle you must n't look so self-conscious. That 's just like a woman. She 's always ashamed to do what she 's ashamed of."

"You need n't be so superior. I believe you 've tried it, and that 's why you know so much," said she. I changed the subject, without jar, by remarking

"Here are our guards. How I shall hate to leave them behind when we reach Cérbére. They only go as far as the border, and I 'm sorry to say they are not a French institution."

"What are they, anyhow?" asked my friend, as we stopped at a little station, and the two vigilantes walked slowly past our window with their alert yet stately tread.

"They are the best and most reliable men selected from the police corps, and are sent two at a time to take care of every railway train. In the time of brigandage this used to be a very necessary precaution, and while now, it 's not absolutely so, it 's very consoling to feel we have two brave fellows, well-armed, and always ready to defend us in case of any danger. They 're called *guardias civiles*, and are always civil and pleasant."

"They 're certainly a picturesque addition

to the landscape," said my friend, as we looked at the tall figures in cloaks and cocked hats.

"Look there!" I exclaimed. "There 's a living exposition of the old proverb: 'Quien á buen árbol se arrima, buena sombra le cobija.' (She who leans against a sturdy tree is secure in pleasant shade). Look at that peasant girl against the shade of the olive tree, with the stalwart peasant's arm about her. How happy they both look under that matchless lapis lazuli sky! No matter if they grow old and withered and worn with toil and wind and weather, they 've had their day."

"If you talk like that I shall begin to wish I were a Spanish peasant."

"Many Spanish peasants never see a coin except from chance tourists," I answered. "They raise barely enough potatoes and rye to support life, but they seem contented."

We were nearing Port Bou, the last Spanish town, a rambling village with low picturesque houses and a fine view of sea and mountains.

"The Moors left Andalucia by the Puerta de Despeñaperros (the Gate of Infidel Dogs)," I murmured, "but we seem to be departing from Spain by the Gate of Angels. Between the perfect hues of sea and sky, it 's all so wonderfully fair it is almost as if Paradise lay be-

yond those snowy mountains.   Even music is
not wanting, for

"' I hear
Once more the music of the mountaineer,
And from the sunny vales the shepherd's strain
Floats out and fills the solitary place
With the old tuneful melodies of Spain's heroic race.'"

"What did you like best in Spain?" asked a
sleepy voice, as the Pessimist aroused herself.

"Oh, fie upon you!" I answered.   "That
question 's a crime.   How can I tell, where
each city is so different, each charm so varied,
and all so delightful!"

"Why do you travel at all if you can 't tell
what you like?" she asked, severely.

" 'The universe is a kind of book, of which
one has read only the first page, when one has
seen only his own country.   I have traveled
much, and all the imperfections which I have
seen in different peoples have reconciled me
with my own land.   If I derived no other
benefits from my travels than that, I should
regret neither the trials nor the fatigues,'
Monsieur de Montbrou said.   I confess that
while I have enjoyed every minute of our trip,
that there are some things truly American
which I shall hail with delight—an ice cream
soda, for instance."

"My native land 's the best!" sighed the
Pessimist, waxing sentimental.

"It is the fashion to regard Spaniards as monsters or whited sepulchres or ravening wolves or something unpleasant of a like nature," I said, "but we have traveled from Gibraltar to France, and had nothing but friendliness and courtesy. The country is wonderful. There are mines of literary wonders and artistic delights and exquisite scenery displayed to one's view, mental or physical. I feel as if my Spaniards had opened to me as new a world-as Columbus opened for them."

"With you it is a sort of 'with all thy faults, I love thee still, O Spain!'" said my friend.

"In spite of her faults, not with them," I answered; and then the train stopped, and the guard cried, "Cérbére!"

"Our first French village!" said the Pessimist. "*Vive la France!*"

"Nay," I said—and there was a lump in my throat—"before one cries 'Long live the King!' one should at least say '*Le Roi est mort!*'"

Then I looked backward whence we had come, at the sparkling waters of the sea, the green vales bright in the warm June sunshine, the gay villages where tall spires cleft the cloudless sky, the background of mountains, pure and white. "Farewell," I murmured, "Adios, España! Vaya usted con Dios!"